I0764493

Island Castaways

A Story of Adventure, Intrigue, and a Dead Body

A Novel

By Jesse R. Hale

Published by Shades Creek Press, LLC
Savannah, Georgia, 2011

First Edition
First Printing, 2011

Book design by Jesse R. Hale
Cover design by Jesse R. Hale & John Morris-Reihl

Proof-reading by Fran Johnson, Gil and Barbara Rodriguez
Proof-reading & editing by Marty Hale

Island Castaways
ISBN: 978-0-9838376-0-2

This is a work of fiction. Names, characters, places, and incidents are either the product of the author's imagination or are used fictitiously, and any resemblance to actual persons, living or dead, business establishments, events, or locales, is entirely coincidental. Some references to geographical locations are in part based on factual logistical data and information; however, all characters, stories, and plot detail are purely fictional and the product of the novel.

Shades Creek Press, LLC
Savannah, Georgia 31410
www.shadescreekpress.com

Printed in the United States of America

For Jesse Rudolph "Buddy" Hale, my dad, who I think of everyday. I hope he would be proud.

Chapter

1

The dew glistened on the leaves of the trees that stood along College Street, and only a few people dotted the sidewalk cafés and art galleries. I was sitting down with a large mocha java and a copy of the Asheville Times, when Carl walked up and asked the question he had been longing to corner me on since we had returned. It was Sunday morning here in the mountains of North Carolina in this hidden jewel of a city that had become a melting pot of cultures and life styles. This was the city where Julie and I came as often as we could to escape the pressures of the daily grind, the work-a-day world of traffic, egos, and cigarette smoke, with countless nameless faces of people who were unfriendly either out of fear or their own smugness.

Alas, here I sat, finally back in the Eden of the mountainous world of free America, where freethinking and openness were expected virtues and characteristics of those who resided here or visited this city. And this coffee shop was a great little hideaway, an escape for most. Located in a tiny space between the old

Woolworth's store and the new Urban Cowboy clothing and accessory store not far from the corner of College and Broad, it had developed a loyal following and patronage.

"So, Ethan," Carl said, as he approached, wiping a table or two on the way over to my table, "Tell me what happened. I've been dying to know the details." Carl sat down with me at the small table outside his coffee café with the eagerness of a kid in a candy store.

We had arrived back in Atlanta at Hartsfield-Jackson International Airport just after midnight a few days earlier. We promptly rented a car and drove straight through to Asheville, some two and a half hours north, to our townhouse near the Grove Park Inn. It was like stepping into the most luxurious spot in the world, like the Grove Park Inn was originally back in the 1920's and 30's. Once we came over the mountain and through the pass north of Waynesville on state highway 64 and merged onto I-40, the weight of the world literally lifted. There was finally a sense of peace, relaxation and safety. We could finally breathe.

"Where's Julie?" Carl asked, almost without taking a breath. The thought struck me that his questioning Julie's whereabouts was oddly ironic given the journey we had just experienced. Carl had been a close friend and confidant since our college days. He had finished his MBA at Kennesaw State and headed for the mountains. Ten years later, after waiting tables and tending bar, he had scraped together enough money to open his dream business, a small coffee and book café… a coffee shop, in most people's eyes. For a modest yearly membership fee of fifty dollars, members could have access to books, DVDs, and the internet along with the newly installed SKYPE for person-to-person communication. We had seen a lot of this type of technology in Belize and other parts of Central America where we had traveled.

"She's out shopping," I said, folding my paper. Carl sat down and settled in for what would be an extended conversation. "So, tell me, Ethan, would you do it again? Tell me what happened. I can't wait to hear the story," he said.

"Well, Carl, it was an incredible journey. The island scenery was spectacular, and the people were very gracious. And yes, I'd do it again; but, believe me, having gone through what we went through, we would do it much differently," I said, taking a sip of my coffee.

"But tell me what happened, Dude. I know you guys had an adventure, and I want to hear all about it," Carl said. I began recounting the tale as he threw his questions at me one after the other.

"I never intended to be stranded on a beach, not knowing how I had landed there or what had happened to me. But, that's how it began… with my waking up on a beach with sand and sea water in my mouth," I said. "Only hours before all had seemed well! The voyage over from Galveston Bay was great, a real blast! I suppose it should have been a clue as to what lay ahead. You know, Carl, we will probably have to finish this conversation over dinner and a good bottle of Pinot Grigio… but, here goes," I continued.

"The ride on the windjammer from Galveston Bay was touted to be the best ride in that part of the Gulf, and it wasn't too expensive. We had worked out our schedule and were to meet the others on Ambergris Caye off the coast of Belize. But, nobody knew what would come when darkness engulfed the voyage. Man, was it strange. Many of the details of what happened that night are still unknown. I'm just glad it worked out; we were really lucky," I said, as I began telling the story of our strange adventure to the Central American coast of Belize and the small island town of San Pedro.

"Things took a bizarre turn when I found myself stranded on the beach, not knowing where the hell I was, or how I got there! And, Julie was missing! I had no memory of what had happened... at least, not at first," I said, continuing the story.

Carl issued orders to two student workers who had arrived for their shift at the coffee café. He sat with both elbows on the table, his chin resting in his cupped hands, his eyes eager for the rest of the story. I sipped my mocha java and continued to reveal the saga that would indeed require several bottles of wine over dinner.

*** *** *** ***

Frothy ocean water sloshing around me retreated with the rhythm of the waves crashing on the sand as the sun's heat and brightness broke the darkness. The morning sounds of seagulls and motorboats could be heard in the distance. A misty fog lay over the bay, and the damp salty air served as a reminder of the pitching waves and howling winds of the storm the night before. I lay there feeling every sharp edge of every grain of sand, imagining that it was caked so thick over my body that I couldn't move. The sense of dread was overwhelming. Then, gasping suddenly, I realized that the incredibly salty and foreign taste in my mouth was the gritty taste of sea-washed sand. I had been lying face down on the beach in the darkness; but now, the sun was burning down on me. Every bone in my body ached, and my head ached, and I felt as if I had been kicked by a mule. Where was Julie, I wondered. Realizing the shock of my predicament, I tried to muster the strength to pull myself up from the sand. I thought I would be able to remember what had happened the night before. But, in the blur, clear memories evaded me.

The ocean water rushed over my feet as I stumbled to stand and walk up the beach, panic struck. Julie was missing! What had happened? Where was she, and how the hell did I get into this situation? I couldn't concentrate on anything else; where was Julie? The question burned in my mind. I yelled for her, "Julie, Julie, where are you?" Again and again, "WHERE ARE YOU?" I screamed. It was surreal, like a science fiction movie. I was playing the starring role right there on the beach. To say that I was in shock is probably an understatement.

*** *** *** ***

As I retold the story and recounted the details of the trip, I considered how the experience had changed me... and us. The journey had been nothing like we had expected or planned. It was so much more. Carl was a close friend, and I wanted to share everything with him. I wasn't sure, however, that I could convey the full impact of our experiences.

On the beach that morning, as scared and shaken as I was, I fell to my knees, losing control of my emotions and cried for a minute with my face buried in my hands. I prayed. I pulled myself up from the surf, stood stiff and tense; bewildered and confused. With the details of the night before still eluding me, I just stood there... speechless. The waves were almost knocking me over.

The sun was very bright and hot, and I guessed it to be between 8:00 and 10:00 A.M., just when it starts heating up. The intensity of the heat from the bright sunshine was incredible; sweat was already dripping from my forehead, mixing with the sand and seawater dried on my face. My head was aching. It was one of those migraine-type headaches I sometimes got, and my eyelids were now beginning to become part of that ache.

"What the heck happened?" I mumbled to myself, looking first in one direction then the other, trying to figure out not only what had happened, but where I was, and more desperately, where was Julie? I suppressed my fear and panic and sat down in the shade of some palm trees and began to gather my thoughts... to let my analytical mind do its sorting. It was the kind of thing I was known for. I had made a lot of money playing the role of "problem solver" for corporations and non-profits, working first with consulting companies, and eventually moving out on my own, freelancing in the business of making people in highly competitive fast-paced jobs feel gratified and secure with their jobs and their workplaces. Now, I was faced with the greatest challenge of my life.

I had not eaten since the party aboard the ship two days after we sailed from Galveston Bay. The hunger pains in my stomach broke my concentration. The reconstruction of my memory and the details of the events of the last 24 hours were not falling into place as I had hoped they would. The boat ride had been long and grueling, filled with craziness beyond belief. Had I fallen overboard, or had I been pushed? Was I delirious, or was there something happening that was too crazy and insane to believe?

Standing up slowly, with every muscle and bone aching, I gazed around trying to decide in which direction to begin my course. I remembered that the ship had set sail to the southeast, then turned southwest toward the northern quarter of Belize, sailing approximately 85 miles around and south of the Yucatan Peninsula.

"Well now, Oh, Captain, My Captain, I think I'll face east and turn south," I mumbled to myself, feeling a bit more confident and somewhat less panicky. I kept thinking positive thoughts about Julie, the love of my life. Perhaps she was up ahead. "I'll find her, I know it! I just know it," I whispered to myself as I began walking down the beach, silently. Then, I prayed... *"Dear God, give me the strength to endure, and please keep Julie safe. PLEASE keep Julie safe. Amen."* I looked toward the sky as if asking God directly. Tears filled my eyes.

After walking for what seemed hours, I looked at the sun and calculated it to be about 12:00 Noon, remembering the position of the sun when I began my day's journey. "If I'm guessing right, and if I'm where I think I am, San Pedro should be up ahead... *unless* I landed off the coast of southern Mexico, which was my greatest fear. THAT would be an almost impossible situation, almost as hostile of some parts of Guatemala," I murmured, thinking out loud to myself.

I had sailed around the island of Ambergris Caye years ago while on vacation with my brother-in-law. The caye was north of the mainland of Belize, and I could only hope that's where I was now. If so, then perhaps I could find Julie and the others, and figure out what had happened the night before. What had led to my waking up on the beach covered with dried salt and sand? I wasn't in the habit of drinking to the point that I would pass out and not remember a thing. Rather, I suspected that something more sinister was at play; and, I hoped, more than anything, that Julie was safe. My mood had now transformed from panic and fear, to anger. I was *"mad as a wet hen,"* as my mother used to say. But, I knew I had to keep my cool and stay focused.

Chapter

2

Stopping underneath the shade of some palm trees, exhausted and sunburned from the sun's rays that fell directly on the back of my neck, and with my feet burning from the sand, I paused again to analyze my surroundings. Using my left hand to block the sun, I looked to the south and realized my luck was about to change. "I'll just be doggone! Land Ho!" I said to myself. My lips were parched and I was thirsty beyond imagination, but there was civilization up ahead.

Gathering my wits, I began walking again. As I slid my numb feet through the hot sand, I realized that I would soon encounter other humans, and I thought about trying not to look too obvious. Within a few minutes, I reached the outskirts of what I hoped was San Pedro, the village located on the south end of the caye.

"Right!" I thought, as I further analyzed the situation and predicted the probable coordinates of our boat. My mind kicked in gear. I could imagine someone asking where I had been and wondering why I appeared to be so dirty and tattered. My mind wandered further, "Oh, pardon me, Sir," I thought to myself in a thick English accent, "but I have just arrived on this enchanted island paradise by way of floating like a dead person; darn cheap way to travel, I must say," I thought, shaking my head and feeling confident, but stupid.

In the distance, I could see a long pier that extended far into the gulf. It appeared to be a public dock; and, as I got closer, I could see people standing along the length of the pier, fishing.

"That's a good sign. People are fishing," I thought, as I mentally examined the prospects of having washed up on Ambergris Caye after some mysterious and bizarre events that were locked steadfastly in the fog of my mind. Seeing people on the pier had given me a burst of energy... similar to reaching the trailhead after hiking up the Appalachian Trail some 3000 feet. I felt exhilarated. My gait became more brisk and more determined. Before long I arrived at the steps near the pier, steps that led to the main street in the middle of the village. I grew excited about the possibilities of finding Julie.

Pausing to catch my breath, I tried to take in the scenes around me. I turned from right to left, trying to notice every detail; trying to remember the way the town of San Pedro had looked on my last visit. It had been years since the vacation with my brother-in-law, and we had stayed on the south end of the island. More importantly and even more surprising, Belize and Ambergris Caye had been discovered. The place had changed! For years it had been a well-kept secret spot for divers and underwater adventurers and had avoided the transformations and trappings of commercialism and the resort barrage. Apparently, that era had ended. My mind quickly returned to thoughts of finding Julie.

Whether I was lucky enough to have washed up on Ambergris Caye or not, I somehow did not feel threatened. I felt determined.

"Let's go, mate," I said aloud, as if I had a traveling companion. At the top of the steps I stopped, and surveyed my surroundings slowly and deliberately. In the distance I heard voices and laughter coming from the sidewalk cafes, bars and shops. "What about Julie," I thought. "Where was she? Was she on the ship? What had happened to her?" My mind drifted from panicky thoughts to *damn the torpedoes* to the reality that I wasn't sure what had happened. Was danger lurking around the next corner? I had to stay alert and attentive. Looking disheveled, my clothes torn and stained, and dried in the ocean breeze, I walked toward the voices and the laughter. The surface of the street was a fine dust, and it felt good to my tired bare feet... a sun-warmed powder that soothed and encouraged me.

Turning the corner at the first intersection, I saw tables outside a café. People were seated there, eating what looked like eggs and thick bacon and drinking coffee. The smell of the food was almost debilitating. My stomach growled and churned from the lack of food. To make matters worse, I had probably had too much liquid intake the night before, in addition to ingesting a good deal of seawater. I was starving.

Whispers and surprise glances were relinquished, but I moved forward anyway; slowly... concentrating on acquiring a laid-back appearance and trying not to be too distracted by the smell of the food and coffee. My thoughts ran swiftly from point to point. "What a price to pay for adventure!" I thought, not exactly sure of where I was going or what I would do next.

San Pedro, Ambergris Caye, Welcome to Paradise, the sign read. It hung by two rusty nails on the side of a hardware store. Without thinking, I jumped in the air and yelled out like I had just won the lottery! At least I knew where I was. "Okay, that's one piece of the puzzle," I thought, and felt even more confident now.

The people of the island were friendly. They appeared trusting and courteous toward me, an American who looked like he had been through hell and back. As I walked beside the storefronts, trying to put together the events of the night before... the events that had landed me on this island... my memory began to return, at least in part. It had begun as a perfect evening. Dinner included prime rib with a 1978 bottle of chardonnay from a prestigious New York winery. A friend had given us the wine five years earlier. "That's it!" I said aloud again. This time, villagers turned and gave me strange and curious looks. "It must have been at dinner that whatever happened occurred," I mumbled to myself again. This was indeed, turning out to be the strangest adventure of my life!

Walking over to a table, I sat down feeling relieved but exhausted and tried again to ignore the crowd. Thinking to myself, I recalled how Julie and I had met in college, over a game of ping-pong in the student life center at Jeff State Junior College just outside Birmingham. We had known each other as friends for years before marrying in 1992. As part of the same group, we had even ended up in the same car on several double dates, but we had never imagined becoming a couple. Then, as fate would have it, one evening when we each had planned a double date, we found ourselves without the chosen companions of the evening. On a lark, we decided to go out as a couple; and, before the night was over, we knew without speaking a word, that we were a good fit. It felt natural. Now, here I sat, not knowing where she was or what had happened to her.

The idea of escaping the stress and pointless endurance of city life and corporate ladders to the warm sandy beaches of a Central American island had been a topic of conversation for many years. When my consulting company was bought by a group of German investors, we began thinking seriously about our adventure. We had built our company over a span of ten years, leaning heavily on the marketing expertise of friends and colleagues, and inviting them to work on a full or part-time basis, structuring their compensation and investment in the firm with stock options and shares of the company. When Julie and I were contacted by the corporate attorney from New York about the prospect of selling the company to an outside entity, we were reluctantly excited and recognized that we had a golden opportunity. We called a meeting of partners and colleagues and presented the proposal, leaving the decision primarily with them. A week went by, and the attorney began pressing us for an answer. Julie suggested a weekend retreat at the Grove Park Inn, a favorite of ours as well as many of our friends and colleagues. We had to get to the heart of the matter, to decide to either accept the offer... or turn it down and plan a course of action for the next year. Even though the offer was too big and too good to refuse, no one associated with our company wanted to be the first to embrace a desire to sell. After much discussion and debate, the decision was unanimous. We would accept the offer and divide the assets according to each partner's stock ownership. Everyone would benefit from the transaction.

Julie was the first to broach the idea of the lifestyle change that she and I had dreamed of for years. We had all talked about taking a year off to travel to a remote island, and the sale of the company would enable us to make this trip. So began our journey of adventure and mystery.

There were three couples altogether, friends from school or work who shared the same adventurous idea. Proceeds from the sale of the company and the stock options that had been negotiated as part of the deal, afforded the fulfillment of a dream. We had agreed to meet on Ambergris Caye, with an arrival date set for March 12th. Due to several family-specific issues, each couple had decided to travel to Belize independently by chartered boat.

The San Pedro Café was located just off the square in the tiny village and across from an old Catholic Church that had stood there for a hundred years or more. My mind was racing. Panic hit again. "Julie, where was Julie?" I mumbled. The young girl waiting tables brought me a glass of chilled water, no ice. I drank it without stopping. Then, feeling a bit conspicuous for gulping down the water, I apologized. The young girl stood there, as if waiting for my next request. I asked for more water, and she scurried off behind a curtain to retrieve it.

When the girl returned, I asked about Julie, describing her as an American woman about 5'6" tall with short brown hair, medium complexion, and a British accent. "No, Señor," she replied. "I have not seen her." She turned to walk away, but paused once more to inquire if anything else was needed. "Yes," I replied, "more water, and something to nibble on, please." She smiled and disappeared into the back of the café.

"Señor", a voice came from behind me, "Señor, I have seen an American woman." It was a waiter who had suddenly appeared from inside the café. I sat there, almost paralyzed, as if everything were in slow motion. I watched every step the waiter took toward me, and heard his words in slow motion, as well. "Where? When?" I asked. "Last night," the waiter explained. "She came by looking for her husband. She said something about having sailed here from Galveston. She had brown hair and was so high," he said, indicating her height with his hand."

"Where was she going? Did she say?" I asked desperately.

"No Señor, she did not. Perhaps you might check the church," the waiter said as he pointed across the street. Immediately, I bolted across the street to the church, my heart pounding with anticipation.

Out of breath, I stopped for a second in front of the church doors, with one hand outstretched and somewhat leaning on the door to rest a minute. The doors were old and weathered, daunting and reverent. The outside structure of the church was stucco and had been colorfully accented, and was long faded by the sun. Children played in the courtyard just outside the front entrance.

I eased through the bulky doors, my eyes searching from side to side, as I moved into the vestibule and squinted to see. Someone was praying near the front. The sunlight shone through the stained glass of the church and made it difficult to see clearly. I made my way slowly toward the front of the church, walking deliberately down the aisle. I had a rush of emotions. I felt awkward being in a church... as if I were a kid sneaking into a forbidden place ...while at the same time, I felt a rush of hopeful anxiety. The figure I was looking at, trying to focus on, appeared to be a female with short dark hair. Could it be Julie? "Julie," I whispered. "Julie, is that you?"

"Ethan, Ethan," she said as she turned and ran toward me. "Where have you been? What happened to you? Are you OK?" she asked in her slight British accent. Julie had grown up in Cheshire, England, but at the age of 18, had moved to Birmingham, Alabama to live with her uncle, Jim Buchanan, who was in politics at the time serving as a United States Senator from Alabama.

"I'm fine. I'm Ok," I whispered as we stood there holding each other until we both regained our composure and were breathing a bit easier. We kissed, and tears filled both our eyes. "Ethan, I thought you were..." she couldn't finish her sentence. I gently stroked her hair and placed my finger to her lips. "Shh, Shh, I'm here. And, you're here. That's all that matters right now. I love you so much." I kissed her gently on the lips and we held each other again.

"Come on," I motioned, leading her by the hand. We went to one side of the church to the end of a pew and sat holding each other. With the sun's glare in our eyes through the stained glass windows we were silent and motionless, contemplating what had happened and what would come next. Though much of our ordeal was still unknown, at least we had found each other.

"Come on," I said, breaking the silence. "Let's go over to the San Pedro Cafe. I need some food and some air. Besides, I can't think here. It's too reverent," I said in a low whispering voice. Julie smiled, took my hand, and nodded her head in agreement. We left the church and headed for the café. Sitting at a small side table, we collected ourselves and began to reconstruct the events of our journey from Galveston. I motioned to the young girl who had waited on me before...the one I had asked for food just before I darted out of the café toward the church. The girl smiled and disappeared, only to reappear moments later with a large plate of nachos topped with cheese and chicken.

***   ***   ***   ***   ***   ***

Carl was in disbelief, sitting on the edge of his seat. It was a good thing he had plenty of help on this cool morning. In the span of about forty-five minutes, several people, mostly college students, had filtered in and made themselves comfortable on one of the many leather sofas situated in the coffee café. Carl had worked hard for this little piece of the American dream. He had a connection in Jamaica where he was able to procure a plentiful supply of Blue Mountain Coffee, some of the best coffee in the world, rivaled only by the pure Kona coffee from Hawaii. While he didn't make a lot of money at the café, he was happy and contented, and always searching for ways to enhance his business. "I need to post this on my blog, Ethan. It could potentially be a money maker you know."

"I thought blogs were for politicos," I said, responding to Carl's exuberant interest in our story. "I need another cup of mocha java," I told him, "if we're going to get to a stopping point in this story." And, with a quick motion to one of the girls working behind the counter, a fresh large cup of Carl's famous coffee arrived at our table. And, as usual, it was delicious.

Chapter

3

Julie and I had chartered our boat, the *MISS SHEILA,* out of Galveston Bay, Texas. It was a sailing ship, complete with the basic crew and the look of a 19th century schooner. The captain and four crewmembers had assured us that the journey would be safe and enjoyable as we embarked on our grand plan ...moving to an island for a year. More than ten years of developing the company and building the business and its subsequent sale had paid off. We were making a concerted effort to simplify our lives by giving up the daily grind of big city life in Atlanta for the more relaxed and meager lifestyle of island living. We had paid off our debts, sold our house in Virginia Highlands, a very eclectic neighborhood near the downtown area of Atlanta, and sold all but one car. We had kept our townhouse in Asheville for our future return back into the civilized world. Trusting our financial investments to Mike Henderson, a friend and former college pal who now worked in the banking and financial services industry, we set out on our journey. We left Atlanta and its horrendous road-rage traffic behind. Our plan included utilizing my background in construction, teaching, and working with large groups in the corporate world to pave the way for the next year. Beyond that, we would fly by the seat of our pants, as the saying goes. By design, we had no definitive plan. With $150,000 set aside to fund our adventure, and with Mike's handling the rest of our investments, we were off to paradise!

Back at the San Pedro Café, Julie and I were finally eating our first meal since the ordeal. Aside from Julie wearing her clothes from the night before and looking a little windblown, she really didn't stand out from the crowd. My clothes, on the other hand, looked as though I had been in a fight with a cat. The sleeves of my shirt were torn and shredded. My pants had been soaked, dried, soaked and dried again, and had that week-old look. I felt much better than I probably looked, but I kept my focus, and didn't make eye contact with anyone but Julie. We sat and enjoyed our food and drinks as if nothing much had happened. Besides, we had a mystery to figure out!

"What do you remember, Julie?" I asked as we sipped our coffee.

"I don't remember very much," she replied, speaking with her soft British flair. "I was awakened this morning by the noise of children playing near the church. I guess I had fallen asleep there in the churchyard, right inside the gate, but I just don't remember everything. The morning sun was so bright; it became warm very quickly, so I went into the church to stay cool and collect my thoughts. Oh, Ethan, I was so frightened," Julie said, looking worried.

"I know, darling, I know. So was I. I was more worried about finding you again than anything else."

As we finished the eggs and bacon, and drank yet another cup of coffee, we felt more confident about our ability to take care of ourselves. We telephoned Mike at the bank in Atlanta and arranged for a money wire. Leonardo, the café owner who had befriended us, agreed to assist with the money transfer. We would hang out near the café for the rest of the day until we could secure our money. Leonardo remembered me from my previous trip to Belize, which was a lucky break for us. We were, at least for the moment, literally stranded! We found ourselves in a foreign country with no money, no identification, and no personal possessions all on the cusp of one single mysterious event. We went back to the public pier and dock area hoping to find clues as to the whereabouts of the other couples who were to join us on this adventure. As far as we knew, they had not yet arrived.

Belize was a place we all had visited before, and we were comfortable mingling with the native people. We were also familiar with the island, and knew where to look for a safe and inconspicuous place to stay ... a place where we would not necessarily be noticed and could blend in with the other tourists. While Belize, and Ambergris Caye in particular, had been a divers' paradise since the early 1960s and had only recently become a semi-popular tourist adventure destination, it still offered some unique hideaway spots for those who wished to escape the world of hustle and bustle.

The public pier and commercial docks were located about a quarter mile north of the church and café where Julie and I had found each other and had breakfast. We walked as casually as we could, trying not to cause unnecessary notice. We were not yet able to differentiate with any degree of certainty between our enemies and our friends.

The pier was about 22 feet wide and made of weather-dried planks. Several fishing boats and two rather large dive rigs were moored to the dock posts, tied with large grass ropes worn smooth by many years of use in this semi-tropical climate. To the left of the entrance of the pier was the public rental office, where shirtless men with tanned leathery skin stood talking and laughing. On the opposite side of the counter, a guy checked the schedules for the morning and afternoon dives. Multicolored air tanks lined the wall, and a diver flag was draped across the top of a window.

"My God, Martha Stewart would flip," Julie mumbled, looking at the décor.

"May I help you?" A voice rang out from a corner across the room. He was a rather young-looking fellow: an American with light brown hair, tanned skin, and a slim build.

"Ah, yes, ah… I mean, we're just looking around; killing a little time," I answered without making eye contact. Trying to stay cool and collected was perhaps rather foolish on my part since my pants were ripped from the thigh down to my ankle on one leg, and the other was ripped just as badly, but shorter. Julie's hair was beginning to look like a seagull had roosted in it, and our faces, arms and other exposed areas of skin were smudged and dirty from the night we had just survived.

Rolling her eyes slightly, Julie glanced in my direction, as if she were thinking that I always tried to be the knight in shining armor. This was an odd situation. Julie glanced toward the young man in the corner, the same one who had just asked if he could be of any assistance. Without hesitating ...and to my dismay, Julie charged forward with her direct inquiry.

"Well actually, yes, we were wondering what you charge for dive trips," she imposed.

"The rates are posted on the board behind you," the young man quipped, indicating with a glance rather than bothering to point. He seemed amused as he made a brief attempt to size us up. He seemed, at the very least, puzzled by our appearance, and probably by our demeanor, as well.

Without moving her body, Julie slightly turned her head toward the board in question, and smiled ever so slightly. "Oh, yes, I see," said Julie. "$45.00 per hour, plus equipment, lunch provided on morning dives; night dives -- $75.00 per hour, no food, water provided; equipment rental - $35.00 per day; experienced divers only!" she continued reading aloud. "Yes, well," she said, toning down her English accent, "we are interested in a little snorkeling. Do you provide that service, as well?"

"No. Sorry," the young man responded without elaborating. There was an awkward pause, and suddenly we felt conspicuously uncomfortable. We thanked the young man, turned and left.

"What was that all about?" I whispered to Julie as we made our way off the dock, posing as casual tourists who were just looking around.

"Ethan, the only way we are going to find out about the others is to make contact with somebody we might be able to trust, if only for a little while."

"I know," I said, feeling somewhat foolish, "but...I don't know! Let's keep walking, and maybe we'll figure this out."

My thoughts raced from one scenario to another. We had definitely hit our second wind. Walking along the waterfront, we noticed a vessel with three tall masts docked near the end of the pier. We stopped, looked at each other, and picked up our pace as we eagerly approached the boat. Was this the schooner we had boarded in Galveston Bay? We continued walking, passing a large fishing boat and abruptly gained clear view of the vessel.

"There, look!" I pronounced, holding tightly to Julie's hand. Julie stood silently. The words *MISS SHEILA* were imprinted in large blue letters on the stern.

"I'll just be doggoned," I said. "Look at this. Is this not a surprise?"

"Be careful, Ethan! Make sure there isn't anyone around," Julie said as she glanced behind her.

Suddenly, as the thought of meeting up with the captain and his crew occurred to me, a cold chill ran down my spine. Without saying anything, I took Julie's hand and led her back toward the entrance to the pier.

"Don't look so anxious, Julie," I whispered calmly. "Maybe we can get out of here without being noticed." I couldn't help wondering, however, where the captain and his four idiot mates were hiding.

"You know, darling, this would make a great book!" Julie quipped. "Nobody at home would believe us if we were to phone home and tell them right now."

"Oh, jolly right!" I retorted. "We're having a bloody blast down here amongst the fish and the fugitives. It's a real Moby Dick story, alright!"

Chapter

4

Rounding the end of the pier, we were back on the gravel road and headed south toward the *Victoria House*, a quaint Inn where we had stayed years before. We slowed to a more relaxed gait, feeling less threatened by our surroundings. The walk from the village center to the Victoria House took about thirty minutes. We chattered as we walked on, lost in thought. Seeing the *MISS SHEILA* moored at the wharf was to say the least, unnerving. Almost simultaneously, we looked at each other and breathed more slowly and deeply as if to signal that it was time for a break. We approached the inn in silence, ready for a substantial rest. Victoria House would be our haven for the next few days. It was a clean and fairly inexpensive place to stay and had good food that was safe to eat. We had been in contact with the innkeeper about staying there for a few nights until we could set up our more permanent residence. We hoped the inn might also have a record of our past stays and might allow us to stay the night based on our promise of payment after our money transfer was received at the café.

Luck had finally smiled on us. Francisco, Leonardo's brother, who worked as manager of the Victoria House, was on duty at the front desk. He remembered speaking with me several weeks before about lodging arrangements. And, as we had hoped, Francisco was very willing to assist us with accommodations for the night. We were given a one-room grass hut that had a small stove, a sink, one bed, a shower, and a couple of sitting chairs. There was no air conditioning, which was fine with Julie and me. We were thankful to have a base from which to operate.

Francisco offered to acquire some new clothes for Julie and me, since his sister worked at one of the local clothing stores. We gave him our sizes, and he promised to return shortly with at least one set of fresh clothing for each of us. For now, we were thrilled to have a cold shower, some lunch, and drinks ...a margarita for Julie and a cold beer for me. We knew it would take an hour or more for someone to return with our newly acquired clothes, so we undressed and took advantage of the roomy shower and the coolness of the hut provided by the large ceiling fan hanging from the bamboo rafters. We were asleep on the bed, barely covered by towels, when Francisco returned with a plastic bag filled with clothes.

"Señor Ethan, Ms. Julie, you in there?" he asked as he rapped on the door of the grass hut.

"Yes, Francisco, just a minute," I mumbled sleepily. I threw the bed cover over Julie, who hadn't heard the knock on the door, hurriedly slipped on my pants and answered the door.

"Francisco, hello," I said. "Were you able to get us some clothes?"

"Oh yes, my sister had plenty. She said for you and Ms. Julie to come by the shop, and she will give you more. You can pay her later, Mon; your word is good here."

"Thanks again, Francisco. You'll never know how much I appreciate this."

"No problem, Señor Ethan. Your evening meal will be served in about an hour. What do you and Ms. Julie want for dinner?" Francisco asked in his heavy Caribbean-Spanish accent.

"Ah, Francisco, surprise us. Anything you cook will be delicious!"

With the bag of clothes in hand, I waved as Francisco made his way back toward the main building. Julie had gotten up and was moving toward the shower again. I waited this time, and then showered again myself.

Our table was waiting, complete with a candle, a bottle of wine, and steamy bowls of chowder that proved to be an amazingly satisfying appetizer. Our meal had been specially prepared. Crab cakes and stuffed shrimp initiated the evening, followed by blackened Mahi-Mahi, steamed oysters and black beans and rice. Francisco brought out a freshly prepared cup of coconut custard for dessert. Finally, we were feeling rejuvenated.

We ate until nothing was left, thanked everyone, and excused ourselves from the dining area. When we had walked a sufficient distance, far enough not to be heard, we retreated to one of the hammocks near the beach. We lay there holding each other, listening to the ocean waves, and contemplating our next move.

"Where do you suppose the others are?" Julie whispered. "And we haven't yet put the pieces together from last night," she added. "What do you think happened?"

"I don't know," I said. "The last thing I remember is the party. We were all on the forward deck, along with the other folks who had booked their trips to parts of Mexico and beyond. And the Captain was serving wine ... good tasting wine, but it seemed awfully strong."

"Yes, it did," Julie agreed. "And, my memories of the evening are about the same as yours," she noted, leaning back in the hammock. "I remember chatting with Sarah, the lady from Seattle, about her trips to Honduras. And from there, my memory is quite fuzzy."

"Do you suppose the Captain and his four idiot mates got us so drunk we passed out?" I asked, "then, took our money and passports and threw us overboard?"

"Darling, Ethan, do you really think something *that* sinister happened?" she questioned and then paused. "Well, perhaps though, something of that nature did happen. The guy with the scar on his face was flirting with me; I do remember that. And he was very inquisitive about how we would manage living on the island."

"Sorry dear, I didn't see him approach you. Was he harassing you with questions?"

"No, Darling, he was quite clever in his inquiry, but your suspicion makes perfect sense the more I think about it."

"Well," I said, "we *have to* locate the others tomorrow. They were leaving on Tuesday, so they should all be here before the end of the day."

"Ethan, we should check out the docks again tomorrow. What if the Captain and his cronies have plans for the others? There's no way to reach them by cell phone; there's no way to warn them!"

"You're right, Juls. Perhaps we should sneak away later tonight to have a look, after everyone has gone to bed. We have to be very cautious, however."

"Ethan, how much did you tell Leonardo or Francisco about our state of disarray when we arrived? Is there any possibility they suspect something?" Julie asked, being careful to whisper.

"Can't be certain," I said. "I told Leonardo that we had been fishing and had lost our wallets, and that our luggage hadn't arrived yet."

"Did he buy it?" Julie inquired, glancing around at the other couples strolling nearby.

"He seemed to have; but, at this point, we can't trust anyone, Julie."

"I know," she said, "let's wait awhile, and then we can go. Besides, I'm exhausted," she added, holding and gently stroking my arm. The steady clanking of diesel engines could be heard in the distance as a fleet of shrimp boats moved out of the protective waters of the harbor. The air was cool with a slight breeze. The ache in my shoulders felt as though my muscles were tied in square knots. Julie's head lay on my shoulder, and her leg dangled from the side of the hammock. We had fallen asleep. I lifted my arm to glance at my watch; but, of course, it wasn't there. I had forgotten.

The sky was filled with bright stars against a deep purple background. There were no clouds to be seen. The silhouette of a freighter inched silently across the horizon.

"Julie," I whispered. "Julie, wake up. We've missed it, I'm afraid."

"What?" she mumbled, as she, too, began to feel the stiffness in her neck and shoulders. "What time is it?" she asked.

"I don't know; remember, I lost my watch somewhere in the night."

"Oh yes, that's right. Is it too late to take a look around at the dock?"

"Do you really want to go now? It seems late," I said. "Besides, I don't want Francisco or any of the other workers to suspect what we're doing. And since we haven't moved from this hammock for hours, let's just go to our hut and crash."

"Okay Darling, you talked me into it; but, I'll be worried about the others if they don't show up by tomorrow afternoon." Julie climbed out of the hammock first and began to pull on my hand.

"Yes, so will I," I replied in a low voice as we started walking toward our room.

Chapter

5

The palm trees and hibiscus swayed gently in the morning breeze as the sun rose over Victoria House. Faint voices could be heard in the distance as some of the guests had made their way down for breakfast. The aroma of the breakfast bacon and coffee, however, had not yet made it to the hut where Julie and I were sleeping.

It had rained since we walked from the hammock to the hut, and the ground was damp and the air cool. My arm was numb from lying in the same position for most of the night. Julie had not moved much. She made soft snoring sounds during the night; although, she would never admit it. As I lay next to her watching her breathe, gently touching her hair and being careful not to wake her, I was reminded of her genteel beauty and what a lucky guy I was!

"What time is it?" Julie asked, as she began to wake, turning from her side to her back with her body partially covered by a sheet. Her tanned skin only accented her already olive complexion.

"I'm not sure," I replied in a low voice, my mind wrapped in thoughts of her, "but it's early, I don't think there are many people stirring about."

"Good!" Julie said, easing toward the small bath area and turning on the shower. "Darling, please go get us some coffee and juice, and maybe a newspaper. Perhaps we can begin to figure out this mystery. The coffee will be wonderful! Remember?" she said, referring to her memory of the Victoria House coffee during our last visit in 1996.

I returned with a small decanter of coffee, some freshly baked sweet rolls and a newspaper. Julie was still in the bathroom dressing. "I'm back!" I announced as I struggled to open the door with coffee, two cups, the two rolls, and a newspaper folded under my arm.

"Great, let me help with you with that," she said. Setting the coffee and rolls on the small round table that sat next to the bed, Julie poured each of us a cup of the strong, black coffee we had enjoyed before. She smiled and leaned over and kissed me on the lips. "Ethan, I love you so much," she whispered. Returning the kiss, I took another sip of coffee and retreated into the bathroom for my morning ritual, realizing I had no toothbrush. I washed my face, rinsed my mouth with water and returned to the table. Leaning down to plant a quick kiss on Julie's cheek, I said with one hand partially covering my mouth, "Sorry, Darling, there's no toothpaste. I know my breath is atrocious."

"I love you anyway, stinky breath and all. Sit down and enjoy the coffee; it's wonderful, just as I remembered," she said.

As we ate the fresh rolls still warm from the oven and drank the strong black coffee, Julie and I again attempted to reconstruct the events that had gotten us there, and to examine possible whereabouts of our friends. "O.K., let's lay out the events of the past 48 hours to see if we can connect the dots," Julie suggested, as I was devouring another roll.

There was a loud knock at the door. We gave each other a quick glance, and I said, "Yes, who is it?"

"It is Pablo, Señor Ethan. Papa sent me. You have a telephone call from America. He said for you to come quickly."

"Already?" I asked. But, before Pablo was able to respond, I stood, gave Julie a kiss and rushed out the door. "Stay here, and lock the door behind me," I shouted back toward the hut. "I'll be back in a flash. I hope this is Mike calling to confirm our money transfer."

"Ethan, do be careful, Darling," Julie said, as she watched Pablo and I walk toward the covered pavilion adjacent to the main lodge. Her mind began to wander as she thought of the other couples; and, for a moment, she felt guilty for enjoying the rolls and coffee. What had happened to the others? And, what *really* had happened to *us* on the boat? She poured another cup of coffee, stacked the bed pillows against the headboard of the bed, and sat scanning the newspaper, a week-old Wall Street Journal.

It wasn't long before I returned. Julie spotted me walking along the path leading from the lodge. My gait was almost leisurely. I noticed Julie peeking out the window of the hut, as if she were wondering what could be going on. As I got closer, Julie could see that the expression on my face was one of pleasant stupefaction. The handle rattled as I opened the door of the thatched hut and entered.

"Julie, Mike is a genus!" I said excitedly. "Everything is set. We will be receiving the wire this morning, by noon at the latest. He's sending a packet from American Express containing travelers' checks, two American Express cards, new passports and contact information for the account he has set up for us at the Bank of Belize in Belize City. We're back in business!"

Julie was a bit stunned at the lengths to which Mike, our friend of 18 years, had gone to assist us. "Darling," she said, jumping to her feet and giving me a leaping embrace, "this is great! Mike is a doll, isn't he?"

Her gleeful attitude faded. "But, what about the other couples? We haven't heard from them, and we haven't found our 'friend,' the Captain, either," Julie said with a tinge of worry or dread in her voice.

It was a stark reminder of what tasks lay before us. We had not heard from the others! We had to find them! And, we also wanted ...no, we *needed* ...to figure out what had happened to *us*. Were we in an accident, or was it something more sinister? This had been a long-awaited trip, a trip we had all talked and joked about, but it had always been just outside the realm of reality. Now, since we made a deal and sold the company, it had become real ... VERY real. It was becoming a bizarre story; one I wanted to discuss in detail once everyone in our group had safely arrived.

"Ethan, are you alright?" Julie asked, getting my attention.

"Oh, I'm fine," I said, as reality set in once again. "Let's go by the lodge and ask Francisco if he's heard anything from his circles about the arrival of our friends."

"Maybe," said Julie, "if we explain to Francisco and Leonardo the details of what has happened to us, they'll offer to help in solving this mystery."

"I think you're right, Julie," I said. "We need to trust somebody down here, and I think Francisco and Leonardo are probably the only people we CAN place our trust in, at this point anyway."

"I'm glad you agree, Ethan, Darling. It will make me feel better knowing that the Captain and his crew are not stalking us. I do think Francisco and Leonardo will help us," she said convincingly.

"Do you think the Captain might be around the docks at the pier, Ethan?" she asked. "Would we have any luck snooping around for a while?"

"I'm not sure," I said. "We can head toward the pier and try to find out more about the Captain and his boat. Leonardo said his cousin, Luis, hires out as a fishing and dive guide. If we can locate him, maybe we can uncover more clues. And, our friends should be arriving today unless they have run into problems."

"But, can we get in touch with them if they don't arrive?" she asked. "Do you think there's a way to access their ship's manifest?"

Julie pondered as she was undressing and dressing again, trying to decide what to wear. The selection of clothing that Leonardo's sister had sent was not impressive. Nothing really matched, which was slightly annoying. "How does this look, Ethan? Ah, never mind," she said with a chuckle. "I suppose we won't see anyone we know!"

"I suppose not; but, you look marvelous anyway, my sweets," I said as I wrapped my arms around her waist.

"Ethan, we haven't time for that now," she said, with emphasis on the word *now*. "But you are a darling; how could I ...no, how could we be so lucky as to have each other?" she mused. I said nothing, just kissed her gently on the back of her head. I tried to suppress my emotion.

Clearing my throat, I said, "You're right again! What a gorgeous piece of work you are! And, *you are* a very lucky person!" I laughed.

"Ethan, you are spoiled rotten to the core!" Julie shouted playfully. Her accent was suddenly thickened as she placed emphasis on the enunciation of her words, but with a wily grin. "Ethan, YOU are the one who is lucky, my dearest darling! Think about it!"

"Right O', Right O'," I replied, mimicking her accent. "Let's see if Francisco has a couple of bicycles we can borrow for the day."

"Oh, brilliant idea Ethan," Julie said. With that, we left the thatched hut, walked to the main lodge and secured the two bicycles. Francisco was eager and happy to assist.

Chapter

6

The ride into to town took only a few minutes and was pleasantly cool, although it was not yet nine o'clock. Once the sun began its ascent toward the midday mark, the temperature would quickly climb to a scorching 90 degrees or more. We went directly to the café and spoke with Leonardo, thanking him for his sister's help with the clothing. Leonardo pointed down the street, in the opposite direction of the church, and described his sister's shop. "She's expecting you today," he said. "Stop by, and she will help you with more clothes. And, Señor Ethan, did your friend from America reach you? He called earlier, and I told him you were staying at the Victoria."

"Yes, Leonardo. Thanks," I said. "We spoke with him this morning. I appreciate your help."

I paused.

"Leonardo," I continued, "there's something else we need to discuss with you."

"Yes, how can I help you?" Leonardo asked.

We began telling him the story of my waking up on the beach and Julie in the churchyard. "This is most concerning," he said quietly. "I will discuss this with Francisco, and we will help you, Ethan. You and your friends are welcome here! We will take care of you!"

"That would be great, Leonardo. Julie and I are going to look around at the docks and see what's happening there," I said.

"No problem," Leonardo said, returning to his work as other customers began to trickle in. "I will come to find you later. I will also call Francisco. He knows a lot of people who fish on the water. They will know something, that's almost certain," he said.

"What next?" Julie asked, as we walked out of Leonardo's café and into the street. Several small children were playing kick ball near the entrance to the churchyard, very near where Julie had spent the night two days earlier.

"Julie, look," I said pointing to the children, "I can't believe they're playing kickball."

"Ethan, didn't you play kickball as a child?"

"Oh yes, we played at school all the time. It was one of the major events every day. We couldn't wait until recess. We would run down the hill to the field, choose teams and get into it right away! We played kickball or baseball every day!"

We had left the bicycles at the café in order to survey the docks again. As we made our way along the dusty road, my thoughts began to wander. My eyes moistened as I recalled the day my grandfather took me to the Western Auto Store to pick out my first glove. It was brown leather, with a deep pocket and extra padding. It was a great glove. My eyes beamed as we walked out of the Western Auto and got into my grandfather's old Dodge truck. Life was good indeed.

"Ethan, Ethan," Julie said, noticing that my mind was wandering. "Ethan, when do you suppose the others will arrive?" Julie asked in a low voice as we continued walking. Julie's nudging question quickly refocused my attention on the current crisis.

"Sorry," I said, snapping back and looking quickly to the left and right. "I'm not sure, Julie. Let's go over to the docks and do a little nosing around. And, if we can find Leonardo's cousin, Luis, perhaps he can tell us where to inquire about the other ships' manifestos. In fact, it would be helpful if Luis could accompany us to the International Maritime Office in Belize City. Maybe, if we go there, we can find the approximate arrival times of the other ships," I said.

Looking consumed by a thought, Julie remarked, "Do you recall the names of the other two ships?"

"Yes," I said, hesitating slightly, "I think one is *The Water Crest* and the other is called, um, let me think...*The Sunbeam II*. Yes, that's it." Julie seemed relieved that I remembered the names of the ships our friends had boarded. The ships that William and Elizabeth and Bob and Lindsey had chartered were called 'windjammers' ... boats designed for passengers who worked as part of the crew. They were similar to the *MISS SHEILA*, the boat on which Julie and I had sailed. The boats were designed to function with full flaps of fore-and-aft sails. But, in case the inexperienced crew couldn't get the job done, the boats were also equipped with twin 3.9 Cummins diesel marine engines, and enough horsepower to get you across the Caribbean and up the east coast.

There were people all around the dock area. It was a place of daily commerce, where fishing boats unloaded their daily catch, and where supplies from the mainland came into port. It was also where the clipper ships, large seafaring boats, and charter boats were docked. Some who sailed around the Caribbean often would moor their boats for weeks at a time. Julie and I hoped we could snoop around the dock area and overhear something that might shed light on the events of the past 72 hours. We were also hoping to learn more precisely when the other boats might be arriving. Leonardo and Francisco were now clued in to our predicament and had agreed to help in our efforts to solve at least part of the mystery.

"Julie, do you see those guys in the dive shop?" I asked.

"Yes, and one of them looks like a mate that was on our boat," she said.

"Let's go in for a closer look," I said. "Maybe we can get a glimpse of who he is and watch the place for a while to see where he goes," I said. "Then, hopefully, Leonardo can advise us on how to address the situation with the authorities."

"Ethan," Julie said, her eyes glued on the half painted window in the wall of the dive shop. "Look, Ethan, there," she said, pointing gingerly with her finger. "I believe it's the Captain!"

"Are you serious, Julie?" I asked. "Is it really him?"

"I wouldn't kid you about this. I *do* believe it's him," she said.

"Let's go for a chance encounter," I suggested.

"Oh, I don't know.....Ethan...wait for me," she said.

Our hands were sweaty and our knees knocked as we walked up the boardwalk and entered the dive shop. The door seemed stuck as I attempted to open it; then suddenly, without warning, the door broke loose and we were face to face with the Captain. My chest bumped his, and we obviously startled each other. The door bounced off the wall and swung on its hinges back to the closing position. Without thinking, and in an accusatory tone, I shouted, "Captain, Captain, I've been looking everywhere for you ...ever since you dumped me off the boat! Where is the rest of my money? And, where is my passport?"

This encounter happened so suddenly! My mind was a blur, and I soon realized I was not even hearing what I was saying to the Captain! My outburst, apparently, was a reaction to all the frustration and uncertainty I had associated with my washing up on the beach.

Julie was at first stunned by my newfound tenacity, but quickly became concerned, as my shouting played out.

"Yes!" she joined in, "We need to talk!" she said sternly, pushing me forward toward the Captain as if to ensure the intimidation factor was still present. The Captain began to mumble and stutter, as we all three stumbled backward inside the dive shop.

"Sir, I know nothing about your problem. We docked at..."

But, before he could finish his sentence, I had a rush of adrenaline, and pinned the Captain to the wall with a crow bar. "Oh yes you do, you dirty bastard! Now tell me what happened that night. How did I end up in the water? And where is my money?"

I felt someone tugging at my arm, "But, Sir, I know nothing, I swear." Another crew member was pulling at me, and Julie was swinging anything she could get her hands on.

BANG! A deafening shot rang out! The dive shop owner, Scott, had fired a blank flare gun. "Nobody move!" he yelled, holding a spear gun in his left hand.

"Now, everyone separate; stand on opposites sides of the shop. And, if anybody makes a wrong move, you'll be wearing a designer spear, because I'll shoot your ass!"

Everybody was clear on the directions that had been given. We began to slowly straighten up and move to one side or the other of the tiny dive shop. For what seemed an eternal minute, nobody spoke. We studied each other; and finally, everybody's breathing slowed.

"Remember, nobody moves," he said, as he jabbed the dive spear in the air in a forward motion.

Looking toward the Captain, Scott demanded, "Now, Captain Riley, tell these folks what you just told me this morning about their unfortunate mishap."

"Looking down, then up again," the Captain hesitated.

"Tell them, damn it!" Scott shouted, "Or I'll poke you with this spear gun!"

"O.K., O.K.," the Captain murmured, wiping a taste of blood from his lip. He began to recount the sequence of events that began with their approach to the reefs and the Bay of Belize, just off the northern coast of Ambergris Caye and north of Belize City, the country's largest and most populated metropolitan area.

"Everyone had been drinking and having a grand time," the Captain began. "When we docked, everyone except you two and another couple ...the Sloans, I think ...disembarked."

The air was so tense and thick you could cut it with a knife. "Go on, go on!" I barked, looking the Captain in the eye suspiciously.

"The crew and I left the boat," he said, "and when we returned, all the passengers had gone. The last I saw of you and Miss Julie was down below. When the crew left the boat, I had no idea where you two were. And, I know nothing about your money. I swear!"

An eerie silence filled the tiny dive shop. Scott stood with his muscles flinched and a death grip on the spear gun. Suddenly, without notice, the door of the shop swung open. It was eleven-year-old Pablo, Leonardo's son. With his eyes peering up and glancing from one side of the room to the other, he spoke quickly, "Scott, can I see you for a moment, out here?" He pointed to the other side of the door.

"Pablo..., I'm kinda busy."

"I know, Scott," Pablo insisted, "but I think I can help."

"What? Pablo, tell us, tell us." Scott urged.

"Yes son, tell them now," Leonardo agreed, as he appeared in the doorway behind his son.

"I was playing in the street with Emilio the night the sailing boat came in, and we saw two men board the boat. They came out a few minutes later carrying *her,*" he exclaimed, pointing to Julie.

"But it was not the Captain," Pablo continued. "The Captain would not do such a thing! He is good to me, and I have known him for a long time."

Pablo began to weep, then went on to further describe what he had seen. Pablo's voice echoed through the otherwise silent dive shop.

"I believe what Pablo has described, Ethan," Scott said. "The Captain might drink too much sometimes, but he is not a kidnapper, nor a thief."

These words seemed to relieve the Captain somewhat. He appeared humbled now, his body more relaxed. The tension eased.

After a moment, looking to Julie for a sign, I quipped, "Okay, Okay, but this isn't over. I hope, for Pablo's sake, you're telling the truth."

And with that, we turned and walked out of the dive shop, pausing just outside the door before moving toward the street. The sun was at the baking stage now, and we were exhausted from the confrontation in the shop and the downside of the adrenaline rush.

Looking straight ahead, I said in a low voice, "Come on, Julie, let's go find someplace to get a beer. We've got more thinking to do."

Chapter

7

Friday: 10:00 P.M.

The schooner *Water Crest* was pulling into port at Ambergris Caye. The Captain's announcement blared over the ship's PA system reminding the passenger-crew of a final departure meeting on deck. Bob and Lindsey smiled at each other as both were heavily engaged in reeling in the excess rigging attached to the forward sails. They had boarded the *Water Crest* in New Orleans and were eager to hook up with the rest of their dream-team travel companions.

Bob and Lindsay's trip had been fabulous; everything they had hoped for. Their captain, David Smyth, and his wife, Mia, were extraordinary hosts. Mia, an accomplished chef, kept them well fed throughout the voyage. As members of the windjammer sailing crew, Bob and Lindsey's trip had been part work and part play, but one hundred percent exhilaration. Bob and Lindsey, as well as William and Elizabeth, had opted to sail with a more exclusive schooner and clipper ship company. They had been concerned about Julie and me, since our charter was with a lesser-known company at a bargain price. Julie and I had made the decision to get to Belize as quickly as possible, and we had suffered the consequences.

The final meeting of the *Water Crest's* passengers and crew was somewhat poignant. Captain David began the meeting as he had the first meeting shortly after they set sail from New Orleans three days earlier ...with a toast of cheap champagne purchased at the duty-free shop. He noted that the pleasure had been his and Mia's, for having had the opportunity to work with such a fun-filled and hardworking crew of passengers, each with his own mission for sailing to Belize. The arrival party for the Port of Call to Ambergris Caye continued with a buffet of exquisite cuisine set for a king. The dining crew, led by Mia, had put together a spread of food, wines and exotic beers so delicious that it made some of the passengers reluctant to leave. The party went on for hours.

Bob and Lindsey left the ship around 12:30 A.M. and set out to find their quarters, which had been prearranged before leaving New Orleans. The *Hotel Coral Bay* was a short walk up the beach road. Streetlights, dimly lit, marked their route. The crunching of the limestone under their feet marked a sharp contrast to the sounds of the sea they had heard for three days and nights while sailing on the schooner. Soon they arrived at the *Hotel Coral Bay* and went by the hotel office to find an envelope inscribed with their names. Inside the envelope were two room keys and a note. *"Hope you had an enjoyable trip. Welcome to Belize!"*

Exhausted, they made their way to room 206 and unlocked the door to a cool, air-conditioned room. This was a luxury in itself, since electricity on the Caye was highly controlled by the Belizean government who charged exorbitant fees, except to Americans.

In 1995, the Belizean government created the Foreign Retirement Program, referred to as the FRP. Americans and other foreigners who wanted to retire to Belize, buy real estate there, or live in the country for at least six months out of the year, could do so by providing verification that they had a minimum of $10,000.00 per month of pension or investment residuals. These assets had to be deposited into the Bank of Belize that is operated by the Belizean government. The influx of U.S. currency and U.S. citizens had positively impacted the Belizean economy.

Bob and Lindsey had set up an offshore account in the Bahamas through the use of a Limited Liability Corporation they called B & L Enterprises, LLC. This was a commonly used mechanism through which money, such as 401k funds or other qualified pre-tax assets could be transferred on an as-needed basis to their account in Belize. As a bonus, these funds would be tax-free, since using the LLC in the Bahamas fell outside the provisions of the U.S. Government and the IRS.

Belize, although a popular dive spot with the second largest barrier reef in the world off its shoreline, is largely a third world country. Formerly British Honduras, the Brits left the country in 1982, and slowly Belize carved itself a niche in the world of commerce. Being able to take advantage of the tax breaks and avoid much of the Belizean red tape pleased Bob and Lindsey.

After a quick shower, they fell into a deep sleep. At seven A.M. the next morning, a knock on the door awakened them. Groggy and stiff from their sailing trip and suffering from the morning after effects of their party with the crew, they were not happy to be awakened so early. Bob staggered to the door, looked through the peep hole and saw nothing. Opening the door, he found a note taped to the brass room numbers. It was a hotel envelope with the raised crest of the *Hotel Coral Bay* in the upper left hand corner. Bob opened the envelope and read the note.

> *Bob and Lindsey,*
> *Hope you had a great trip. We are at the Victoria. Meet us for breakfast at 10:00 A.M. at the San Pedro Café ...or call us. Francisco will get us to the phone.*
> *Ethan & Julie*

"Well, well, honey, look at this. It's a note from Ethan and Julie; they're at the Victoria," Bob said as he walked back toward the bed and sat down.

"Really," Lindsey replied, not leaving the comfort of the bed. "Where are they?" she asked with a little more curiosity as she rolled over to face Bob.

"This note says they are staying at the Victoria. I thought they had a different place arranged for their temporary accommodations," Bob said, scratching his head and rubbing his eyes.

By this time, Lindsey was in the shower. Bob wandered over to a table near the dressing area in their room and surveyed the wide selection of coffees. Each room at the *Hotel Coral Bay* was supplied with several bags of coffee, each labeled as a different strength. Bob started a pot of the strongest blend. He knew he would need all the caffeine he could drink. Soon they would be on their way to meet Julie and me, and would begin to hear the story of our mysterious adventure.

* * * * * * * * * * * * *

Bob and Lindsey met in 1978 at a Bee Gees concert in Asheville, North Carolina; both were in college at the University of North Carolina at Chapel Hill, and both had a free-spirit approach to life. Lindsey majored in business and marketing, while Bob pursued a degree in political science and finished with an MBA before leaving the university setting. Bob and Lindsey were married in Asheville, in 1982, at the Grove Park Inn. The old resort hotel that overlooked the city in one direction and the Blue Ridge Mountains in another had become their favorite place to visit.

They moved to Asheville in the summer of 1988 and Bob opened his restaurant, *La Saveur de Asheville*, in the downtown area. The restaurant offered fine dining in the midst of the art galleries and boutiques just off Market Street. Lindsey worked in the banking industry, and was in charge of corporate lending and development at a prominent Asheville bank. Asheville had become a Mecca for people from all types of backgrounds, cultures and ethnicities. It had become cosmopolitan with a Smoky Mountain flair. Attracting eccentric and unusual people to the area had begun when the Vanderbilt's built the now famous Biltmore Estate, and had continued later when the Grove Park Inn was constructed.

Bob and Lindsey met Julie and me at Bob's restaurant in 1990, when we were in Asheville on a weekend excursion. We became friends quickly and a steadfast friendship began developing. In the spring of 1997, Bob and Lindsey, along with William and Elizabeth, formed a consulting company with Julie and me. Soon after, Julie and I bought our townhouse in Asheville. The six of us began discussing the idea of leaving the country for a year to take a break from the hustle and bustle of life in the city. Once, Bob had even tacked a picture of a tropical island on the wall behind the bar at his restaurant. It was a random picture; but, he would tell everyone it was his retirement destination. The photo became THE conversation piece at the bar with the regular customers. The idea of living on an island for a year was an intriguing one. But, once it became a reality, it would require more than any of us expected. It would endanger our lives and force us all to refocus and reprioritize.

* * * * * * * * * * * * *

We had just ordered coffee when Bob and Lindsey walked up. Julie had managed to put together a matching outfit of pleated yellow shorts and a white blouse with embroidered flowers around the shoulders. The tail of her blouse was cinched around her waist, and she had found a pair of white sandals and tied a piece of yellow ribbon in her hair. She looked great.

"Ethan, Julie, how are you guys? We made it," Bob announced as he and Lindsey joined us at the small table outside the front door of Leonardo's café.

"Great! Great to see you guys," I said standing and shaking Bob's hand.

"We're so glad you're here. How was your trip?" Julie asked, giving Lindsey a slight embrace.

"Sit down," I said. "Julie and I have just ordered coffee. Let me get the waiter's attention so you guys can order."

The waiter had already noticed that another couple had joined us, and he hurried over with coffee for all of us. He took our orders for breakfast, and our conversation resumed.

"So why are you guys staying at the Victoria?" Bob asked with great curiosity. "I thought you were going to stay on board the ship or some other place until we arrived? And, have you heard from William and Elizabeth? Have they made it down yet?"

Glancing at Julie and pausing momentarily, I began to reconstruct the events of the past four days. Pausing for refills of coffee and mango juice, Julie and I laid out all known details. Taking a napkin, I drew a series of boxes, abbreviated an event in each one, and drew connecting lines with arrows from each box to the next, identifying the known sequence of events. Then, in the margins, I listed other extraneous details; those that didn't particularly fit on the continuum of events. I had created a storyboard of sorts, perhaps clarifying for myself as well as explaining to Bob and Lindsey.

"That's amazing! I can't believe it! I'm glad you two are okay," said Lindsey. "And thank God for Mike; he came through in a pinch. So, when are you guys going to the police about the Captain?" Lindsey asked, shocked about the ordeal Julie and I had been through.

"We thought about that, and we have considered registering a complaint with the International Maritime Office in Belize City, but we're also working a different angle," I replied. "If the Captain or any of his crew really took our money, then it will show up eventually. Somebody will want to spend it. And between Leonardo and Francisco, and all their cousins, maybe we'll discover the truth. If the Captain and his mates are guilty, then we'll have our proof. Americans seem to have a good deal of clout down here with the government officials, especially if they think you're loaded."

"What about William and Elizabeth?" Lindsey asked again, reminding the group that their *La Troika* was still missing a link.

"We're hoping they sail in today," Julie answered. "Remember, they were in the last group to leave."

"What was the name of their ship, Julie? Do you remember?" Lindsey asked.

"It was the *Sunbeam II*," Julie said, her British accent glaring a bit.

"That's it, the *Sunbeam II*," Bob said, repeating the name.

"Should we check with the Port Authority to see if they have heard from the *Sunbeam II*?" Lindsey suggested. "Maybe they can give us an approximate arrival time," she added as they rose from the small table. The sun was bearing down on eastern wall of the small cafe, and the temperature had begun to rise. It was going to be a hot day in San Pedro.

"I'll catch the tab," Bob said, reaching in his wallet for a twenty-dollar bill. "You guys have been through enough. You deserve a break."

"Okay," I replied, "I'll let you get it this time."

Bob paid the waiter, included a generous tip, and we began the short walk north, along the docks toward the Port Authority Office.

Chapter

8

The Port Authority Office was filled with people, mostly locals who were waiting for the ferry to complete its hour-long trip from the mainland. A lot of the local residents of Ambergris Caye made the trip over to work or shop the markets, or to get medical treatment whenever necessary. There was no public medical clinic on the Caye. If medical emergencies arose, a small piper cub was on standby for the short thirty-minute flight to Belize City.

Waiting outside the Port Authority Office, we sat on a bench looking out toward the Gulf of Mexico. Bob, Lindsey, Julie, and I began to plan our next moves, assuming William and Elizabeth would agree. As soon as they arrived, we would all go to Victoria House and secure accommodations for all of us. Given the circumstances, and the unresolved mystery surrounding our ordeal, we agreed that safety in numbers was a good idea.

William and I had met in college at Vanderbilt University while we were both working on our graduate degrees. We had roomed together for two summers, focusing on intensive work and study, both of us having cleared our calendars of work and family play in order to complete the coursework leading to our terminal degrees. William had grown up in rural Illinois and worked for a small college in the southern part of the state. He was on a career track that would eventually lead to an executive position with the college. He and I had hit it off right away. When our wives finally met, the journey of their friendship began.

William's wife, Elizabeth, was his high school sweetheart. They had been married almost all their adult lives and were a delightful couple. Elizabeth was a school teacher and was interested in archeology and the unspoiled Mayan ruins. William and Elizabeth were also founding partners in our consulting company. Given both their backgrounds and career areas, the partnership served them well, allowing them to pick up contract consulting in areas related to their professions.

We had all converged in Asheville and met at Bob's restaurant to first discuss the idea of going to live on an island. It became a game-like activity. Instead of Monopoly or Clue, we would meet in Nashville or Asheville, and play our version of Let's Make A Deal on a 'Fantasy Island' trip. When the conversation became more serious, both William and Elizabeth were reluctant, but later decided to take the sabbatical.

* * * * * * * * * * * * * * * *

The door of the Port Authority Office squeaked as a young Belizean boy opened it and stepped over to Bob and Lindsey, who were sitting on the end of the wooden bench closest to the office.

"Señor," the boy called. "Señor, your friends, they are on that ship over there," he said, pointing toward the east to the horizon.

"The Captain has just radioed in and given his position and course settings. They should arrive in about an hour," the boy repeated, and then disappeared back into the Port Authority Office.

Looking silently at each other, there seemed to be a long pause, as if each of us was trying to decide the next move. We didn't want to scare William and Elizabeth.

"Ethan," Bob said, breaking the silent stares and listless cloud of apprehension that seemed to have come over us. "I thought you had made arrangements for a house down here. Are we on track for that?" Bob asked, leaning forward slightly to make eye contact. The wives said nothing, but waited for my response.

"Yes Bob, but we need to wait on William," I answered. "The house is owned by the law professor William had at Vanderbilt. William and I made the arrangements on my last trip to Nashville."

"So we're good to go there?" Bob asked, needing reassurance that the arrangements for accommodations for the next twelve months had not vanished the same way our money had.

"We're good to go, Bob. Relax," I reassured him. "As soon as William and Elizabeth arrive, we'll get everybody checked in at the Victoria, and then we'll phone the caretaker of the property. Leonardo can help us with getting everything moved over to the house when we get the key."

"How far from the Victoria is the rental house?" Bob asked. I sensed a little testiness in Bob's questions. Lindsey gently slid her hand underneath his arm and around his elbow and forearm in an effort to calm him. She knew full well that the Bob's persistent questioning was due to his chronic frustration and lack of patience.

"It's less than a mile actually. They're expecting us in fact," I said, never looking up.

"Bob, don't worry," I encouraged. "Unless some strange events have happened to William and Elizabeth, Julie and I are the only ones to have had a little bad luck. And, after all, you and Lindsey tried to convince us not to contract with the lesser-known charter company. Remember?" I knew I had regained Bob's confidence once I saw his reaction to this reminder. It was like someone had released the pressure valve.

"You're right," Bob said, smiling. "Besides, we're supposed to be letting go of expectations, right?"

Everybody nodded and began to laugh a little.

"Let's get out into the sun. I think this small and crowded building is getting to us," Julie said, turning on her British accent and hoping for a favorable reaction.

"You are absolutely right, Julie," Bob said, rising to his feet. "Let's get a cold beer. Come on, we have an hour according to what the boy said."

It was the right suggestion at the right time. The ordeal of the journey and the uncertainty of our situation, along with a lack of initial enthusiasm had momentarily caused Bob to become distracted from our purpose. He had just experienced his first battle with the difficulty of 'letting go' of the trappings of his old world. I was very confident of the arrangements, but also knew that if we needed a back-up plan, Francisco's Victoria House could serve as a temporary base until other arrangements could be made. What Bob and

Lindsey had not realized was that Belize, and especially Ambergris Caye, had become very much Americanized. The government of Belize not only wanted, but desperately needed the infusion of U.S. currency; therefore, the real estate market was particularly slanted toward the needs and wants of wealthy Americans and other foreigners who were coming to Belize to retire or take long sabbaticals. Besides, in my opinion at least, if we had to adjust our plans, it would add an element of mystery and intrigue to our adventure.

Chapter

9

Back at Leonardo's place, the San Pedro Café, Bob and Lindsey, Julie and I ordered a round of cold beer and a plate of quesadillas. We had been enjoying the opportunity to relax and unwind when the young boy from the Port Authority Office found us and announced that the *Sunbeam II* was about to dock.

"Wow," Bob said looking surprised, "that was a quick hour."

I motioned to the waiter and Bob reached for his wallet, "What's our share, Ethan?" Bob asked.

"Not to worry my friend; I told you at breakfast that the next one was on me." I reminded him. Julie and Lindsey had excused themselves to the restroom to freshen up and returned just as the waiter was taking my payment.

"Ready to go, girls?" I asked, looking shyly at Julie. She was radiant. Lindsey was straightening her blouse as Bob reached around with his right arm and embraced her. She cocked her head, looking up at him with a smirk, as if to suggest that he was acting strangely.

"Linds," Bob said in a relaxed voice after having consumed several glasses of Red Label beer, "You are gorgeous and I'm glad we're here. I haven't felt this adventurous since we first moved to Asheville." Over the years, Bob had become more influenced by the grinding corporate world than he realized.

"Well, I'm glad Bob, because we *are* here for a *year*!" Lindsey said in a giddy voice. The Red Label beer had loosened Bob's anxiety about striking out on such an adventure. He hoped Lindsey would become a bit more amiable later ...when the evening sun collided with the horizon.

Walking back to the Port Authority Office, we could see the mast of the *Sunbeam II*, which stood just on the other side of The *Water Crest*. It was moored at the end of the docking pier. People were busily disembarking the ship and loading the nearby ferry. The loading dock was a busy place, especially when ships arrived. A steady line of people, all residents of the Caye, hurriedly walked to the ferry, which was filling fast. It was the second ferry of the day, and the next would not run until 3:00 P.M.

Lindsey could see William's head over all the others in the Port Authority Office. William and Elizabeth were making some last minute currency exchange transactions before departing the dock, not aware that we awaited them outside the Port Office. A stack of luggage and boxes sat next to a bench outside the dockside door, and attached was an American Airlines tag that read "*ORD*", "This must be theirs," I said, since it's tagged from Chicago.

"Do *all* these belong to William and Elizabeth?" Julie asked. She leaned down to examine the stack more closely, her hair falling down atop her shoulders and exposing the brown skin on the nape of her neck.

Just then the door of the office swung open, "Hi guys! Whew! We made it!" William shouted while at the same time reaching to shake hands and exchange hugs. "Hi guys!" William said again, taking my hand, "Damn, it's great to finally see you all and to actually *be here*! I'm glad to be on solid ground again."

"Lindsey, Julie, how are you guys?" William asked, making his way around the group. He was clearly ecstatic about his and Elizabeth's new adventure.

"How was your trip?" Julie asked, "Wasn't this your first trip on a sailing ship?"

"Oh, it was great," Elizabeth answered. "William enjoyed himself too much last night and woke up this morning with a slight headache, but other than that, we're good," she added. There was something in her voice, however, that made it quite obvious that the trip had not been as enjoyable for her as it had been for William.

"Are you ready? Everything clear here?" I inquired.

"Yep! Let's get going," William replied, bubbling over with excitement like a kid with a new toy. That was his personality, fun-loving and gleeful. William enjoyed life, although he had a serious side and was very smart. Elizabeth, on the other hand, was a bit more reserved. She would loosen up eventually, once she had time to re-ground herself and adjust to a slower, less formal lifestyle. She was always reluctant in making changes to the 'norm' ...just the opposite of William, who hit the ground running and then made adjustments.

Elizabeth grew up in Louisville, Kentucky, in a rather affluent section of town. Her father was a successful businessman and had accumulated a number of well performing investments. The family had a big house on a small horse farm, and held partial interest in several businesses around Louisville. Elizabeth had grown up in the world of high society and Bluegrass money. She and William had gone to high school together, although he moved away during the summer of his junior year. His family had moved to southern Illinois. Though William has a charismatic and verbose personality now, he was very shy as a young man.

William grew up on the poor side of Louisville, actually just outside the city limits, in a small blue-collar neighborhood. His mother worked two jobs, and had divorced his dad when William was a child. As a young man, he too, worked several jobs, but managed to play sports and was popular with most of the other kids in school. William had been an intelligent, suave and debonair young man, and sometimes had an air about him, which was mostly a disguise. He was actually shy and reserved, and knew full well the differences in his family and the wealthier families of the sometimes snobbish town girls. He and Elizabeth met in the school library while both were doing research for a class. He was a sophomore and she was a junior, but when their eyes met, it was all over. It would take several years for them to fully realize their love for each other.

* * * * * * * * * * * * *

"So, where do we go from here, guys?" Elizabeth asked, looking like she could use a shower or swim. She and William were both exhausted from the three-day sailing excursion.

"Well, that's a detail we need to talk about," I said. "While waiting on you guys to get here, we had discussed the idea of everybody staying at one place until we get the house secured. So, what do you guys think about hanging out at the Victoria House? We can stay there for a few days, maybe even a week or ten days. That would allow us plenty of time to become acclimated to the area, as well as get the big house ready. Bob and Lindsey have agreed to move their stuff over, and Julie and I are already staying there. Besides, we need to bring you guys up to date."

"You got that right," Bob mumbled. "You're not going to believe it."

"What? What? What's happened, Buddy?" William responded, chuckling as he spoke, and knowing that I was always covering an angle.

Turning toward Elizabeth, William looked to her for approval and agreement, "Sure, that's fine with us. Besides, this is supposed to be an adventure, right?" she said, and began to snicker. Julie and Lindsey helped her with her bags while the guys picked up the boxes.

"Let's take this stuff down to Leonardo's and see if we can borrow some hand trucks," I suggested.

"You know, maybe Leonardo will just give us a key since we've been there so much," Bob retorted. He grunted as he lifted a box marked *"Personal"*. "My God, Elizabeth, what do you have in here, rocks from home?" he exclaimed! He grunted again as he lifted.

"No, Bob, it's just a year's worth of books," she responded with a smile, as she, Julie and Lindsey began walking ahead of us down the dusty gravel road. With the sun high above, it was scorching hot. We couldn't wait until we reached Leonardo's for a break and a good dinner before moving on toward the Victoria House.

Chapter

10

"Leonardo," I called as I stepped up onto the wooden veranda adjacent to the open-air bar and restaurant area.

"Yes, Señor Ethan. Your friends finally made it from America?" Leonardo asked, as all six of us gathered amidst our collective belongings brought to hold us for a year. Introductions were made, and Bob, William, and I went aside with Leonardo and Francisco to discuss arrangements for another few days of lodging for all three couples.

"No problem Señor, no problem whatsoever! It is my pleasure to take care of your friends," Francisco said in a pleasant tone. He seemed genuinely happy to be able to assist us with our accommodations. Francisco was Leonardo's brother, and they were inseparable. Both had grown up on the island, and both ran businesses there. I had managed to establish a strong rapport with Leonardo, and I was quickly becoming friends with Francisco, as well. Leonardo also agreed to assist us with getting the rental house cleaned and set up for our move.

Bob and Lindsey walked back to the *Hotel Coral Bay* to retrieve their belongings while the rest of us sat down with Leonardo to have some refreshment. "Does either of the other ladies need clothes, Señor Ethan?" Leonardo asked. "My sister has a new shipment. I can get her to bring some samples by in the morning if you would like," he said with a smile as he looked toward Julie, Lindsey and Elizabeth.

"No, thanks," I said, "not at the moment Leonardo, but I'll be sure to let you know if we need clothes later."

"What was that about the clothes, Ethan?" William asked when Leonardo left our table to welcome some arriving restaurant patrons.

"I'll explain later," I said, "better yet, ask Julie if she would like for Leonardo's sister to bring her some *more* clothes," I added with a chuckle. "She had a challenge finding a coordinating outfit." William looked at me with a quirky look, and laughed. "Seriously, you know how picky Julie can be with her clothes, and Leonardo's sister was being very generous, and we truly appreciated that," I said, trying not to give William the wrong impression.

"Nope, Buddy, I smell a trap here," he said, "but I'm curious as heck!"

By the time Bob and Lindsey returned, William and I had consumed three bottles each of Red Label beer, and William was working on his fourth. Julie and Elizabeth were nursing their first Piña Coladas. Dinner would consist of fried chicken, island-style, which was an attempt by Leonardo to make us feel at home. He had also included a sumptuous dish of black beans and rice, and fried plantains topped with powdered sugar. It was needed nourishment for the task ahead.

On arrival at the Victoria House, Francisco provided the other two couples with keys to their own thatched huts, adjacent to ours. By the time we reached our huts, we were exhausted from carrying all the luggage and boxes in the extreme heat. We had also had several beers, which intensified our physical exhaustion. Bob and William crashed as soon as their luggage was brought inside; and, I was already dozing as Julie undressed and stepped into the shower.

The night sky was clear and the stars were plentiful. With her hair wet from the shower, Julie grabbed her brush and pulled on my foot. Glancing back over her shoulder, she walked out into the darkness and found an empty mesh hammock hanging between two nearby palm trees. She was wearing nothing but an oversized t-shirt as she sank into the mesh netting of the hammock. I quickly joined her, and we lay there snuggled together until the late hours of the night, until all the background noises and laughter from the bar had long gone silent.

Chapter

11

The house was enormous, built in the early 1950s in the height of British control of the area, when the country was called British Honduras. It was lined with heavy, dark mahogany paneling, polished to perfection to yield an amber glow aged by time. The entry doors were adorned with stained leaded glass, imported from Havana when the house was built. The transit window served as the crown of the entry, with a cut glass cross slightly tinted for effect. The entry was filled, from one side to the other, with dark oak flooring that spanned across two rooms and was lined with old fluffy couches and stuffed chairs and accented with side tables of the same dark and polished mahogany. The tall curtainless windows ushered in dim sunlight and framed the house in simple island elegance. We stepped into the house, as Miguel and Fernando, Leonardo's two young cousins, brought in our luggage. They set the pieces down just inside the doorway, and waited.

We all just stood there, in awe, as if time had suddenly stopped. Each of us examined, with deep contemplation and reverent stares, every inch of the large expansive room. It had an old elegance. We had stepped back in time ...to a time when world travelers of the day knew this place where a friendly game of cards, a smooth three fingers of scotch, or a delicious evening meal could be found for those who were acquainted with the home's owners. Yes, there was an aura about this place.

Without moving a muscle, Bob said in a monotonic voice, "Holy Moses, what have we here? Have you guys ever seen anything like this?"

One by one, our feet began to shuffle as we turned our bodies ever so slightly from left to right, as if following a line of circumference.

"This is grand," Lindsey remarked, bending down to grab a bag, but not taking her eyes off the ornate crown molding and the large paintings that hung around her. For a moment, she thought of the galleries in Asheville, off Market Street.

Bob and William were taking care of the two young porters with a tip of crunchy dollar bills and change. The boys preferred the coins over the bills. The rattle of the coins seemed to provide an element of entertainment, as well as some level of clout among the youngsters in the area. The boys scampered away, as if they were running away from a haunted house, jingling their coins as they ran.

"Shall we explore the house?" I asked, hoping to break the awestruck silence, as I had sensed the effect of the house on our group.

"Yes, yes, let's do," Julie quipped. "Come on, you guys, snap out of it. Let's go explore the other rooms," she said again, and off she went. She disappeared through the doors leading from the large living room. Looking around with a quick glance, Lindsey and Elizabeth smiled, and hurried to catch up with Julie.

Elizabeth turned without stopping and said, "Come on, boys," as one corner of her mouth curled up in a devilish grin.

The kitchen and dining areas were located to the rear of the house. The kitchen was lined with cabinets, and counters, and a large copper sink, positioned in front of an expansive rectangular shaped window that offered a panoramic view of the woods to the back of the house. The dining room was adjacent to the kitchen, and contained an old oak dining table with hand-sculpted legs. The chairs that sat around the table were an odd assortment, some matching the obvious ornate style of the table, others being of an odd lot. Two hand-made corner cabinets occupied the two inside corners of the room, while a curio cabinet and hat stand filled the remaining corners. It was as if the former occupants had just vacated the room. The dark, amber colored oak flooring gave the room a soft glow.

A rather roomy study and small bedroom and bathroom separated the dining and kitchen areas from the large front room that had captured our imagination when we first entered the house.

"What's in this door?" Bob asked, as he opened a small, narrow door. At first, it looked like a closet door, but, to his surprise, it wasn't.

"Look guys, it's the stairs," Bob exclaimed. Each of us took a turn looking up the narrow stairway, which was dimly lit and smelled musty. We all hesitated to ascend.

"Who'll be first?" I finally asked.

"I will," Elizabeth said and stepped forward. Bending over, she began to climb the stairs. As she reached the top of the stairway, she turned and yelled, "William, are you coming?" Laughing and shaking his head, William leaned forward, twisted his upper body and took the first step.

"Come on, you guys. It's beautiful. You're not going to believe it," rang Elizabeth's voice. Looking a little surprised, we all crept up the stairs, one by one. And once we reached the top, each of us had the same response.

"Wow!"

"Man! What a place!"

"What a view!"

"Can you believe it?"

The upstairs was expansive with a roomy sitting area and a full bathroom complete with a large claw foot tub. Beside the tub, a large stained glass window overlooked the gulf and the lawn area between the house and the beach. There were four bedrooms off the sitting area, each with a dormer window, a small closet, a full-sized bed, a small dresser and a wash table and mirror.

The sitting parlor, which served as a common area connecting the four upstairs bedrooms, was filled with stuffy chairs and side tables, two legal bookcases and a humidor. A pole lamp stood beside each chair. This was obviously the place where guests or family gathered before retiring for the evening. It was quaint. It was charming. It was definitely old world. And, it would become our refuge, our safe port in a storm.

Chapter

12

In the back of the house, our wives had assembled in the kitchen and were discussing which couple would move into which room when we walked through the door.

"What are you three scheming?" William said through his famous grin.

"Yeah," Bob retorted, "What are you girls planning now?"

I looked toward Julie, who wasn't saying anything, and who smiled when our eyes met, as if to say *I'll explain later*.

"Come on guys," I finally said, "Let's go get the rest of the stuff. Where do you want us to set up the computers?" I asked, looking toward Lindsey, knowing that she had emerged as the technology guru of the group.

"In here, let me show you," she said, as she led me from the kitchen toward a corner of the front room near a large window overlooking the gulf. The others stood there looking at each other.

"Then, where does the rest of this stuff go?" Bob finally asked, after a rather long and awkward pause.

"Put the books upstairs, I guess," Julie said, but in a reserved way, glancing toward Elizabeth for a response. "Is that O.K. with you, Elizabeth?"

"Sure, Julie that would work out great I think. That way, if someone wants to read or work on anything, the upstairs area will provide a quiet nook."

"Great, upstairs it is," Julie said, looking toward Bob and William, who then proclaimed that they had become indentured servants on Ambergris Caye, laughing and repeating their retorts all the way up the stairs.

"As soon as you guys finish setting everything up, perhaps dinner will be ready," Julie called out. She, Elizabeth and Lindsey had gone out to the market in San Pedro to buy fresh vegetables and fish earlier that morning. They had gotten lucky; a fresh shipment of assorted fruits and vegetables had just arrived from the mainland, and the fishing boats had brought in a bountiful catch, as well.

"All right, all right," Bob called back, and then asked if there was wine to accompany the dinner.

"Yes, Bob, you know we have wine; YOU brought it," Lindsey answered from the front room, looking upstairs with a frown on her face. Bob had insisted on bringing a case of his finest wine from the restaurant, a Sonoma Valley Pinot Noir dated 1992. It was his favorite.

A short time later, after all the boxes were delivered to their assigned places, and each couple had unpacked and set up a bedroom, we gathered in the dining room for the first official meal and marked the beginning of our journey.

"Let's drink a toast to our friendship," Bob said, raising his glass and smiling. "Whose bright idea was this again?" he continued. "To Ethan," he said, looking straight at me.

There was something communicated with that toast, something significant but subtle, between Bob and me. Neither of us would understand it for a time, but we would experience it in the days and months to come. Neither asked nor acknowledged the connection, but we both knew this would not be an ordinary adventure.

"Yes, to Ethan," William repeated, "thanks Buddy!" William continued as our wives looked on at this strange ritual in which we were now very much engrossed.

"There they go again," Lindsey said, looking at Julie and Elizabeth. They shook their heads and refilled their wine glasses. We continued to celebrate our official 'first meal' until 2:00 A.M., when our wives finally insisted we come to bed ...which became a comical event in itself.

After a slow start the next morning, William, Bob and I began inquiring about the tidal cycles and what fish were biting when. We would spend the next several days setting up the house and fishing off the dock that came with the property. We had decided to relax and not worry too much about solving our mystery. We would allow Leonardo and Francisco to work their magic! After all, we were beginning to feel very comfortable and secure on the island.

The local people were extremely friendly to us, and we trusted Leonardo and Francisco. We had decided to start enjoying our newfound freedom instead of obsessing on trying to understand one weird incident. Soon, our routine had become like clockwork. We would awake early, have coffee and breakfast underneath the palms and begin our day of fishing. Some days, we would fish from the dock entirely, while on other days, we would venture out in the small skiff that was available to guests at *our* house.

Since moving into the Big House, we had discovered the joy of eating outdoors under the large tropical trees, and lounging in the hammocks that were stretched between palm trees around the property. This was beginning to feel like the paradise we had all envisioned.

Chapter

13

The clock on the bedside table next to William and Elizabeth's bed ticked loudly, and seemed to get louder as the night passed slowly. The numbers and hands on the clock glowed in the dark like a stage prop from a Star Wars movie set. William began to toss and turn, then suddenly screamed out, grabbing his side. With a groan, he tried to sit up on the side of the bed, but fell back to his side, still moaning. Slowly, he began to slide out of bed and place his feet on the floor.

"William," Elizabeth said in a startled voice, as she realized that something was wrong. "William, what's wrong? Is it your stomach?"

Glancing over toward her, he groaned, "Yeah. I feel like I've been kicked in the gut. Help me to the bathroom, Elizabeth."

They stumbled and slowly made their way to the bathroom. William didn't know which to do, kneel or sit. So, he just stood, leaning against the closed door.

"William, are you Ok in there?" Elizabeth called to him from outside the door.

"Yes, I think so. The pain is subsiding, but I feel really dizzy. Elizabeth, come in here and help me back to the bed," he continued in a voice that was barely audible. Within a minute, William and Elizabeth were back in bed. With Elizabeth cuddled snugly against him, William lay on his side until he finally fell asleep.

Elizabeth was awakened by the brightness of the morning sun as it shown through the window of their bedroom. William was still lying on his side, in the same position he had settled into after crawling back into bed. His painful battle with his stomach did not seem to keep William awake for long, but Elizabeth had not slept well at all, and had tossed and turned the rest of the night.

Elizabeth heard the others rustling around and making their way downstairs. She knew if Bob and Lindsey were up, that coffee would soon be made. They had been here for only ten days, and William had had intestinal issues almost from the beginning, she thought. He wasn't a big complainer, but this particular time had gotten his attention, as well as Elizabeth's.

"Okay, William," she whispered, slipping out of the bed trying not to wake him. His hand was wrapped around the pillow he had grabbed getting into bed. "Rest easy my big guy. I'll check on you in a few minutes," she said, leaning down and kissing him softly on his forehead. His forehead felt very warm. "I think you may have a bit of a fever, Love," she whispered, standing next to the bed, puzzled about what ailment could have knocked William out like a light.

Downstairs, coffee was indeed ready, and Bob and Lindsey were already preparing a breakfast of fresh fruit and banana nut bread sprinkled with lumpy sugar and cinnamon. It smelled heavenly.

"Where's William?" asked Bob, looking curiously over the lip of the cup of coffee he was sipping.

"Elizabeth, is there anything wrong? You look awful," Lindsey remarked, having noticed the gaze in Elizabeth's eyes.

"William isn't feeling well, I'm afraid," Elizabeth said without making eye contact as she poured herself a cup of coffee. "He was up during the night complaining of severe abdominal pain. He hasn't moved all night. And his forehead feels very warm. I'm really worried," Elizabeth said, glancing over toward Lindsey.

"Have you taken his temperature?" Bob asked trying to think of what William could have eaten that might bring on this type reaction. "Elizabeth, I don't mean to alarm you, but has he broken out with any rashes? Has he ever had a reaction to seafood, like oysters or shrimp?" Bob inquired.

"None that I can think of, Bob. Do you think Ethan would know a doctor here?" Elizabeth asked, looking at Lindsey. "I'm really concerned. He hasn't moved all night. He's just lying there, groaning in his sleep," she continued.

"I'll go wake Ethan and Julie," Bob said without hesitating. Lindsey refilled her cup of coffee and placed her arm around Elizabeth's shoulders in an attempt to console her.

Bob and I went directly to William and Elizabeth's room, where William was still lying on his side. His bed sheets and blankets were piled high, and his face looked flushed. "He's burning up with a fever," I said to Bob, in a low voice. "We need to get him up and moving. He needs fluids no matter what this is," I said, turning to Bob.

"Help me roust him up," I said. Within a few minutes, William was sitting on the side of the bed, feeling weak and dizzy, and complaining of nausea.

"What happened, you guys?" William mumbled.

"We're not sure, but you've got to get up; you need to get some liquids in you, William. Whatever this is, you don't want to get dehydrated," Bob said.

"Okay, Bob," William said, as Bob and I lifted William from the bed to his feet. Once downstairs, Elizabeth washed his face with a damp cloth, and Julie was on the phone to Leonardo.

"Okay, great, Leonardo. Yes, that will be fine. Okay. Okay. No problem. I'll pay him there. Okay. Great! Yes. Si, many thanks, Leonardo," Julie said.

"We can fly to the clinic on the mainland in one hour," Julie said. "That's the quickest way to see the doctor," she added, "unless we want to wait until tomorrow afternoon for the doctor to come here."

"My suggestion is that we go now, without hesitation," I said.

"Okay, Buddy," William responded, taking a sip of water, "you won't get an argument from me."

"Thank you, Ethan." Elizabeth said with a smile and a relieved look on her face.

An hour later, we were all at the small airstrip, where William, Elizabeth, and I boarded the small single engine plane. Leonardo met us there as well, and gave instructions to the pilot. "I called ahead, Ethan," Leonardo confided, "I told the head nurse at the clinic that your friend had severe stomach pains, and that this was not related to bad food or drink."

Smiling back at him, I responded, "Thanks, Leonardo."

"You think he's trying to protect his business?" William said laughingly, after we were safely in the air. "Maybe so," I chuckled, shaking my head.

The head nurse at the clinic met us at the door. I paid the taxi fare and soon we were in the small exam room, waiting for the doctor. The nurse had ushered us quickly through the crowded lobby filled with local people, adults and children, some of them moaning from their discomforts. The fact that we were Americans on a year- long respite was no secret. It earned us preferential treatment, which bothered Elizabeth immensely.

"Mr. William, it appears that you may have some sort of stomach virus," the doctor said. "Perhaps it is a reaction to your recent change of diet; perhaps something in the food or the water. I am going to prescribe for you an antibiotic, enough for ten days. Take all of it. If you do not improve within a few days, I will also consider some tests for you. I will be traveling to Ambergris Caye on Thursday. Please come by the church if you are not feeling better," he continued in an extremely monotonous voice. "Do you have any questions?" the doctor asked.

We were stunned. The efficiency and thoroughness had been a surprise. The doctor had prescribed a high-powered antibiotic and had the nurse bring the medicine directly to us in the patient exam room. Before we could exit the room, an attendant appeared at the door and instructed us to follow him. We exited through a back hall and out the back door of the clinic, where a taxi was waiting to take us to meet our plane. The same single engine Cessna that had carried us over from the island was waiting.

Once we landed, Pablo met us at the airstrip with a note.

Hope all went well. If so, meet us
at the Victoria House under the palms.
If not, send a message by Pablo.
Bob

"They're at the Victoria, William. Do you feel like meeting them there, or do you want to go back to the house?" Elizabeth asked, as we climbed out of the plane and began to walk toward a small four-person golf cart Leonardo had just received from Houston.

"We can go to the Victoria," William answered. "Maybe the salt air will make me feel better."

We found Bob, Lindsey, and Julie sitting at a table under a canopy of palms beside the huts where we had stayed a few weeks earlier.

"Well, what's the verdict?" Bob asked, trying to keep the conversation light.

"I think I'm going to make it," William replied, as he and the others sat down at the table. He was already feeling stronger since taking the first round of meds at the clinic.

"That's good, guys, because we have some more news," Bob said. They looked at each other with hesitation. "We have a tropical storm coming our way. It's skirting the southern coast of Cuba as we speak, but the meteorologist on CNN is predicting that it will strike somewhere between here and the Yucatan," Bob further explained. William, Elizabeth and I were stunned. We stood silently for what felt like an eternity.

"How fast is it moving," I finally asked.

"Right now," Bob said, clearing his throat, "it's moving at about 35 miles per hour. If it keeps moving at that speed, we have a week to ten days, maybe a little more. If it picks up speed once it hits the warm gulf waters, maybe less," he continued. "Then there's the question of where it will hit," Bob kept talking. "If it's a direct hit, the island could flood. If it hits to the south, then we'll get the counter kick of the storm, which will be mostly wind. If it hits to the north, then we'll get a lot of rain and squalls. So, any way you look at it, we're in for a ride."

I posed the question, "Did any of you guys ever see that John Wayne movie where he played the part of a fisherman who was in love with ... the character played Elizabeth Allen? They were on an island in the South Pacific and were caught in a typhoon. I think the title was *Donovan's Reef*." The others looked at me as if I had completely lost my mind. "Well, -- anyway," I continued, "they rode out the storm, and I think we should, too." Now the others were truly stunned.

"Are you serious, Ethan?" Julie asked, looking straight into my eyes.

"Yes, yes, I am serious. Think about it, you guys. Either way we go at this point, we're screwed. We have to deal with this storm, no matter where it lands. Besides, all of our stuff is here. If we leave, we can kiss it goodbye! If we stay and survive, maybe we'll be able to help these people recover from the storm. If you think about it, it really befalls our lot to ride this one out. It's La Troika time!"

After a few minutes of discussion and shaking of heads, William finally replied, "I think Ethan's right. We should ride this thing out."

"I totally agree," Bob said.

"What do you ladies think about this," William asked, looking over to Elizabeth, Julie and Lindsey.

"Let's go huddle, girls," Julie suggested. And they walked off to the side, whispered among themselves a while, and then returned with their collective answer. "You're on, you three, but when this is all said and done, you guys owe us a cruise," Julie announced, as Elizabeth and Lindsey looked on with supportive resolve. Laughing and smiling at each other, Bob, William, and I all agreed that a cruise would be in order, perhaps in the spring or early summer. But for now, we would turn our attention toward the storm.

Chapter

14

Bob, William, and I left the table underneath the palms and walked down toward the beach and began contemplating the potential impact of the storm, regardless of its identified category. If it hit the island, there would be devastation everywhere.

Elizabeth began to recount the situation at the clinic as Julie and Lindsey listened. She told them how we were provided preferential treatment and were ushered in like royalty.

"You guys should have seen it. It was unlike anything I had ever experienced. Not even in Bangladesh were we given such treatment. We were escorted in without waiting; William was examined by the doctor almost immediately and was given a medication to take care of the virus and upset stomach. It was awkward," Elizabeth said.

"What about the people in the clinic?" Julie asked, with great eagerness.

"Yes," Lindsey agreed, "tell us about the conditions in the clinic and the people there. I've always heard that the medical conditions were absolutely horrid."

"I couldn't agree more, Lindsey," Elizabeth said, pausing for a moment as if she were searching for the right words to describe what she had seen. "First of all," she began, "the area outside the clinic was surrounded by people and animals. It was like looking at one of those posters depicting a third world country. Many of the children were malnourished, but seemed happy, except for the ones who were sick. They were dirty and obviously have very little. Then, in contrast, a few of the people around them seemed to have plenty. And, inside the clinic, the waiting rooms were filled with people, mostly women and children; many who looked too weak to stand. The main waiting room was dark and dingy. The paint on the walls was faded and peeling. The floor was dirty from all the foot traffic, and it was crowded and hot with no air circulation. It was sad, truly sad."

"My gosh, Elizabeth," Julie replied in a somber tone of voice, "it sounds very much like the scenes I was jolted to when I arrived in South Africa on school holiday," her British accent thickened as she recalled her earlier school days in England. "How many physicians were working at the clinic?" Julie finally asked, after listening intently to Elizabeth's description.

"I'm not sure, Julie. I only saw one doctor and two nurses. It was quite crowded," Elizabeth said. All three began to silently absorb the images she had described, when a waiter approached their table with a fresh pot of coffee, "More java, ladies?" He asked, mimicking an island accent. "It's freshly made." They all, of course, reacted with the same measure of enthusiasm, "Yes, please, by all means." The waiter poured the coffee and returned to the main dining room.

"You know, if that storm hits this little island, the medical needs could be staggering," Lindsey said, sipping her steaming cup and changing the focus of their conversation.

"Yes, and here we sit, just talking about it. We should do something... in anticipation," Elizabeth remarked, looking at Julie for additional support.

"Yes, I quite agree," Julie responded firmly. "In fact, what do you girls think about this idea..."

As they moved toward the middle of the table, Julie began to lay out her idea for assessing the medical needs and readiness of the island. Elizabeth and Lindsey listened intently and agreed. It was perfect; just what they needed to give this adventure a sense of purpose. The girls had almost finished listing and prioritizing their tasks when William, Bob and I returned from the beach. Our conversation had strayed from hurricane preparation to planning our next dive trip with Leonardo.

"It's just like you guys to be completely oblivious to what's about to happen here," Lindsey said, looking right at Bob, who knew by the look on Lindsey's face, that she was serious.

"Ethan, darling, you guys sit down and hear us out. We think there's a real possibility that the devastation will be enormous if the storm hits Belize," Julie said, motioning for me to sit in the chair beside her. "And the medical needs following the storm could be overwhelming."

"And besides," Elizabeth added, "we have decided to ride out this storm, and we all wanted an adventure with a humanitarian twist. So, this twist is off the southern coast of Cuba."

"According to the CNN report, it's predicted to hit somewhere between the southern coast of Belize and the Yucatan Peninsula, right? That puts us right in the center of the projected path," William added.

"Even with a 10-day window, that doesn't leave us much time. So, what plans have you girls devised?" I asked.

"Yeah, let's hear it," Bob added. "I'm surprised you girls hadn't found a humanitarian issue to focus on before now."

"Well, it's just that the opportunity is about to be dropped in our laps, so to speak," Lindsey replied, giving Bob an inquisitive look.

"I love it!" William said chuckling. "I think this will be awesome, just awesome. I mean, where else could we have gone to take a sabbatical and end up being in the middle of a potentially deadly storm and in a position to help these people? It's great! I love it!" William always saw the positive side of every situation, no matter the circumstances.

After discussing the initial idea of bracing for the storm and making sure that William had overcome his bout with the bad fruit, water, or wine, whichever it may have been, we moved to the dining area of the Victoria House and discussed our plans with Leonardo. We watched CNN for updates and continued following the tracking information on the storm.

"Here's the phone, Señor Ethan. Hopefully you can get an operator. The lines will be very busy with the storm coming," Leonardo said as he placed the old black AT&T phone on the counter.

"Cross your fingers, my friend. Hopefully, I can reach Mike in Atlanta," I said, as I dialed the number for an international operator.

Chapter

15

"Ethan, good to hear from you," Mike said. "Have you seen a weather report? There's a tropical storm in the Gulf, and it's headed right for you guys. If it's a direct hit, the island may flood, so what are you guys thinking? Are you considering leaving or seeking higher ground inland?"

Smiling and glancing over to William and Bob, I finally spoke into the telephone receiver, "Mike, Mike, take a breath. As William would say, we're all over it! We're staying," I said.

"What? Are you guys nuts? No, don't answer that. I already know the answer. What can I do to help?" Mike finally asked in retreat.

"Okay, here's the plan; it's hot of the press," I said, as I sat up in my chair and focused on the details of what the group had just discussed.

Then, suddenly, it was as if the air had been sucked out of the room. Silence, like a thief of attention, filled the space, as everyone turned to stare at the television.

"Hold on, Mike. CNN is giving an update on the storm," I said.

"Okay, but let me know what you guys need and when. I'll have my buddies with the International Red Cross on stand-by. I'll check back with you later, Ethan," Mike said, and hung up.

New updates on the position of the storm were being explained. The storm had picked up speed, and its direction had become more defined. Ambergris Caye remained its direct target.

"My God, guys," Bob gasped, as he realized the seriousness of our decision to stay. "It's going to be a wild ride. We have a lot of work to do," he said.

I spoke up, trying to keep focused and moving in the right direction. We had made the decision to stay and ride out the storm, partly out of crazy reasons related to our egos, and partly because we knew that if the island got a direct hit, the devastation would be big, and the need would be serious. Mike would be on standby in Atlanta, ready to sound the alarm. Within hours of our request, life-saving and life-sustaining items would be flown down. Perhaps, this was our chance... our opportunity to make a difference; and, if so, it was a hell of an ego trip. But our intention was more serious and purposeful, rather than caviler. This was a major storm, and would likely be a category 3 or 4 hurricane before it made landfall.

I suddenly had a sick feeling in my stomach. This would be a test and may be life threatening one. For a moment, I thought about what I had in place, documents, a will, things that would be needed just in case Julie were to...

The CNN reporter blared on, "Tropical Storm Henrietta, as the storm is now called, should strengthen overnight, probably gaining hurricane strength as winds increase and the eye of the storm intensifies. This is nothing to take lightly; it will be at least a Cat 2, and perhaps a Cat 3 hurricane according to all the scenarios from NOAA," the reporter continued. None of us could break the silent choke-hold. We were all mesmerized.

"I need more coffee," William exclaimed as he got up from his chair and headed toward the kitchen. I noticed Elizabeth was looking toward the sky with a worried look on her face.

Suddenly the commercial ended, and there was more commentary about the storm from the news guys. Because the cayes are so vulnerable to a major storm, worldwide organizations refuse to support the construction of hurricane shelters on tropical islands. The presence of a shelter on an island might give a false impression of a potential safe haven, and possibly encourage people to stay rather evacuate.

"They do not want to give a false sense of security," said Jose' Gonzales, a local news reporter now appearing on the television screen. He spoke in English, and then, repeated himself in Spanish. "The best protection is to get off the island when you can," he stressed. "Of course, we will assist those who do not make it off the island or choose to stay for whatever reason. What we are saying is that people should not count on this type of support, and instead should make a plan in case an evacuation must occur," he said.

Of course, this got my attention; and, as they continued, I began to concentrate on our plan for us to stay and ride this thing out. Maybe it wouldn't be as severe as they were reporting, but the intensity had changed. There was a level of seriousness in the air that had not been there before. We knew from our research that during previous storms the Catholic Primary School on Ambergris Caye and the Community Center on Caye Caulker had been used as a shelters, but there was certainly no mention of this now.

The reporters continued... "Historically, 90 percent of all hurricane casualties have occurred from drowning and 10 percent from other causes. Therefore, it is imperative that all persons evacuate the cayes, beaches and other locations that may be hit by high tides, storm waves, or storm surge. The highest tide occurs during the second half of the storm. The rise of the water may take place very rapidly immediately following the eye of the storm or the time of the lowest barometric pressure. If your only passage to high ground is over a road subject to flooding, leave early. Do not run the risk of being marooned or having to evacuate at the height of the storm amid flying debris. It is important to have a planned place to go. Hotels and motels quickly fill up during these times," he said with emphasis.

We looked at each other as if each was reading the other's mind; our resolve strengthened. We would definitely stay. Perhaps this was to be the purpose for our excursion, taking a year away from the hustle and bustle of the world we knew and had grown tired of. But, it would also be a test.

"Let's do it," William said, breaking the silence. "What do we do first?" he continued. That was all that was needed to get the group ignited and going. We paid our tab and made our way back the "Big House," as we called it. It was a truly BIG house, one that had weathered many a hurricane. It was built like the strong seafaring ships that were designed for the rough waters around Cape Horn. The frame was built from old ship timbers, and every major joint and beam was secured with huge wooden pegs. Perhaps, subconsciously, this provided a mental feeling of safety for the group, knowing that the Big House itself had survived worse storms than the one that was about to hit the area.

William, Bob, and I gathered around the dining table and began to map out our plan and priorities. We listed the people we needed to contact first and made note of our own safety issues, developing a contingency plan. We, too, might be ordered from the island, and our offer to help not necessarily welcomed.

The storm, not yet officially a hurricane, was tracking southward of Cuba, but was expected to take a turn to the northwest. Just how far north and west was the big question. It could hit the island directly, which would cause catastrophic damage and loss of life; or, it could skirt the edge of the area, and bring only high winds and rain. Another factor was *when* the storm hit. If it struck during high tide, there would certainly be flooding and some expected structural damage.

Suddenly, there was a knock at the door; it was Leonardo with word from town. "The officials have just ordered an evacuation of the island within the next 48 hours," he said desperately. "There are only two ferries at the docks, and the townspeople are gathering their belongings and dragging them down the street. It's chaotic! I think you should prepare to depart. I can have your plane ready on your order," Leonardo finished.

Again, there was a momentary silence as Bob, William and I stood at the doorway to the kitchen. Looking at each other, we all three said in unison, "We're staying, Leo, we're not leaving."

Looking stunned and confused, Leonardo begged, "But, Señor, you must leave. It's an order from the authorities," Leo pleaded, but quickly recognized our resolve, and stopped in mid-sentence.

"Okay," he said, "so, what's your plan?" By now, Leonardo had learned that we crazy Americans were on a mission, although he wasn't sure what. In spite of our craziness, Leonardo knew that our intent was genuine and that we were serious.

"Come on in, Leo," I said, and waved him in, "and join us in the den. We'll tell you our plan and purpose for staying." And with that, we all walked through the kitchen and into the den beside the bank of windows that framed the ocean and the sky... the horizon that would eventually yield clues as to what fate would be bestowed on this island, its people, and those who stayed.

Elizabeth brought in a fresh pot of coffee and some oatmeal-raisin cookies, which seemed to be needed fuel for the conversation that ensued. Lindsey and Julie waited in the kitchen, half listening, yet trying to carry on their own conversation, as well. They were trying hard to absorb what we were about to experience. They were, after all, on an adventure, and had set aside this time in their lives to complete a journey, no matter where it led them.

Elizabeth rejoined them as Leonardo, William, Bob, and I were discussing the plan and rationale for staying.

"I think Ethan really wants to make a difference," Julie said, her eyes intently focused on the group in the den.

"Yes, I agree," said Lindsey. "And I think William and Bob are spinning off Ethan's adrenalin and enthusiasm. I just have to take a deep breath and hold on, I suppose," she added.

Lindsey was probably the most conservative of the ladies in the group. She was certainly the more motherly, more cautious type, although she was about the same age as Julie and Elizabeth. They listened for a while and then turned their attention to the NOAH weather radio that sat on the kitchen counter next to the coffee pot. Bob, William and I, along with Leonardo, joined the girls in the kitchen for the latest update, then decided to check on the townspeople and secure more provisions in preparation for weathering the storm.

Chapter

16

The streets of San Pedro were filled with people, pulling their belongings behind them, rushing toward the docks at the end of town. Panic seemed to fill the air. "Leonardo," I asked, "It occurs to me that the evacuation order was given a bit early. The storm is parallel to the south of Cuba. It may be a week before it is within striking distance of the Caye, and may even miss this place altogether."

"Yes, I agree, but it is the decision of the authorities," he responded.

We parked the jeep in front of the San Pedro Café, went inside and sat down with our notes in hand. We began to check over the list of needed items. Leonardo disappeared into the back of the restaurant through the curtained doorway.

Meanwhile, back at the house, the girls were worried. They looked at each other in silence, each sipping a glass of wine or staring out the window or at each other. There was no conversation. The deal had been struck. We were staying and would ride the storm out to whatever end, with the ultimate goal of saving lives. But, for a moment, time stopped and thoughts flooded their minds, causing tears to gently fall, but in an odd sort of way. They communicated with each other, without words, and their resolve was unified. And, then, slowly, they began again to prepare for what they could not anticipate.

Would all of hell's fury be thrown at them? Would one or many tidal surges or walls of water slam against the shore? Against the house? They could not predict, but could only prepare for the worst.

Their thoughts became focused on the maps of the Gulf of Mexico, as they marked the coordinates from the NOAA radio. Outside, the wind blew gently through the palm trees, and the waves that rolled onto shore seemed usual and fairly non-descript...unlike the harshness of the pounding surf that would be crashing into the sand only days from this moment.

"The storm seems to be arching in a northwesterly direction," Julie said. Elizabeth and Lindsey moved closer to the map.

"How far is it from Cuba...or, really... Haiti?" Lindsey asked.

"It looks to be about 50 or so miles west to southwest of Santiago de Cuba, but the cloud swirls from the storm pattern show a better picture," Elizabeth said, pointing to the computer's screen.

"My God, it's enormous, and it's moved in our direction," Lindsey said, her eyes fixed on the screen. All three moved in closer, and all three suddenly fell silent again as they marked the track of the storm with a yellow highlighter.

"The storm originally formed from a tropical wave that emerged from the west coast of Africa on 18

August and moved steadily and uneventfully westward across the tropical Atlantic during the following several days," the weather reporter explained. "On 23 August, however, convection associated with the wave increased, and satellite classifications from the Tropical Analysis and Forecast Branch (TAFB) of the Tropical Prediction Center/National Hurricane Center (TPC/NHC) began when the wave was located about 500 nautical miles east of the Lesser Antilles. As the wave approached the Lesser Antilles, a surface low formed near the southern Windward Islands. The system soon acquired enough of a circulation to be designated a tropical depression on 24 August while centered about 40 nautical miles north-northwest of Grenada," he continued, as he explained the original formation of the storm.

He continued to explain that the storm was likely to sweep by Cuba and brush the coast of Jamaica, near Kingston. He reminded the listening audience that all indications pointed toward the storm intensifying and picking up speed. This mere fact heightened the level of anxiety with everyone. A direct hit by a hurricane with a high tidal surge would decimate the island.

Chapter

17

Julie and Lindsey were the first to react when we arrived back at the Big House. They winced at each other as they began to read through our notes. Our priorities included such questions as... How would we acquire fresh water? A human being could live several days, even weeks, without food, but not without water. It was crucial. Other questions... What would we do with any dead bodies? Disease and decay could also become a high-alert concern. Our survival and the survival of others would hinge on having the essential resources needed to wait out the storm and to begin any rescue that might follow.

"What do you think of all this?" Julie asked. She began wiping off the tables just to keep busy as Lindsey paused and thought about the question. It was obviously weighing heavily on her mind, as it was with all of us. But we didn't have time to think about our feelings. The time had come to plan and act in a deliberate and calculated way.

"I think we're in this for the long haul, whether we want to back out or not," Lindsey said. Her voice reflected a serious mood, which gave Julie some pause as well.

"I take it that you and Bob need to hash this out?" Julie said. Ethan and I have been together long enough to develop a sixth sense about each other, in a way, like we know what the other is thinking.

"Julie has always supported my adventures," I said. "This time, though, the stakes are a bit higher."

"You might say that," Lindsey replied. "Bob and I are committed, but I guess I have a bad gut feeling about all this. It's just a little scary. It really hadn't hit me until I saw the storm on the computer monitor a few minutes ago, before you guys returned from town. I just had a sick feeling in my gut," she said. Lindsey had been agreeable to the adventure, but her life experiences were less adventurous than Bob's. She hadn't expected to be the target of a major hurricane on a tropical island.

Elizabeth bounded through the kitchen doorway bearing all smiles and very rosy cheeks. Julie and Lindsey just looked at her in wonderment, then glanced at each other, each remitting a sheepish grin.

"So, Elizabeth, what have you to say about our little predicament," Julie asked, employing a little heaviness with her British accent. Elizabeth, bouncing on her toes and reaching for a glass, said without looking or making eye-contact, "Oh, I'm game; aren't you?"

Pouring herself another glass of margarita from the freshly made pitcher, she took a sip, and sat down in one of the tufted leather chairs. She looked directly at

Julie with her eyebrows raised incredulously as if to ask what had been discussed around the coffee table.

"Lindsey and I were just discussing this part of our adventure. I think we are all in… committed I mean. Would you agree?" Julie asked, looking directly at Elizabeth and waiting for her to answer.

Elizabeth seemed to be chugging the margarita as she wiped her mouth and raised her glass. "I think we should party on and prepare to kiss our asses goodbye," Elizabeth said. Julie and Lindsey were stunned, but then realized that perhaps Elizabeth had taken some of her anxiety medication, washing it down with her second tall margarita. They were just seeing the effects kick in.

"Elizabeth, are you okay?" Julie asked, as she and Lindsey became a bit more concerned about her demeanor.

"Sure, I'm fine, you guys," Elizabeth said. "I just needed this margarita to calm my nerves. Aren't you guys nervous?" she asked.

Relieved, they took her by the arms and moved her to the table where they began talking intently and seriously among themselves. They finished off the remaining portion of the margarita pitcher Julie had made earlier and were now laughing and more relaxed.

William, Bob, and I, hearing the laughter in the kitchen, met each other in the upstairs hallway. It was a wide hallway with ceilings at least 10 feet high and exquisite crown molding adorning the ceiling. Six-inch baseboard painted a glossy white lined the darkened wooden floors like a runway in the desert. The old house was about 70 years old and had never sustained any severe damage from storms or hurricanes. Bob, William, and I looked at each other then glanced down the hallway toward the stairs. We each emitted a low laugh, almost a giggle, which only added to the laughter still spewing forth from the kitchen. Like three kids waking up on Christmas morning, we ran downstairs to see what was happening.

Entering the kitchen, we stopped at the swinging door, and began to laugh. Looking at the girls, who by now had turned and were staring at us, we all began to laugh uncontrollably. The silliness continued for what seemed to be forever, and then we finally sat down at the table. "What is so funny?" William asked, giggling to himself.

"We have drowned our apprehension with margaritas," Lindsey said, motioning to Elizabeth and Julie for support and affirmation.

"Wow, so you didn't save us any?" William asked, looking over at Bob and me. Bob rose to make another pitcher of the juice, the television still broadcasting hurricane updates in the background... more of the same information... the same forecast tracks for the storm and the same possible scenarios for landfall. But, it was no longer a tropical storm; it was now a hurricane.

"Get the salsa and chips," Bob said, as he began to pour the mixture into the large pitcher, adding some ice, and stirring until well mixed.

Chapter

18

Darkness came a little earlier, it seemed. The wind was noisy, and the sea birds seemed more nervous than usual; but the crashing of the waves was unchanged. We ate without concern or dread and could not predict what veracity the storm would slam our way. It had been 48 hours since the evacuation order was given, and the storm now seemed within striking distance. No one really slept much that night. The wind began to howl around 1:00 A.M., and I could smell the aroma of coffee brewing downstairs. William and Bob were both in the kitchen, talking quietly, and obviously discussing the weather and the impending arrival of the storm. The glow of moonlight through the fog made the waves seem bigger and the sounds of the wind and water seem more deafening.

"What's happening, guys?" I said as I walked into the kitchen. They stopped talking almost as if they were a couple of schoolboys who had just been caught by the principal.

I asked again, "What's going on, dudes?" I tried playing this off as a passing coincidence, but I knew what I had noticed, and I also knew that there was a heavy fog of doubt suddenly in the room.

"We were just talking about our adventure here, Ethan," William said, looking me square in the eyes, with Bob quietly observing our interaction. "We have some concerns," he said. Bob said nothing, but just looked back and forth between me and William. William had that cold, chilly, interrogative gaze he always got when he was questioning the circumstances of any situation. It was one hell of a poker face.

"And, what are your concerns, William?" I asked, looking at Bob, and then back to William. I waited for an answer, but he paused to collect his thoughts. It was obvious that I had interrupted their conversation, but I couldn't determine where each stood. It wasn't like we could change our minds at this point, or at least I didn't think so.

"I tell you, partner," William said, laughing a bit, more like a half-hearted chuckle, "I'm not so sure we've made the right decision."

"What do you mean, William?" I said. "We had this discussion, all of us, and we all agreed. What's changed your mind?"

"It's... it's just that there's been a lot of crap happen down here. First, you and Julie had that strange thing happen to you where you were separated. Hell, you don't even know yet what happened to you or who did that to you! Then, I had that stomach virus thing... and now this storm. Doesn't all that make you want to run like hell?" he asked.

I paused before speaking, "Bob, how do you see it?" I wanted first to let what William had said settle and sink in, and then to give Bob a chance to respond or add to what William had said. "What are your thoughts, Bob?" I asked.

"I do have my concerns, Ethan, but I'm with you. I know you've been through hell just getting down here," Bob said, "and I know you and Julie planned for this little adventure for a long time. But I have to say, I see William's point, also," he said.

"So, just what is your point, William?" I said sharply, looking him straight in the eye. I was pissed. We had made this decision together. Nobody had coerced anyone, and we had all allowed each other plenty of opportunities to back out without regret. Where was this coming from, I wondered.

"We discussed this, William," I said. "And what is this, Bob? This 'you're with me' shit?" I questioned. "Look, you guys, we made this decision together. I know it's not the best situation with the tide about to rise to who-knows-what level, and we're stuck here on this sandbar of an island about to take a direct hit from a hurricane! It's daunting," I said, trying to sound more empathetic, "but we made this decision together!"

"Ethan," William said, "I know we made this decision together, but..." he trailed off.

Suddenly, I knew what the issue was. It had to be Elizabeth!

"Look, William, if you and Elizabeth want to get off the island, I understand. I can respect that, and it has to be your decision! Julie and I are staying," I said.

William sat there staring at me in deep thought.

"Same goes for you, Bob," I continued. "Same deal. I respect and love you guys. We've been through hell and back together and have known each other a long time. But, if this isn't the gig for you, then go with our blessing. It's no big deal, really," I urged.

"No, we're in. We're staying," Bob said. "But I agree with you, it has to be each couple's decision, and none of us could have predicted this situation. Hell, life's an adventure. But I also see William's point, that..."

"William's point that I haven't yet heard," I interrupted. "So, William, what gives? Come on, man, give it to me straight," I said. I knew this was serious for William, and I thought I knew why.

Chapter

19

The darkness of the night surrounded us as we moved from one chair or sofa to the next. The wind had begun to howl its haunting rhythm around 3:00 A.M., as the conversation dropped off and we moved on to the subject of survival and what to do next. I sat there, motionless, listening to the wind and the surf as the waves crashed against the beach with a new found fury. They were more frequent, more furious, and the wind seemed to blow in cadence. Without moving or lifting my head, I glanced around the room, studying each body closely, watching the breathing, listening to the sound of gentle snoring, and noticing that we had fallen asleep in such odd positions. I wondered how we could sleep at all. None of the wives had joined us; and, I heard not a footstep from upstairs, although I expected one of them to come creeping around the corner at any time.

With as little noise as possible, I repositioned my arms, hands, and legs, and eased myself up from my chair. I moved slowly across the room to peer out the window. There was no moon, but there was a lightness outside that was eerie. It was shadow-like, with the trees blowing one way, then, yanked in the opposite direction by a strong, unseen force with the accent of a lightning bolt. The surf looked enormous now, as if it were crawling closer and closer to the shore. With each directional change of the gusting wind, the old house would moan and creak a little, as if it were bracing for the onslaught to come. But this old house had been through many hurricanes and tropical storms. It was reinforced with cable stretched diagonally across each side and anchored to pylons buried deep in the ground. I reminded myself again that the house had been on this island for 70 years and had never been badly damaged by a storm. Its finish was like that of a fine sea-faring vessel, painted with an impregnable sealant and paint that would make any sailor proud.

Deep in thought, I didn't notice that Julie had come downstairs, and had eased up behind me. She placed her hands around my waist, and I jumped a little as I glanced around and her eyes met mine. Placing my finger to her lips, I smiled. We were both thinking the same thing... be careful not to wake anyone and just enjoy the moment. We stood there for a few minutes, and I thought about our next move. What would be thrown at us? What really did William think? And, what did Elizabeth think? What was all that really about? I had my ideas. I assumed it was simply 'cold feet' or something akin to buyer's remorse. Perhaps Elizabeth now wished they had left the island and not chosen to stay. But it was too late. We were here to stay, and we had to ride this thing out.

"How soon do suppose the storm will hit land, Ethan?" Julie whispered, staring out the window.

"If I had to guess," I said, "I'd probably say that landfall will be within the next 12 hours. I'm just hoping it veers northward and skirts the island," I added. "Then, we'll just get a lot of wind and rain."

"What about the people who didn't leave the island? What about them?" Julie said, her voice steady and low.

And for a moment, my mind wandered in thought, racing down a checklist of conversations I had heard about the evacuations.

"Julie," I said, "as far as I know, the island has been evacuated with the exception of us... and maybe Leonardo... although I may regret that decision."

"No Ethan," she said, now glancing upward and making eye contact, "not everyone left. There are people on this island in the village near San Pedro." Then it hit me. In that instant, I knew what our mission would be... our next move. The shanties and shacks in the small roadside village located about a half mile from the town of San Pedro would take a big hit if the winds were above 60 miles per hour, and God help them if there was a tidal surge.

Patting her hand and deep in thought, Julie knew my thoughts. Nothing more needed to be said. We just stood there, locked in our stance, watching the wind and the rain. Julie melted into my body as we both contemplated in silence the events that were about to unfold.

"Let's move into the kitchen," I whispered and motioned toward the kitchen. We crept like kids sneaking around a corner for a glimpse of Santa Claus.

"Let me kiss you," I said. She didn't say a word. She just smiled, leaned in, and kissed me. The glimmer in her eyes told me all I needed to know... that she had my back. She was with me, no matter what happened. Although I could not have possibly anticipated the events thus far on this adventure, I knew without a shadow of a doubt that I was where I wanted to be, and with the people I wanted to be with, my friends in the other room notwithstanding. I glanced at the clock. It was now 4:20 A.M. It would be daylight soon.

Chapter

20

The crash of the shutters against the side of the house jolted me out of bed. Julie and I had made our way back to the bedroom and fallen asleep watching with awe as the clouds sliced through the night sky. The wind was whipping now, probably gusting around 40 miles per hour. I figured the storm was coming in sooner than anticipated. I had no idea where the others were, and listened for a moment, but heard nothing.

"Julie," I said. "Let's get up. The wind is blowing hard, and I think the storm may be coming in sooner than we thought it would."

Groaning a bit and rolling over on her side, she mumbled, "Ethan, darling, will you please make some coffee? I'm in need of a jump start."

"Of course, I will," I said. "But we need to get about prepping for the storm; and, don't forget about the people in the village. We need to get a head-count as soon as we can," I said.

"Okay, Okay," she said, somewhat exasperated, but knowing we had our work cut out for us in getting things ready for the storm, and reaching the people in the village.

I made my way downstairs where William and Elizabeth, Bob and Lindsey, were sitting around the dining table discussing the storm.

"Morning, Mates!" I said, springing into the room. "How is everyone this morning?" I asked. "Bob, is your neck stiff this morning?" I asked, grinning toward him, trying to test the waters with the group.

"We were just talking about what we need to do first, Ethan," Bob said. William said very little and didn't make eye contact with me. Elizabeth was silent after I entered the room. She was reserved as part of her nature, but I sensed something was amiss, especially given the strange conversation we had had only hours before.

"We want to run a few things by you, Ethan," Bob said, "and then we want your input and Julie's too," he said.

"Okay," I said, sitting down with a cup of strong coffee, having forgotten about Julie. She would figure out soon enough that I had been re-directed somehow, and would join the group armed and ready. I had filled her in on the earlier conversation. She, too, had noticed a strange distancing from Elizabeth, but dismissed it as nervousness from the potential danger we all had voluntarily placed ourselves in.

I sat there, sipping the coffee as if it were the last cup, and it very well could be. Bob seemed to be the newly appointed spokesperson of the now dissimilated group. For the next 20 minutes, Bob unveiled what could only be the thoughts, fears, and desires of William and Elizabeth, probably more so Elizabeth. There were few surprises, but they lacked the potential for probability, since the storm was almost here.

"What do you really want to do, William?" I asked. "What exactly can you do at this point? I mean, we all agreed to be here, to do this, and to ride this storm out. If anyone is having second thoughts, then go. Get off the island. I'm sure Leonardo can make the arrangements. It may be a bumpy ride, but you can probably get off and be back on the mainland before the storm hits," I said.

"No, now don't take this the wrong way, Ethan," William said. "We just have some concerns, and ..."

"But, William, we all agreed," I interrupted. "I can understand being suddenly scared shitless with this storm literally about to knock on the front door," I said. "And, I'm sorry to interrupt, but if you and Elizabeth... if you guys want out, then by all means, let's get on that right away, because the window for getting back on the mainland is rapidly closing," I reminded him.

There was momentary silence. William and Elizabeth glanced at each other, and Lindsey studied everyone at the table. I had come to the conclusion that Elizabeth had given William so much hell that he had decided to capitulate. My assessment, in short, was that he really wanted to stay and play the game of hurricane survival, but fear had overcome Elizabeth. I couldn't fault her for wanting to get out. It was a scary situation. The surf had advanced some 10 to 15 feet inward, and the eye of the storm hadn't even hit yet; it was still 80 or 90 miles out. According to the NOAA radio, the storm was linear in shape, and ran about 130 miles north to northeast, and was about 65 miles wide, stretching in a southeasterly direction. This was, perhaps, a positive aspect of the storm, in that we may not get a direct hit; rather, the storm may slice its way across the Belizean and Mexican gulf coasts. Our greatest hope was the possibility of the storm being overcome by the warm gulf waters, which would pull it toward the northeastern coast of Texas, and would greatly lessen its impact on Ambergris.

"William, what are your thoughts?" I asked, looking straight at him. My question caught him by surprise, I think, and he hesitated a second or two, but answered in that confident, but low voice.

"Ethan, I really think Elizabeth and I would feel better if we were more inland a little," William said, reaching over slowly and taking Elizabeth's hand in his.

"I understand, William, I really do," I said. "What do we need to do first? Tell me what you need or want me to do," I said, trying to sound empathic, and meaning it of course, yet feeling a little perturbed with Elizabeth.

I guess this drove home a point, one that I had not considered before now. This adventure was more mine and Julie's, and maybe Bob's and Lindsey's, too. But, as for William and Elizabeth, I had now realized that once they left the island, they would not return. I saw it in their eyes. I felt it in William's voice inflection. And, as an extra garnishment, Elizabeth had still made no comments at all. I had to honor their decision, however...William's decision. It would make the challenge a little more difficult but certainly not impossible.

"Bob, I guess we need to contact Leonardo. Where are the ..."

"I already have, Ethan," Bob said, getting up from the table, and glancing at William.

"Right." I said. "I guess I should have anticipated that." I looked at William, giving him a quick smile that was meant to convey that all was okay. Elizabeth blushed a little, but still said nothing.

I didn't notice, but Bob had answered a knock at the door. It was Leonardo, dressed in full rain gear, with a walkie-talkie in his hand.

"Come in, Leonardo," Bob said, shaking Leonardo's hand and gesturing for him to come in out of the storm.

"Mr. William," Leonardo said, "Are you ready? We must be quick. The surge is coming and the surf is getting fierce. It will be impossible to get across if we wait any longer. We must go now if you want to make it to the mainland," he insisted with an urgent tone.

"Okay, Leonardo, we have a bag packed. Hang on and I'll get it," William said, running quickly upstairs to their room.

"Elizabeth, are you okay," Leonardo said in a low voice. At that moment, I glanced over to Elizabeth, whose eyes looked like a dam about to overflow.

"Elizabeth," Julie said, moving closer to her, "it's okay, and it will continue to be okay. You'll feel better once you're on the mainland," Julie comforted.

"I know," Elizabeth mumbled, "I just need to be in a different place, Julie. Really, it isn't..." Her voice trailed off as she choked up and leaned into Julie's embrace. She was visibly shaken, and I knew there was more to this conversation than we knew, or perhaps would ever know.

"Okay, we're set," William announced, as he bounded down the stairs, seeing immediately what shape Elizabeth was in. He walked directly to her, and held her for a moment. Julie backed away as William took her place.

"Leonardo, how are you going to do this?" I asked.

"My friend has a fishing boat, and he has been thinking about mooring it inland, up in the mouth of the

Belize River, for safe harbor," Leonardo explained. "He had not made a final decision until I called him this morning. He has been nervous, too, and wanted to get his boat out of here," Leonardo said. His comment about "being nervous, too" caught my attention, and I glanced at Bob. I knew from his response that we would talk later, and that there was another side to this sudden departure. In an instant, William and Elizabeth were out the door, following Leonardo to his truck. Bob, Lindsey, Julie, and I crowded at the side door leading from the kitchen and watched them get into Leonardo's truck, then pull away. We all waved heartily, but William only offered a slight gesture and Elizabeth offered nothing.

I didn't like what had just transpired, not because William and Elizabeth had decided to seek some other means of safety, not even because they both had seemed elusive and had avoided a direct conversation other than a defensive one the night before. We had all been friends for years, had been through some difficult times together and had supported each other in times of loss. This departure was strange. It was different. I didn't know whether to be worried, pissed-off, or both. And, I didn't have time to be either. Julie and I had a new mission, one we had not even discussed yet with Bob and Lindsey. I decided to ask for boundaries. That was the best approach to take with Bob. He could be reserved from time to time, and would act only in his due time.

"Bob," I said, "What the heck just happened? What was all that really about? But... before you answer, let me ask a more important question... have you seen the latest weather report or heard an update from NOAA?" I asked.

"Yes, I have heard the weather updates, Ethan, and we have very little time," Bob said, "and as for what just transpired, let's save that for later," he said. This is not the time to discuss it.

Perhaps looking surprised, but not really being shocked at the questioning from me, he added, "I'll explain. I promise. But, we have to get hopping if we're going to be ready for this storm!"

"Wait," I said, "I have to ask one question, Bob. Do you and Lindsey want to go too? If so, there are no hard feelings, really," I said. But, before I could say anything further, Bob threw up his hand in retort.

"Nope. We're in, Ethan. Seriously," Bob said firmly. "Now, let's go man, we have a lot to do."

"Julie, you'll have to explain to Lindsey what we talked about last night. Bob and I will be back later, and then we can go from there," I said, giving her a peck on the cheek.

"Love you, darling," Julie said in a low voice. With that, Bob and I were out the door, and had jumped in the golf cart, driving toward the storage shed a quarter mile down the road. We had to board up the windows on the house and check the anchor cables. Next, we would gather all the items necessary for survival at night: flashlights, radios, canned food, bottles of water, floatation devices, beacon signal igniters, flares, knives, and scuba gear. We would position most of these supplies in the attic of the house, just in case the storm surge was more than predicted. By nightfall, all hell would begin to close down upon us.

Chapter

21

As the evening became late, the winds grew stronger, and the sky even more greenish, like a sparkling emerald amongst the clouds. The air was as thick as the heavy humid air of August. The ocean raged with fury, as the waves crashed closer and closer to the grass, having long since engulfed the beach. The crow's nest at the end of the dock walkway was the only thing visible from the second floor windows. The overview of the scene outside the Big House looked as though the sea itself was rising up to swallow the entire island whole. The storm seemed to rage against any obstacle in its path, and with seemingly little effort removed the object with formidable power, thrusting it in the air. As I watched through an opening out the side window, I saw boats as big as tractor trailer rigs being thrown about, their nets and riggings ruined and flailing in the wind. Sections of boardwalk and dock timbers were hurled through the air as if being shot from cannons. Palm trees were uprooted and became orphaned battering rams, smashing whatever crossed their paths.

Looking over the second floor balcony railing, I discovered that water had already made its way into the first floor of the Big House. The power to most of the island had been shut off earlier in the day, and we maneuvered by candlelight and flashlights. The water swirled with its black hue, and the shear darkness and the sounds of the wind, rain, and water, made it all the more eerie. The old house seemed to creak and moan with each gust of wind, almost as if it were flexing to resist the powerful forces that were challenging its structure. The water from the ocean covered the lawn and surrounded the house. The steps leading up to the front porch were gone, apparently falling victim to the rushing currents of wind driven water. Winds had reached 80 miles per hour and were ripping and claiming anything that would give way. The house shook with every gust. It reminded me of flying through a thunderstorm and feeling the air currents slam against a jet as it cruised at 600 miles per hour or more, its pilots pushing it through down drafts and air pockets as the plane lunged and jumped from side to side. It was the kind of flight that made you pray to God to let you touch the ground or caused you to reach over to the person next to you with a reassuring gesture of unity, as each of you silently acknowledged that the end may be near. On this night, as pitch black as it was, the most sinking thought was that it was early, and the storm was moving methodically parallel with the island. At the last moment, it turned northward just enough to spare the island a direct hit; but the side swiping and slicing that was occurring was every bit as daunting.

"Ethan, I'm scared," Julie said in a low and shaky voice. I reached over and pulled her closer to me. I patted her forearm as we sat there huddled against the inside wall of our bedroom closet. Bob and Lindsey were in the next room in their closet. We had decided to separate just in case one of us got in trouble; or, in case the house began to break apart. It was our best hope of at least one couple making it out alive. A somber calm had come over us, as we planned for a half dozen scenarios. We were as ready for this as we could be, given the fact that we were surrounded by the gulf, with our sole existence hanging on the foundations of a 70 year old house. It scared the hell out of me if I let myself think about it. I could only wonder how Bob and Lindsey were fairing in the next room. I wondered what they must be thinking. I hoped they were staying strong. As intense and harrowing as this storm was, not knowing how this would play out made it even more frightening.

The Big House was made for this sort of storm; the kind that hits hard and fast, and brings with it an ocean of strong currents that cut through the trees and vegetation and whatever else is in its path. The bones of the old house were designed with parts that were removable, like sections of flooring, planks of the wallboards, and even certain sections of the copulas on the roof. All the removable sections of the old house lessened its resistance to the tidal surge and the back surge that would come as quickly and with as much force… only in reverse, sucking the already weakened structures, trees, and other miscellaneous objects and the pieces of humanity that once inhabited the island right out to sea. The storm was like the angry arm of Aegaeus, the Greek God of the angry seas, who would unleash great storms at the whim of the Titans. The wind would gust and strike with fierce velocity, provoking fear in its wake.

Then the wind stopped. The water covering the lower floor of the Big House glimmered, as if part of a glass lake. The silence was deafening. There were no birds squawking. There were no distant sounds of motorboats or shrimp boats making their way along the length of the island, and no planes flew overhead. It was an island isolated from the trappings of the 21st century, but with obvious reminders that civilization was only a 20-minute flight in the Piper Cub, or 45 minutes on the ferry. But now the air was soundless, void of any discriminating undulations or the clanking of diesel engines in the distance, of any reminders of human presence.

In the haunting stillness and thick air of the eye, we sat there. Our bodies relented just slightly as we relaxed from bracing against the walls of the closet. We were half way through this hell we had volunteered to endure. The backside of the storm might be worse, unless we were lucky enough that the storm veered northeastward toward Baton Rouge and the Texas-Louisiana gulf coast. Time would only tell, but with no further warnings. It would hit harder and more quickly. I hoped that the Big House would hold.

Looking southwest in the direction of the Great Blue Hole and the other cayes that dot the coastline of Belize, the storm's cover loomed heavily, with its layers of clouds folding and rolling into themselves. I could see the intensity of the storm, and hoped that the backside of this thing would be not as dramatic or horrific as what had just passed over us.

For what seemed like hours, time crept slowly, as the darkness that hovered tightly against the horizon began to loosen its grip. The blackness of the storm appeared to be rolling out and away from our line of vision. Without much notice, the water that covered the first floor and the grounds surrounding the Big House disappeared as quickly as it came. In my mind, this was a good sign, a positive. We sat, not moving a muscle. Our breathing had eased a bit, and we listened.

"Ethan," Julie finally whispered, "what do you think has happened to the villagers?"

"I don't know, but it can't be good," I said, glancing at her and seeing how worried she was. I knew Julie's concern was genuine, but it was also a defense mechanism for her. It was her way of coping with the situation we were in currently, the stress of the moment, not knowing what would happen next, or if we would survive.

"We'll see about them as soon as the storm has completely passed," I said. "I don't want to get caught out in the open when the back side of this storm hits us," I reminded her.

Just then, Bob and Lindsey emerged from their safe place. They stretched and looked around, in awe of the remnants of the storm. It looked as if a giant bucket of water had been thrown across us. "Good God," Bob said, "What a damn mess!"

"Julie, Ethan, are you guys okay?" Lindsey asked, as she sat down next to Julie and they hugged like long lost friends.

"Yes, I'm okay, as much as I can be, but I'm afraid of what's to come, Lindsey. What if the back side of this storm is worse? What will we do?" Julie said.

Bob and I looked at each other, each of us raising our eyebrows like a secret signal to not show panic. We both knew the next round could be worse.

"Oh, Julie, don't worry so much," Bob said, "We made it through the front side, didn't we? We'll make it through the back side. Besides, this old house is built like a tug boat, tough and seaworthy, strong as an ox," Bob continued.

"And besides, Julie, I think there's a chance that it will stay in the gulf. I think we just got a swipe from the outer bands of the storm," I said.

"Oh Ethan, you're always the optimist. Just look at the storm there, on the horizon, how it's bellowing and rolling. See the lightning strikes? See the waves crashing?" Julie said, in her most pronounced English accent, which is what she slipped into when she was mad, concerned, or irritated.

"Yes," I said, smiling, "I guess I am the eternal optimist, but that's better than crying in your beer."

"Oh shut up," she quipped, and made a growling, fluttering noise. "I am just concerned, Ethan. I just want this to be over. I want to check on the villagers."

"I agree with Ethan, Julie," Bob said. "There's a good chance this thing could miss us. Look at the direction of the clouds. The winds seem to be carrying them more northeastwardly. If it catches the gulfstream, it just may suck it on out of here," he said.

"Do you really think that, or are you trying to make us feel better?" Lindsey asked.

"No, no, I'm serious. Ethan's right. The back side of the storm could miss us. We'll get some wind and rain, maybe a flash flood, but the worst part could be over," Bob said.

"I hope so," Lindsey said, looking out toward the clouds and white capping surf.

"Water anybody," I asked, handing out bottles of water. We sat there drinking our water and staring out toward the sea. "It is awesome looking, isn't it," I said. And everyone nodded in agreement.

After what seemed to be a long while, I looked southward, and the brightness lifted suddenly from the farthest point on the horizon. The dark bellowing layers of clouds seemed to leap off the water. The contrast between the dark blue-black clouds and the lightness of the sky behind the storm became more apparent.

"Look, look," I said, excitedly, and pointed toward the light sky. "I think it's leaving the coastline. It's taking a more northeastwardly turn," I said, almost leaping with joy. "We have just hit the lotto," I exclaimed.

"I'll be damned," Bob said, standing up as he gazed toward the light. Julie and Lindsey stood slowly, as well, and we were awe struck for a moment.

"I wonder how William and Elizabeth are," I asked without turning away from the light that entranced us. "I hope they are okay," I said. "By the way, Bob, while we have what seems to be a reprieve from the storm, let me ask you, what the hell was that all about with William and Elizabeth anyway?" I asked. "It was strange, just strange, and I got the feeling that he had confided in you, and that you knew more than you were saying. So what's the deal with them," I asked again.

Glancing down at me, Bob said, "How well do you really know Elizabeth, Ethan? And, you DO know William; he's putty in Elizabeth's hands, like melting butter. Bottom line is this: she got scared, and she's too damn sophisticated to admit it when she's scared. Hell, we were all scared, too, or at least highly concerned," Bob continued. "We all were in the same boat, you might say, and we..."

I interrupted. "And we all agreed to come down here and do this gig," I said. "I have to tell you, Bob, I got the feeling that she was very upset with me because they were here facing a storm. Talk about getting the cold shoulder, it was like an iceberg! Hell, I couldn't have predicted that a hurricane would hit us on this island," I said firmly.

"Yes, but I think she blames you because she has to blame *somebody*. It's in her blood. Remember, she's from high Louisville breeding stock, a real blue-blood from Kentucky. I don't know how much money her daddy has, but apparently it's enough," Bob said.

"Yeah, yeah, I know," I said, "but it's frustrating when I think about it. I wish William had more balls when it came to that," I said.

"When it comes to what," Julie quipped, "and just what kind of balls do you think he needs, the kind you have?" she said laughing. Lindsey was laughing, too. I looked over at Bob, and he was chuckling as well. I felt my face turning red.

"She's gotcha, Dude," Bob said, laughing. The laughter seemed to be a good pressure relief valve. The relief was obvious on each of our faces. We needed that moment, and as embarrassed as I felt, I was glad that the moment had come, and we had laughed. It was a pointless argument. William and Elizabeth would either come back to the island or fly home. I suspected they would fly home. It gave me a sinking feeling in my gut. I wondered what this would do to our friendship.

"Ethan," Julie said, "bring me the camera, please. I want to take some photos."

We had failed to think of this, of pictorially recording our experiences. "Great idea," Lindsey said. And as quickly as I had the camera in her hands, Julie was snapping pictures.

"I left the wide angle lens on, is that alright," I said, as Julie was firing away.

"Of course, darling, it's fine," she said, back to sounding like her old self. "I love it," she said. She was in her element now, taking pictures and recording the events of the moment. We all stepped back and gave her room, as she worked the angles like mother wolf watching over her babies.

"See, score one for the optimist," I said, making a mark in the air with my finger, and smiling. Julie smiled, but kept shooting.

"These should be beautiful," she said, as she pulled the camera down and examined the rear view window to check the last two or three photos. "Yes, yes, those are good. Now let's see what I can do," she said, now totally enthralled.

"Let's go to the village," Julie said, looking up from the camera. It was obvious that she had gained a second wind, a renewed sense of advantage on the game of survival.

Chapter

22

The village was devastated. The wall of water that came through when the storm blew over the edge of the island had brought with it enough hydrologic power to essentially level the front section of the village. The village itself was a collection of small wooden shanties that were situated along a hillside. Additions to the structures had been added through the years as the families grew in number or other family members moved in. The layout of the village was circular in design, in that the houses of the leaders of the village were situated toward the back-center of the circular layout. The older members of the village, especially the more elderly people who had lived in the village the longest, were also situated toward the back-center. The younger couples with children filled the outer circle of shacks; all painted in the faded colors of blue, green, red, and an occasional burnt orange.

What looked like the first three or four rows of shacks had been wiped out; they were gone, as if wiped away with a wet cloth, leaving debris and remnants of the pieces of their lives scattered everywhere. Pieces of splintered wood lay along a path northeastward across that part of the island. It was as easy as tracking an animal in the sand or snow. The visible swipe across the village had been highly destructive.

We stood briefly and surveyed the scene, taking it all in, as we searched the hillside for any human survivors. Slowly, we began walking into the village proper, stepping over broken glass, pieces of wood siding, household debris, clothing, and children's toys. There were children everywhere, all slender and round-faced, with their faces and hands filthy from playing in the dirt. The outer edge of the village was gone, destroyed. Nothing could be more sobering than looking and walking in the middle of what was once, just a day earlier, a thriving community of people; poor and basic, but thriving. The children ran up to us as we walked through their domain. Some of them stood and waved, smiling as we passed. The women of the village, some with babies on their hips, stood in the doorways and looked sheepishly toward us, only occasionally yielding a smile. It was as if they wanted to be friendly, but were wary of strangers.

Any American in this part of the world was considered wealthy. We certainly were not wealthy, but when compared to their standard of living, I guess we were. Here we were, two couples from America, living on an island for a year without having to work, with what must have seemed like endless resources from the states. The people of this island were, of course, use to Americans or Caucasians from other countries visiting the area and spending money on food and drink. Many that visited were divers, who were not your typical tourists, but were attracted to Belize for two primary reasons: the second largest barrier reef in the world, and the Great Blue Hole located just southeast of this island. The Great Blue Hole stretches more than 300 feet across, has a depth of 412 feet and is a perfect circular shape. It has been a famous spot for diving enthusiasts for years... a hideaway of sorts.

The four of us spread out walking through the village. Without discussion, it was obvious that we all were looking for survivors and victims. Bob and I lifted sections of siding and planks of wood, tree limbs, and sections of roofs that lay across the front of the village where the wall of water made its way through. We could only hope that the villagers were safe, and that no one had been killed or badly injured.

"Over here," a voice came from the back of the village, where some of the more sturdy structures were left standing. "Over, here, señor, come, come," the voice said again. We all began moving more quickly now, with more haste, toward the voice. It sounded like that of a young adult male. Suddenly, as we came around a washed up pile of debris, the voice was closer, clearer, and we saw a young boy. He looked to be about 12 or so.

"Over here," he said again, motioning us to come in his direction. It was apparent that he was concerned. Perhaps, someone was injured. As we got closer to the shack, more of the villagers began to come out of their places of refuge. They had gathered on the highest points and in the sturdiest of the houses. I was amazed that some of the small houses had withstood the high winds. Many of the shanties had debris stacked against the leeward side of the structure. As I studied this odd stacking of wooden fencing and pieces of housing, I realized that the piles of debris provided additional structural mass, which I guessed added protection for the pounding wind gusts. These 'fortified' structure became the villagers' safe houses through the storm.

"Ethan, Bob, come quickly," Julie called out. She and Lindsey had followed the young boy into the shack, and now needed our assistance. When we arrived at the door, we saw an elderly woman lying on a small cot with blood soaked bandages wrapped around the calf of her left leg. A closer look revealed a piece of splintered wood stinking in her leg. It was a tapered, but jagged piece of wood. It looked clean and free of any dirt. The woman did not make a sound, but the expression on her face told us she was in pain.

"Ethan, what can we do?" Julie said in a calm low voice, as she consoled the woman.

"Bob, can you and Ethan remove this piece of wood from her leg?" Lindsey asked. Bob and I looked at each other, knowing that we were about to attempt the removal of the splintered and nasty looking piece of wood from this woman's leg.

"Yes, I think we can do that, don't you think, Ethan?" Bob said, looking at the woman.

"I agree, my friend, but we're going to need some of the liquor from the house to use as an antiseptic; and some rags or cloth of some kind that's clean to use for a bandage," I said, bending down slowly to look at the leg and the stick of wood protruding from it. It wasn't going to be easy to extract it, but it needed to be removed before the skin and tissue began to swell and tighten around the object. There was no time to waste, and no one else to hand this off to, and no way to communicate with the outside world. We were on our own.

"Julie, Bob or I can go back to the house and gather something to use for bandages, and get the liquor," I said. "Whoever stays behind can construct a table outside where she can be situated for the procedure. We have to get her outside where we have better lighting."

"I'll go get the bandages and the liquor," Bob said. "You stay here and get the table ready. I'll take the boy with me," Bob added.

"I'll stay with Julie and help her with getting the leg area clean," Lindsey said. Another young boy brought a bucket of water inside the shack and gave it to Julie. Julie looked at Lindsey, and after examining the water for cleanliness, began gently washing the woman's leg from her knee to her ankle, foot, and toes. The woman grimaced when Julie came close to the piece of wood. The splintered wood looked to be about four to six inches long from the point of entry in the skin to the end of the stick. It looked perfectly splintered from a larger piece of wood. It was from an old piece of wood, probably from some part of one of the shacks or the fencing that surrounded many of them. The entry point of the stick of wood appeared to be clean and exact. There were no jagged edges, although the piece was irregular in shape. It was tapered in its linear shape and seemed somewhat pointed at its end. This was a positive observation, since removing the piece of wood would be aided by the fact that the fat end of the piece was on the outside, and the tapered end was inserted into the skin. The unknown factor was how deep the splinter was in the leg.

"Can you feel the end of it," Lindsey asked in a low voice, keeping her eyes on the woman, wary of her going into shock.

"No, I really can't tell. Every time I get near the entry point, she tenses up, and acts like she wants to move her leg," Julie said, as she continued to wash the leg and wipe the woman's face and forehead.

"We're back," Bob said as he and the boy entered the shack. He knelt down beside Julie and Lindsey, sat the assortment of pillow cases and hand towels down and began cutting the pillow cases into strips. "I brought the gin and the whiskey," he said.

"Okay, I've got the table set up outside," I said, "How are we going to move her out of this place?"

"I'm not sure," Julie said, "she grimaces at the least little touch. The leg is very sensitive. We may have to do this in here."

"But the lighting is so dim," I said, "I don't ....."
Julie interrupted.

"But the last thing we need is for this poor woman to go into shock," Julie said, "and I'm afraid of what might happen if we try to move her."

"No problem," Bob said with some confidence. "I brought the flashlights, too; thought we might have a situation like this."

"Bob, you are a crafty guy," Lindsey said.

"That's great, Bob, you're a genius," Julie said.

"Well, I am impressed, but I'm not saying anything more, Bob, your head might get too big to get out the door," I said.

"Kiss my ass, Ethan, besides, I brought your liquor," Bob said with a chuckle.

We set up the flashlights and gave the woman some of the whiskey to drink. Julie and Lindsey gently poured some of the gin over the area of the leg where the splintered piece of wood had entered the skin.

"Do either of you have a pocket knife?" Julie asked, looking at Bob and me.

"Got that too," Bob said, grinning at me as he handed Julie the knife. She cleaned it by pouring some of the gin over it, and wiped it with one of the pieces of pillow case Bob had ripped.

"I have to see if the skin has attached itself to the wood," Julie said in a low voice, as she began to push the edge of the skin around the surfaces of the wood. Lindsey continued to wipe the woman's face, trying to console her. The woman didn't speak English, but uttered moaning protests a broken dialect of Spanish.

"Keep the boy close by, just in case we need him to translate," Lindsey said to Bob, who by now had made a new friend of the boy.

"Oh, I don't think he's going anywhere," Bob said. "I think this is his grandmother. I believe his parents are either dead or away working on the mainland," Bob said.

"Okay, Ethan, can you position yourself on the other side of me?" Julie asked. "As soon as I can determine that her skin is not adhering to the wood, I want you to begin to gently pull this stick out," she said.

I got myself into position with a good view of the entry point on the leg. I could tell that the skin was not affixed to the wood, but we had no time to waste. My thought was that we would get the wood out of the leg, disinfect it with the liquor, and bandage it as best we could. Then, we would get her as comfortable as possible before making our way to San Pedro, which wasn't far. Hopefully, we could find Leonardo, and get some help.

"Okay, Ethan, I think it's time," Julie said slowly.

"Okay, here goes," I said. I moved my hand slowly to the stick, wrapping my fingers around it in a gentle grip, trying not to make any unnecessary moves.

"Bob, can you shine the lights on this side," I said.

"Yep, tell me where," Bob replied.

We all were now in full rescue mode, fully focused on this raw but serious procedure. I examined the angle of the piece of wood, taking into account the entry point, trying to envision the piece of wood. It would get narrower, I thought, as it gets closer to the end.

"Julie, as I pull it out, pour some of the gin around the exit point," I said. "It will burn, and she will scream, but maybe that will mask the pain from the extraction."

"Got it, will do," Julie said. And with that, I began to pull the piece of wood out of the woman's leg. Julie poured the gin from the bottle all around the wound, as Lindsey kept the moist cloth on the woman's forehead. Bob kept the lights in place so I could see the opening of the wound as I removed the stick. Amazingly, as soon as it broke free of the oozing surface of the skin, it came out quickly and easily. The woman did not scream. She only breathed heavily and with a cadence I recognized. Then, in a flash of a second, it hit me that these people never had any pain reliever, no antiseptics to speak of, and she gave birth naturally. So this, while painful and uncomfortable, she was accustomed to enduring pain.

"I think I got it all," I said to Julie. "Can you see anything more?" I asked.

"No, I think it's all out," she said. "Bob, can you shine the light all around and let me get a look?" she asked.

"Yes ma'am," Bob said, pointing the light in the exact area she needed.

"Yep, it's all out. Now, let's clean it and get a clean bandage on it," Julie said.

The woman seemed less tense now. The stressful look on her face had disappeared, although Lindsey continued stroking her head with the moist rag.

"I think we're in good shape, gang," Julie said, sounding very satisfied.

"Tell the boy how to look after her for a while, and remind him to come find us if her condition worsens," I said. "We can check on her when we come back through, or send someone from town."

"I think we're it," Bob said, with a-matter-of-fact tone. "There's no telling what we will find in town, and besides, think of the tasks they will have on their plates," Bob added.

"You're right," I said, "we'll come back by and check on her."

Julie and Lindsey made the woman as comfortable as possible. We asked the boy if anyone else had been injured, and shockingly, no one had. They were all safe; shaken, but safe.

"Do they have any food?" I asked. The thought suddenly occurred to me that these poor people might be without food. "Ask him, Bob, about their food storage," I said.

Bob asked the boy, who indicated that the elders in the village had buried the food supply and some water, but that they would need more water soon, since their cistern had been destroyed by the wind from the storm.

"Tell him we will work on some water," I said to Bob, who relayed the message. Bob and the boy had bonded. Their interaction was personal.

As we made our way through the remains of the village back to the road that led to San Pedro, even more of the villagers began to come out of hiding. They began to pick up the scattered debris, in an effort to reconstruct some semblance of their former village from the chaos left behind from the storm.

It would take about 20 minutes to walk the short distance to San Pedro. We had walked it before, and sometimes had ridden bikes into town for dinner. San

Pedro was a small town, consisting of three or four streets lined with shops and restaurants and the old Catholic church that stood stoically in the center of town. It was the same church where I found Julie after I woke up face down on the beach... a mystery yet unsolved.

Chapter

23

The view of San Pedro was uplifting. All the buildings seemed in place and unharmed. There was debris strewn along all the streets, but the structures were in place and the people were busily working, gathering the items that had been tossed about in the storm. San Pedro was a welcome sight.

"Let's find Leonardo," I said, as we got closer to the edge of town. People were buzzing around, surveying the damage; you could see relief on their faces as they realized the damage was not as severe as they had feared.

"I don't think the town has much damage," Bob said, as he looked around. "There's no apparent major damage. The wall of water must have taken a turn when it rounded the front of the village and hit the drainage ditch that leads to the main channel between the Caye and the mainland. Good golly, were they lucky," Bob said.

"I think you're right, Bob," I said. "The buildings don't have much wind damage either."

"Ethan, there are more people here than I expected to see. Remember, there was a mandatory evacuation order from the Belizean government. Apparently, more people stayed than I thought. I wonder where Leonardo and his family are," Julie said.

"Julie, guys, let's split up and walk separate streets in order to get a better idea of the damage. We can meet back at Leonardo's place," Lindsey said.

"Good idea, Babe," Bob said, pulling her close to give her a quick kiss on her head. "Ethan, you and I can go down these two streets to the left, and the girls can go to the right," he said.

"Good idea, Bob," I said. "We'll see you girls at Leonardo's." I gave Julie a quick kiss on the cheek, but she grabbed my arm and pulled me back.

"Oh, no you don't," Julie said in her heaviest British accent, "I need more than a peck on the head, dear sir," she said, pulling me toward her and kissing me on the lips. "There!" She said, "That should get you down the street and back," smiling as Bob and I trotted off toward our side of the town, laughing like two kids who had stolen their first kiss.

As we walked down the street, most of the businesses were boarded up, but others had been reopened by their owners. The people of San Pedro were proud and independent people and very hard working entrepreneurs with their own businesses, some of which had been passed from generation to generation.

Ambergris Caye has a rich history that dates back to the 14th and 15th centuries with a lot of pirates, privateers, and explorers from Spain, England, and France. Belize was also a British colony from 1632 until

1982, when Great Britain granted Belize its independence. So, the people of Belize, and especially the people who called any of the Cayes home, were survivalists who had a very independent spirit.

When Bob and I arrived at Leonardo's, Julie and Lindsey were standing near the entrance talking with Leonardo. He had not only re-opened the restaurant and had food cooking, but was providing people a place to get water to drink and food to eat.

"Hello, Ethan, Bob," Leonardo said, shaking our hands in greeting. "What did you find on your walk," he asked. He motioned for us to step in under the canvas umbrella covering a large round table. "Did you find anyone in need of serious help," Leonardo asked, with his Spanish accent obvious with every word.

"No, everyone seems to be in good shape," I said. "In fact, we're all surprised that there is so little damage, Leonardo. You should see the village. It was destroyed."

"Yes, Julie and Lindsey were just telling me about the woman with the stick in her leg, and the loss of houses there. Sounds like you guys did a wonderful thing. I told Julie and Lindsey that I will send my sisters and my wife to the village to check on the woman and the other families who live there. I will send some food, too," he said.

"That's sounds great, Leonardo, can we help with anything?" I asked.

"Can you cook?" he asked as quickly as I could finish my statement.

"Well... yes, I can...if it's not too complicated," I said, looking at Julie and feeling Bob slapping me on the back and hearing his chuckle.

"Heck, Leonardo, Ethan can cook with the best of them," Bob said. "What else can we do to help?" he said.

We were all eager to help, and Leonardo took us up on the offer. While I was assigned to the kitchen cooking tortillas, beans and rice, Julie and Lindsey were setting up tables and chairs, wiping them clear of the dirt and debris from the storm, and Bob was setting up umbrellas that would provide shade to the people who would no doubt stop in and eat the free food. Meantime, Leonardo instructed his sisters and wife to go to the village and check on the woman we had told him about. They carried with them huge baskets of food and water.

"Tell them to send someone with their water containers. We will fill them," Leonardo said, as his sisters and wife left walking toward the village.

"This is very kind of you, Leonardo," Bob said, as he raised another canvas umbrella.

"This is what we islanders do, Bob. We take care of each other," Leonardo said. "While the Belizean government is not oppressive, they expend very few of the government's resources for solving problems on the islands. The mainland will get most of the resources. We have to depend on ourselves to survive," he said.

"Believe it or not, it's not too different in the states, Leonardo," Bob said. "Whenever a disaster hits, people get crazy and greedy," Bob said, continuing the conversation.

"You mean like what happened in New Orleans with Katrina," Leonardo said. They both were working feverishly to get all the tables and umbrellas set up. Leonardo was making a special sign with chalk on a small black slate that was normally used for announcing the daily specials.

"Exactly!" Bob said. "That's a perfect example of how greed and incompetence can prevent the necessary assistance from getting to the people who really need it. The people who were left behind were the ones who needed help the most. Hell, Leonardo, there were people dying on the streets, and nobody gave a damn. They had no water, no food, nothing. It was total chaos and a total embarrassment for our country as far as I'm concerned, nationally and internationally," Bob continued ranting.

"I agree 100 percent," Leonardo said. "You want a cold beer, my friend?" he asked Bob.

"You got cold beer, Leonardo?" Bob asked, surprised at the possibility that with no electricity on the island, Leonardo had cold beer.

"Yes sir, cold beer here!" Leonardo quipped with an obvious sense of pride. "I told you we islanders take care of each other. Where would we be as an island without cold beer?" he laughed, smiling and disappearing into the back. "What kind you have?" Leonardo yelled from the back of the storage room.

"Cold...anything cold," Bob said, as he sat down, still amazed that Leonardo had cold beer.

Setting the cold bottle on the table and smiling ear to ear, Leonardo proudly pronounced, "Here you go, Bob!"

"Leonardo, how the heck did you keep this beer cold...ahhhh, with the storm and all?" Bob asked, astounded, but taking a satisfying gulp from the cold glass bottle.

"Island secret!" Leonardo said, laughing as he turned and walked toward the kitchen and called for me to come out front. "Ethan, come out here for a moment, I have something for you," he shouted, chuckling. Bob was still drinking and savoring every swallow of the cold brew.

As I ducked through the curtain that separated the public areas from the kitchen and storage room, I saw Bob sitting at a table. "Hey, no sitting down on the job, bud row, or your pay will be docked," I said, as I walked toward Bob. I noticed that Leonardo was smiling, too, and had one hand behind his back. "What?" I asked.

"You can dock my pay all you want, Sergeant," Bob replied, holding up his half empty bottle of beer.

"Where did you get a cold beer," I asked, turning toward Leonardo. "Leonardo, where..."

But, before I could finish my sentence, Leonardo had placed a cold bottle of Stella Artois beer in my right hand.

"Drink up, Ethan," he said. "It's an island secret!" He laughed along with Bob, who motioned for me to drink up. So, after giving a toast, I turned the bottle up and drank about half of it before sitting down.

"Now that's a good beer," I said.

"Hell, any beer that's cold right now is a good beer," Bob said, chuckling and amazed. "Leonardo, you are the King of this island! Here's to you my friend," Bob said, lifting his bottle, and downing the remaining bit of beer in his bottle.

"I second the motion," I said, following in full step with Bob, finishing my beer in one gulp. "Damn, that was good."

The three of us resumed our work setting up tables, preparing and cooking tortillas, black beans and rice. One of Leonardo's daughters had cut up tomatoes and onions, and placed them in a large wooden bowl. Another wooden bowl, one that looked 100 years old, held lettuce. Both bowls were sitting on top of a large rectangular metal container that stood approximately four inches high, and had condensation beading on the outside. As I examined it, I realized that it contained water and ice, which provided the level of coolness needed to keep the lettuce and tomatoes fresh. I stood in amazement that Leonardo had apparently figured out a way to preserve ice and water during emergencies. He was amazing!

When Julie and Lindsey returned from their trip down the street, we reassembled outside at a large round table. The girls had been to check on a shop owner where they had purchased clothing and jewelry days before. The owners of the shop were an elderly woman and her daughter. The daughter had been educated in the states, but had returned to live with her mother and help her run the business.

"You guys look happy and sassy," Lindsey said, glancing at Bob. "What have you boys been up to?" she asked, as if she knew we had gotten away with something.

"Yes, Ethan, what are you hiding?" Julie said, getting into the action. Leonardo began to laugh and disappeared behind the curtain, only to reappear in seconds with two more bottles of cold beer.

"Oh, my Gosh," Lindsey said, taking one of the bottles and admiring it before taking a sip.

"My, my, what have we here?" Julie said, employing a bit of her British humor, and then taking not a sip, but a huge gulp. "Oh, I'm sorry," she said, "I don't usually behave this way. I mean…" Julie laughed and gave up explaining.

"Don't worry about it Jul's," Lindsey said, as she took another drink of her beer. "Besides, we're on island time, and the customs are different," she said, laughingly.

"You're right, Linds', you're right. Here goes, cheers everyone," Julie said, turning the bottle up and downing the entire bottle with one turn. We all stood in awe.

"Julie, I don't think I've ever seen you do that," I said, amazed, looking at a petit and beautiful woman who just downed a full bottle of Stella Artois.

"Well now, this sets a new standard, I believe," Bob said.

"We can drink with the best of them, right Julie," Lindsey said, placing her now empty bottle on the table.

With the beer all consumed, we compared notes about the damage or the lack of. Leonardo's sisters and wife had returned from the village, and reported that the woman we had helped was resting well, in good spirits, and very grateful for our help and concern. I went back into the kitchen, where Leonardo's wife and sisters had taken over their spots, and were now preparing a tray of food for us. His wife motioned for me to go back out to the table. The food was coming momentarily. "Un minuto," she said as she motioned me out. I followed her command and returned to the table where the others were sitting. About that same time, Leonardo returned with another round of beers, and Maria, Francisco's wife appeared with a large tray of food. She put it on the table and motioned for us to eat, and we did.

Chapter

24

The walk back to the house took a while. We stopped by the village again, and to our astonishment, the members of the village had almost completed the task of clearing away the debris. It looked messy and torn, but at least the front part of the village had been mostly cleared. There were now cooking fires going, with large pots hanging over them, cooking whatever they could gather. Leonardo and some of the other restaurant owners had sent out food for the villagers to cook and eat. We supposed that they were cooking a broth or stew of some type. Some of the men of the village had returned from a short fishing expedition. We were told that after every storm, the fishing is always good. The people of the village were very resourceful, and they served as a stark contrast to the rest of the civilized world, in the art of survival not only in daily life, but during a disaster. It made a definite mark on Julie, Bob, Lindsey, and me. We each vowed not to complain ever again about having to do without some convenience.

Clean-up of the house took that evening and most of the next day. The house was designed to allow rising water to flow through the structure without making the house buoyant. This feature probably saved the Big House from the many storms that have passed over Belize and its Cayes through the years.

Since the walls were made of the same type of planks as the floors in the house, it was a matter of cranking up the generator that pumped water from and underground aquifer, in order to wash out the mud and slime from the house. The smell was horrific, and it required plain old back-breaking scrubbing. Most of the furniture was made of wood. The sofa pillows had to be tossed, but Leonardo said he would order some new ones for the house. He had been appointed by the present owners to oversee and manage the house. Within a few days, we had the house back in ship shape, although we all were exhausted. We hadn't left the house since returning from our original recon trip into town that threw us into a role of playing field medics. We all suddenly realized that we hadn't thought about William and Elizabeth either.

Sitting around in the chairs under a cluster of palm trees, sipping on some margaritas Bob whipped up to go along with our lunch of conch salad, pineapple, chips and salsa, Julie suddenly asked, "Has anyone heard from William and Elizabeth?"

"I don't think so, Julie," Lindsey said.

"Bob, have you heard from William…or Elizabeth," Lindsey asked, directing her question to him.

"No, I haven't. I thought about while we were in the village yesterday, but none of us has had time to inquire, and how would we anyway? All the phone lines are either down or out of service," Bob said.

"I know. I thought about them, too. But I don't even know where they were staying? Do you have a clue, Bob?" I asked. "They didn't tell me. In fact, as we were discussing the other day, I felt like I was getting the cold shoulder," I said.

"Well, you were, Ethan, to put it bluntly. Elizabeth got scared and wanted to leave right then, no discussion, no questions, period. And I think William was embarrassed," Bob said.

"And that's fine, I guess, I just wished that he had been a little more open with all of us. We all made this decision independently to come down here," I said.

"Yes, we did, and I don't regret it one bit, and neither does Lindsey," he said. Lindsey shook her head in agreement, while Julie just sat and listened.

"I mean, we've been here for six months or more, and now it's hurricane season, and hell, the island is on the receiving coastline of Central America, and has a rich history of hurricanes throughout the last 100 years," I said.

"I know, I know," Bob said, "but I'm telling you, and you know Elizabeth and how she gets when she makes up her mind to do something contrary to the group. She'll get her way. That's the way she was raised, and William knows this. Hell, he has to live with her, not us," Bob said.

"Yeah, yeah, I know. Do you suppose they went to the Biltmore Hotel in Belize City?" I asked.

"Don't know. Maybe we can ask Leonardo to find out. It would be good to know they're okay, and what they're going to do from here," Bob said.

"What do you suppose they will do?" I asked.

Bob thought for a moment, then, looked up, "I'm not sure, but I bet they catch a flight out of here. I just hope they let us know," Bob said. I nodded in agreement, and we all sat there eating our food and catching our breath. We had been going non-stop for three or four days courtesy of the storm. It had been a stressful time, and we ached all over.

"Why don't Lindsey and I bike into town and asked Leonardo if he can contact someone on the mainland, maybe even call the Biltmore Hotel," Julie said.

"That's a great idea, Jul's," Lindsey said quickly. "You guys stay here and put the finishing touches on the clean-up, and Julie and I will make you dinner, maybe even open a bottle of wine for your troubles," Lindsey said.

"That's enough to convince me," Bob said.

"Same here," I said, "and see if Leonardo can find out through one of his cousins where the driver may have taken them," I added.

With that, the girls were off down the road on their bikes. Bob and I finished cleaning the small pieces of furniture, tools, and the steps of the house. We had finished the inside earlier and were trying to get all the slimy mud off the legs of the end tables from the living room. The other furniture had come clean fairly easily. We had learned that by applying a thick coating of surf board wax after cleaning the surface of the wood with Murphy's oil soap or Teak oil that the finish of the wood came back with a rich and aged patina.

"I have an idea, Bob," I said, as we were putting away the tools for the final time, with our chores completed.

"What's that, Ethan," Bob said, not breaking stride with his work detail.

"Let's do a dive. We both have our PADI certification. We've had this on our list of things to do down here. Besides, from what I've researched on the net, this place is rich in pirate history," I said.

"I know, I know," Bob said, "I've been doing some research myself. This place is loaded. Have you read about the Santa Yaga?"

"Yes, I have, and the Oxford as well," I said.

"Yeah, that one, too," Bob said. "Let's talk to Leonardo about arranging a dive for us. Maybe this storm uncovered some never before sunken treasure," he said.

"Man, wouldn't that be cool," I said. "What if we found the mother-load," I said, my voice showing excitement.

"Don't count your chickens, Ethan," Bob quipped, "But that would be cool, wouldn't it?" Bob said, sounding as giddy as I did with the possibility of finding something, anything out there from an ancient shipwreck.

"We need to talk to Leonardo," Bob said.

"Yep, let's go see him tomorrow morning, first thing," I said. Bob agreed, and we both grabbed a lukewarm beer and headed for the hammocks that were strung out among the palm trees.

"Right now, I'm gonna just dream about it, Dude," Bob said, getting into the hammock, and taking a long sip of beer.

"I'm with you, Buddy," I said, following Bob's actions and climbing into my own hammock. Soon, we were snoozing to the rhythm of the ocean waves crashing on the beach only about a hundred feet away, as the sea birds sounded their return to the palms.

It wasn't long before Julie and Lindsey returned from town. As they dismounted their bikes, they began to look around the grounds, but saw nothing. "I wonder where they are, Jul's," Lindsey said.

"I don't know, but let's look around on the ocean side. Maybe they're working around there, or fishing or something," Julie said.

They rounded the corner of the house, glanced over toward the tool shed, and saw the shovels and heavy whisk brooms hanging in there places. "Well, the tools are there, in place. I guess they've quit for the day," Julie said.

Just then, Lindsey spotted the hammocks. "Looky, looky, looky," she said. They trotted across the back lawn, motioning to each other to proceed quietly, and they walked right up to the hammocks. Then, Lindsey motioned to Julie to back away from the hammocks, where Bob and I were sleeping, soundly. "What do you suppose we should do, Julie," Lindsey asked, "should we wake them or dump them out?" she said.

"Oh, Lindsey," said Julie, "I have a splendid idea. Follow me," she said. The two of them scurried off to the shed, grab a bucket, filled it with water, and began carrying it toward the hammocks. "This is going to be so sweet," Julie said, trying to giggle quietly, as they struggled with the bucket of water.

Motioning to each other and raising three fingers, as if to count down a one, two, three, go signal, Julie and Lindsey pulled back on the bucket and lunged it forward with a girlish grunt and squeak, and in one huge motion, Bob and I were doused with five gallons of very cold water.

Bob and I rolled out of the hammocks, not knowing exactly what was happening, except that we were suddenly all wet and disoriented. The girls turned and ran, laughing so hard they fell over their own feet and rolled around holding their stomachs.

Once Bob and I realized that we'd been had, and saw the girls incapacitated by their own laughter, without a word, we signaled each other, and ran toward the water hose. I turned the water on, while Bob grabbed the end of the hose with the sprayer, and the water pursuit was on. Julie and Lindsey struggled to get up, which gave Bob and me time to get into position.

"Ethan, don't you dare," Julie commanded, but it was too late. The full force of the water hit her square in the chest, soaking her from head to toe. "Ahhhhhh, crap, crap, crap, Bob!" She screamed and ran.

"Okay, Lindsey, you're next," Bob exclaimed, laughing the whole time. "Where are you Lindsey," Bob said.

"Bob, you two, I can't believe it," Julie said laughing now as she lay on the ground.

"Now, now, now, Julie, all is fair in love and war, and getting doused with a bucket of cold ass water is war in my book," Bob said, laughing just as hard. "Seems like your partner in crime has fled the scene, Julie," Bob said, "but don't worry, she'll get hers when she least expects it," he said.

"Julie, you knew we would get you back. There was no way we'd let this go," I said.

"That's right, Julie," Bob said, "and, pardon me for saying, but you look pretty good in a wet T-shirt," Bob retorted, and chuckled as he turned off the water.

"Oh shut up, Bob, and look the other way," Julie said, chuckling as I helped her to her feet.

"Lindsey, come on out, the water war is at a truce for the moment," Julie said in her British accent.

"I don't believe you. Bob and Ethan will lure me into their trap," Lindsey said from inside the house.

"No, really, Lindsey, we've called a time out," Bob said, "but I owe you a soaking, my dear," he said.

Lindsey came out and we all sat around the patio deck of the old house, and laughed and giggled for a good half hour.

"So, what is the plan for dinner, girls?" Bob said, looking back and forth at Julie and Lindsey. "You guys cooking, or shall we go into town?" he said.

"No, we can cook, I think," Julie said. "What do you think, Lindsey, cook or town?" she said.

"It doesn't matter to me. If we go back into town, though, Bob, you're doing the peddling, or carrying me on your shoulders, take your pick," Lindsey said.

About that time, Leonardo's son, Eduardo, wheeled into the driveway. The crunching of the seashell drive caught our attention. "Eduardo," Bob said, "what brings you out here?"

"Hello Ms. Julie, hello Ms. Lindsey," said Eduardo, greeting the ladies first, and then turning to Bob to address his question, which was also the task his father, Leonardo, had sent him to complete. "I have a message from my father. He wishes for you to join him for dinner at the restaurant. Here, I have a written note for you," Eduardo said, and handed a folded piece of paper with a note written on it.

Join me for dinner at 7:00, I have
something I wish to discuss
something with you.
Respectfully, Leonardo

Bob handed me the note. I read it, and handed it to Julie and Lindsey, who were suddenly quiet, as they were studying the situation with a quizzical aura. "Tell your father we'll be there, Eduardo. Thank him for us for the invitation," I said.

"I will. Thank you, sirs. Good bye, Ms. Julie, good bye, Ms. Lindsey," Eduardo said, as he jumped back on his bike and peddled down the gravel road.

We all sat there for a moment and looked at each other. Finally, Bob broke the silence, "Wonder what this is all about?"

"Beats me," I said. "I guess you girls are off the hook," I said, looking at Julie and Lindsey, who had serious looks on their faces.

"Bob has to do the peddling, and there will be no negotiating," Lindsey quipped.

"You're not off the hook either, Ethan," Julie said. "I'll think about your penance while we are at dinner," she said.

"Penance, for what," I asked, knowing she was yanking my chain, just trying to get a reaction.

"Oh, you'll figure it out. I'm going to take a bath and get dressed. You boys find yourselves something to do," she said, as her voice faded the more into the house she went. Bob and I looked at each other, shrugged our shoulders, and went back to our hammocks. They would call us when it was our turn to get dressed for dinner at Leonardo's.

****

We arrived at Leonardo's at about 6:50, and were greeted graciously at the door, and escorted to a private, out of the way table to the side of the dining area. The lighting inside the restaurant was dim, cozy even, but also on this night, there was an air of covert intent that made it exciting.

Leonardo came right over and welcomed us to our table. "Leonardo, this is lovely, but what's the occasion?" I asked. "We were here earlier this week."

"Yes, but you four have been working so hard for the people of the island, besides the huge job you had of your own cleaning out all that mud and slime. We wanted to show our appreciation," Leonardo said.

"That's great, Leonardo, but I, we consider you guys family. Taking care of family is what we do. We're like family," Bob said, waving his hand back and forth toward Julie and me, and him and Lindsey.

"I know. I know, but what you did for the elderly woman in the village was special. You have no idea what an impact you have made on that village. A message has been sent to the Governor in Belize City about your heroic efforts. This dinner tonight is my personal act of appreciation for you all. You are truly *Islanders* now, one of us," Leonardo said. We were all shocked, speechless.

"Thank you, Leonardo," Bob said. "We are honored to be your guests tonight," Bob continued. We all nodded in agreement.

"Wow," I said. "I'm shocked. I had no idea. All we did was helped the elderly woman with getting the stick out of her leg."

"Yes," Julie added, "but Ethan, no one probably would have gotten to her in time to remove the stick. She would have been at a high risk of developing gangrene, and possibly would have to have her leg removed. This is really special for Leonardo. You can tell he has been really touched by our efforts," Julie continued.

"I agree," Lindsey said. "It feels odd, being honored like this. We would have done that for anybody," she said.

"Yes, but there wasn't anybody else but us to do what was needed and had to be done," Bob said. "I guess this is a big deal for this little island of survivors."

Dinner was ordered and served, and was delicious. Dessert and coffee followed the four course main meal accompanied by a mariachi band of local musicians. The storm had indeed passed, and things were getting back to normal. This is what we came here for, I thought, as we all had our coffee, and were sitting in the opulence of the moment, soaking it all in for pure enjoyment.

"Ethan," Bob said, once again breaking the silence, "let's tell the girls about the dive trip we want to go on," he said. Both Julie and Lindsey sat up with attentive ears.

"Okay," I said. "Bob and I want to do a dive trip to a sunken wreck, if we can find one. Do you girls want to go?" I said, as quickly and to the point as I could be, in order to take advantage of the shock of the idea. Actually, I knew that Julie and Lindsey would not want to go, but they would negotiate something for themselves.

"No, I don't think we'll want to go, Ethan," Julie said.

"Naahhh, me either, Bob," Lindsey said.

"But, darling," Julie said. "Lindsey and I will go shopping while you mates are under water. Is that okay with you dear?" She smiled knowing she had me. I did not want to play hard ball. Bob busted out laughing, "She's got you again, dude."

"Oh, you're not off the hook either, remember Bob..." Lindsey said, reminding Bob of his earlier retorts and soft threats of retribution from the water bucket.

Holding up his hands in surrender, "You win," Bob said. "Go shop all you want, and no water battles."

"You're a love, Bob," Lindsey said, smiling and blowing him a kiss across the table.

"We have to talk with Leonardo, though, to set the trip up," Bob said.

"And to see what he suggests for a dive sight as well," I added.

We had about finished our dessert and coffee when Leonardo came back over to our table. The restaurant had been crowded and busy with most of the customers being local residents or business people who either didn't leave the island, or had made their own way back from the mainland after the storm. Resumption of open transport from the mainland had not yet been approved by the Belizean government, but locals with their own boats had made their way back in order to check on their businesses and secure their property.

"Leonardo," I said, as he walked toward our table. "Bob and I need to talk with you. Can you sit for a minute," I asked.

"Sure, sure, what can I help you with, my friend?" Leonardo asked.

"Bob and I want to go on a dive trip, and we were hoping that we could dive an old wreck. Can you help us with that?" I asked.

"That should be no problem, Ethan. Do you have your PADI certification information with you?" he asked.

"Yes, Bob and I both have all our credentials," I said.

"Then, it will be no problem. In fact, if you want to dive a really old wreck site, where maybe you could find some ancient treasure, I think I can arrange it," Leonardo said.

"That would be super," I said, "that was exactly what Bob and I were hoping for. Now that the storm has passed, and things seem to be getting back to normal, maybe we will get lucky and find something worthwhile."

"Maybe so," Leonardo said, looking anxiously around at the restaurant. "Let me work on it tomorrow. I'll come by your place at the house, okay?" Leonardo said. "I have to get back to work now. My second round of customers is coming in."

We thanked him, and began to make our plans for the gear, maps, watches, dive knives, and all the rest. Julie and Lindsey had excused themselves to go to the restroom. When they came back, we suggested that we go back to the house for a nightcap, and that we would relate our conversation with Leonardo there.

Chapter

25

The next morning, Leonardo drove out to the house. We had coffee, eggs, bacon, and toast on the table and invited him to sit and eat while we discussed the basic idea for our dive trip. The coffee was black and hot, and the eggs were brown eggs from yard chickens that had been gathered by an islander who lived a short distance from the old house.

"Come on in, Leonardo," I said. Julie and Lindsey were putting the jelly and honey on the table.

"Ethan, good morning, good morning," Leonardo said, his Caribbean-Spanish accent sounded more heavy than usual. "How are my island castaways this morning?" he asked.

"Oh, Leonardo, you're a jewel," Julie said, giving him a kiss on the cheek. "Come in and sit down. Do you want any coffee? We have some hot eggs and rolls, and some fruit. Eat with us Leonardo," she said.

"I really shouldn't, Ms. Julie, but I cannot resist the coffee, and if I have the coffee, I must have a hot biscuit, and if I have a hot biscuit, I guess I will have some eggs," he said as he chuckled and sat down.

"Good choice," said Lindsey, "you won't regret it, Leo."

We all sat and chatted as we ate the freshly cooked eggs, bacon, hot biscuits and fresh fruit. It was a breakfast meal that would rival any four or five star hotel resort. It was delicious!

"So, tell me what you are thinking about the dive trip? What is it you are wanting to do?" Leonardo asked.

"Bob and I have had this idea about...well, first diving an ancient shipwreck. Then, as we began researching the area, we had the idea of trying to find some ancient sunken treasure. That's all, Leonardo," I said zestfully, as I signaled to Bob to jump in the conversation.

"That's right," Bob said. "We really want to find some sunken treasure, some really old, ancient stuff. Leonardo, what do you know about the wrecks that are supposedly out there, off the northern tip of the Caye?"

"There is so much to know, Mr. Bob," Leonardo said. "But I will tell you, I know an old man who can tell us where to look, where others either have not looked before... or where they've looked but did not find anything. This could be troublesome for all of you, you know," he said.

And, indeed, we had researched quite a bit about the supposed sunken treasure off the coast of Belize and northern Mexico, near Corozalito Province. We had discovered that the Spanish and English Privateers and Pirates were among frequent visitors to the more than 200 islands scattered along the coast of Northern Mexico and Belize. The waters are clear blue, and fishing is bountiful. The coral reef along this stretch of coastline is the second largest in the world, and the islands are situated between the reef and the mainland. This made it convenient and strategic for pirate hideaways, as the trading and looting heated up among the Caribbean Islands of Haiti, Cuba, and Jamaica. They clamored to conquer the Mayans, who inhabited the islands and mainland in the early centuries until about the 1400's with the arrival of Columbus and subsequent explorers, conquistadors, privateers, and finally the pirates themselves.

"I can take you there today," Leonardo said. "The old man will see us as long as I am with you."

"Okay, we can do that," Bob said, nodding at me for agreement.

"Yes, oh yes, we can do that. When, what time?" I said.

"Let's go now," Leonardo said, laughing at our enthusiasm.

"Julie, do you and Lindsey want to tag along?" I asked.

"No," she said, looking at Lindsey, "I think we'll leave you boys to your adventures and go help the villagers or something more humanitarian," she said, trying to get a reaction from me. "Or, maybe lie around in the sun and drink margaritas all day long, and wait for some fisherman to come up and rescue us from the beach chair," she said again.

"Oh Julie, you are a genius," Lindsey said. "Bob, you and Ethan go do your thing, and we'll order out," she said. She and Julie were laughing now, and clearly not interested in chasing possible ancient sunken treasure.

"Come on, Leonardo," Bob said, "let the three of us leave now before they change their minds," he said, laughing and shaking his head.

I leaned over and kissed Julie and whispered that I loved her, and told her not to get too wasted. She slapped me on the back of the head.

"You goof. Go do your treasure hunting," she said. Then, she whispered back, "I love you too, don't be gone too long tonight."

Leonardo, Bob, and I loaded into the Leonardo's old Willis Jeep. It was a 1955 model, faded green, no top, no windshield, and had the hardest and roughest riding tires I'd ever seen. It was like riding on an oak board behind a truck with nothing but a rope to hang onto.

"We'll have to take the old beach road up to Rocky Point where the old man lives," Leonardo said loudly over the noise of the gravel and the jeep's roaring engine. "We'll stop by the café first and pick up some water and food for the trip," he said.

I looked at Bob through the dust. We both had conflicting feelings of excitement and uncertainty. We were completely dependent on Leonardo, which wasn't a problem. We had done our research, and had many questions about the supposed sunken treasure, some of which was reportedly buried near Rocky Point. It was exhilarating. It was also a mystery that would bring with it more danger than we expected.

We stopped at the café and waited in the jeep for Leonardo to retrieve some bottles of water and a couple bags of food; mostly tortillas, tomatoes, peppers, some beans, and mangos. "Some of this we'll eat, but most we'll give to the old man," Leonardo said, as he jumped back into the jeep. He cranked the Willis and we sputtered off toward the northern tip of the island about 15 miles away. The island of Ambergris

Caye is about 25 miles long and 5 miles wide at its widest point. About half of the island is covered with jungle vegetation and shrub trees common to most of these islands that dot the coastline through Central America.

We stopped to pick up Francisco and two of their cousins, as well as the scuba equipment we would need for the first dive of this trip. When Julie and I were last here in Belize, Leonardo arranged a weekend resort dive for us. Bob and Lindsey had taken some lessons back in Asheville before coming on the trip, in anticipation of doing a little scuba or snorkeling along the inside of the barrier reef. The reef itself is the second largest and second longest in the world, and snorkeling or scuba diving inside the reef is quite pristine. Diving outside the reef, however, is an entirely different experience. This dive for ancient treasure, while it may have seemed at first like a lark of an idea, would be froth with danger and surprise, and totally unexpected consequences.

"Do you remember how to breathe underwater, Ethan," Leonardo asked. "You remember how quickly you sucked the air from those tanks last time? Man, you didn't stay down long, and you were below 85 feet. It could have been serious," he said.

Bob was laughing so hard he almost fell out of the jeep. "So, Ethan, how long were you down?" Bob quipped. "No, don't answer that," Bob continued, "how long was he down, Leonardo?"

They were both laughing now. "Now, Leonardo, how long was my lesson?" I asked in an attempt to save face and dignity, since the dive instruction was a "Resort Course" and lasted perhaps a couple of hours. Bob and Lindsey had gone through a six-week course, and had an actual PADI certification. Julie and I had, in anticipation of this trip, gotten our PADI certifications, as well. "It was almost as long as my resort dive course," I said, slapping Leonardo on the shoulder as we traveled quickly down the gravel road, spewing dust behind us like we were at a Death Valley test track.

"I have to admit, I sucked the oxygen pretty fast while I was down there, but the ten minutes or so was worth every minute. It's an absolutely awesome experience," I said.

"Well, I'm looking forward to it, Ethan. I'm pumped!" Bob said.

We received word from William and Elizabeth that they had decided to fly home, back to Illinois. We knew that the next time we met would be awkward at best unless we passed along our blessings and understanding approval. It was gesture rooted in Southern aristocratic nomenclature passed down through the centuries when the South was more genteel and honored disagreements with less fanfare. The sudden and abrupt departure of our partners on this adventure was acceptable only if we, the remaining two couples, acknowledged their decision as being proper. It was kind of like the old southern saying heard around the south now and again, "Bless their hearts, they had to make that awful and difficult decision to return home and leave that God-awful place..." as many older southern matriarchs might dispense as approval of actions taken, no explanation needed. Elizabeth had become disenchanted with the idea of living on an island without certain conveniences, and William could only do one thing, fly back to the states. And they did.

"If we find a galleon of gold and silver," I said jokingly, "I guess we could include William and Elizabeth."

"Yeah, even though they were a bit chicken to stay," Bob said, "I guess it would only be right to include them."

"Would you actually do that," Leonardo said, looking back at us, as the jeep jumped from one side of the road to the other. "You guys would actually share your bounty with them?" he asked again.

Looking at each other, Bob and I both responded simultaneously, "Yes, we would. It's La Troika," I said. Leonardo looked puzzled, shook his head, and said, "Gringos!"

Chapter

26

The water was warm and clear. You could almost see the bottom, 85 feet down. The waves rocked the boat back and forth outside the reef. It was the spot that the old man from Rocky Point had described. A sunken pirate ship from the 1700's lay somewhere beneath us, and many a man had tried find it. Diving the treacherous waters outside the reef, however, was extraordinarily challenging, and the wreck remained undiscovered. Leonardo's brother and cousin had gathered our dive equipment. The boat was fueled, loaded and ready to go. Bob and I looked at each other but said nothing. This dive was what we had dreamed about, what we had talked and joked about, but most of all, it was what we came here to do.

"We should keep eye contact with each other," Leonardo said; "the currents can sweep you out before anyone notices you're not there. In fact, Ethan, you and Bob should stay close to Francisco or me on this first dive. Let's play it safe and take a look around. Kind of survey the bottom. You okay with that?" he asked.

"Whatever you say, Leonardo, you're the boss. Point us in the right direction," I said. Bob nodded in agreement, but didn't say anything.

We got into our gear, checked the regulators, and one by one, fell backwards into the water. The adventure had officially begun. The storm, the illness, and the unresolved mystery had been a prelude to now, this moment. This was what we were after. Once we were in the water, the world changed. We had talked about the descending rate and the breathing rate, and we knew that we had to control our excitement, or we would quickly use all our air and would have to ascend. And, coming up too fast could potentially be dangerous.

As we drifted downward, I glanced up to see the silhouette of the boat sloshing on the surface like a leaf in the fall of the year. It got smaller and smaller. I turned and looked, and was awe struck. I was floating in the crystal clear water, the white sandy bottom approaching, and becoming larger and more expansive. I saw Leonardo to my left, along with Bob, as Francisco and I were tethered together by a rope that also held a mesh bag for gathering any artifacts.

We reached the bottom and landed softly as a puff of sand dust bellowed upward from the floor some 85 feet below the ocean's surface. Leonardo gave us hand signals as he oriented us to the bottom, pointed to the surface, and then to our gauges that indicated the oxygen levels in our tanks. We all had double tanks; which, under controlled breathing, gave us about 40 minutes of bottom time before we had to make the 12 minute ascent to the surface.

The view from down below was like nothing I had ever experienced. Although my peripheral vision was limited, it was like viewing a massive aquarium filled with tropical fish, underwater plants, and the glistening underwater currents flowing like wind currents during a spring rain. The fish rode the currents for a few seconds and then, with a flurry of fins, they made their run in an attempt to escape the ribbon of water that kept them from gathering their food. They rode the invisible ribbon of water like rodeo clown fish, fluttering their colorful fins and striped bodies like surfers on a giant wave. The sand on the bottom was like extra fine sugar.

Leonardo motioned for us to swim over to a spot on the bottom near a large rock. It looked like a giant crustation buried in the sand, with barnacles covering the very top of the outcropping. Leonardo pointed to one side of the rock, then pointed with his arm in a north east direction, and held up ten fingers. He motioned for us to follow him, pointed to the surface, and pointed to his air gauge, and then motioned again for us to check our gauges. We had used 20% of our oxygen and were breathing too fast.

We swam behind Leonardo, glancing to our left and back to the right. I noticed that Bob was doing the same thing. We caught a glimpse of each other, and it was obvious we were both excited but also cautiously concerned. We were underwater 85 to 90 feet, and had limited air and limited time to spend under water. "Where was the wreckage," I thought, as the four of us swam over a large rock formation that contained what seemed to be indentions. Then, as we topped the largest rock yet, we were suddenly looking at a drop to the floor of the ocean. It looked like the wide-open door to the vastness of the undersea world, and it stopped Bob and me cold. I noticed Bob's eyes were as big as half dollars. I motioned for him to settle down. He shot me the finger, and signaled for me to do the same. We both knew that we were about to go exploring. I checked my gauges. I had used another 20% of my air. I would need 10% minimum to return to the surface. I figured we had about ten minutes. Leonardo descended downward straight toward the bottom. Bob and I hesitated. Francisco stayed with us as we watched Leonardo descend slowly. When he reached the bottom, he turned and looked upward, and motioned us down. It was another 30 feet down. "This would be challenging," I thought, and followed Francisco to the bottom. Bob swam beside me, and we swam behind Francisco. When we reached the bottom, I waved to Leonardo and pointed to my gauge. He signed for me to turn around, which I did. He checked my gauges from the back. Suddenly, I felt coolness in the air I was breathing. He had adjusted the richness of my oxygen. He did the same for Bob.

Leonardo pointed to an indention in the bottom of the ocean floor. He instructed for Bob and me to go there and dig. Leonardo made a digging motion with his hands, like a dog would dig in the dirt. Francisco watched the area around us and above us. "I wondered what he was concerned about," I thought, but only for a second. Without checking my gauges again, I turned and pointed my head down toward where Leonardo had directed us to dig. Bob arrived only seconds behind me. We both sifted through the sand gently at first. Then we heard Leonardo grunt. I turned, and he was making the digging movement again with his hands. Only this time more emphatically. I looked at Bob, and shook my head. We both started digging in the sand, and immediately a cloud of sand-dust engulfed us. "Good God," I thought, as I felt panic flood my mind. I couldn't see a thing. Suddenly, I felt a hand on my arm, but I couldn't see who it was. "I hoped it was Leonardo, but then where was Bob," I thought.

The dust began to clear, and I saw Bob's hands digging in the sand. I went immediately to the area beside him. Almost at the same time, we both felt something hard and slick. Then, we saw it. It was a shiny yellowish piece of metal, an object 18 to 24 inches in length, and about 2 ½ to 3 inches wide. It was partially buried. Where the hell are Leonardo and Francisco, I thought. Without thinking about my air, I continued to dig and tug at the object below us. As quickly as I saw the full length and shape of the object, I felt myself being jerked backwards. What the hell, I thought, and in an instant, I saw Bob being flung backwards as well. There was a huge sand cloud that surrounded us, and panic really took over. I felt myself breathing heavily. I couldn't see. I looked up and around, but was disoriented. I tried to look at my gauges, and couldn't see them, either. I was in trouble, I thought. Then, I felt a large hand grip my arm and I began to be pulled upward toward the surface. In a short few seconds, I saw that it was Leonardo. Bob was on his other side, and as soon as we had cleared the cloud of sand, he motioned for us to ascend slowly and to breathe slowly. I checked my gauges and almost swore out loud. I had 5% of my oxygen left. It would be barely enough to reach the surface. I looked at Leonardo, and held up my hand indicating a five count. I glanced over at Bob and he held up 4 fingers. I looked up toward the surface and prayed. Then, I noticed that Leonardo was carrying the mesh bag, and it contained the shiny yellowish object.

The surface of the water seemed so close and was yet so far away. I wondered if we would make it before running out of air. Leonardo controlled the pace of our ascent. It was imperative that we not ascend too fast, even if we ran out of air. We had practiced holding our breath, and had conditioned ourselves to not breathe for two minutes. That might be enough to get us to the surface, I thought. I was sure as hell hoping so.

As soon as we broke the surface, our masks came off, and we were gasping for air. The boat was bobbing up and down with the wash of the waves. One by one, we all crawled back in the boat, stowed our gear in the bow, and began to gather our thoughts. Leonardo held onto the mesh bag that held the shiny yellowish object. Was it the same one? It had to be the same one Bob and I found, I thought. Francisco began steering the boat back toward the direction of the shore. Nobody spoke. Leonardo, who was holding tight to the mesh bag, was looking in all directions.

"What are you looking for, Leonardo," I asked.

"I want to make sure there isn't anyone following us, Ethan. Believe it or not, it doesn't take long for word to get around that you're hunting for treasure or diving old wrecks," he said.

"We spoke to the old man this morning," I said. "Do you think people would know already?"

"Oh yes, my friend," Leonardo said. "I can expect that there will be a greeting party at the docks," he said. "Francisco," Leonardo said, "let's head toward the Victoria House dock. They won't be expecting us to go there," Leonardo said. And in an instant, Francisco turned the boat slightly, and we were headed for the Victoria House. This route would actually take us further south of the island and closer to Caulker's Caye, and then we'd slowly make our way up the southern edge of the Caye and eventually to the dock at Victoria House.

After what seemed to be an hour or so, we finally pulled into the dock. The lights around the pool and outdoor deck were on, the tiki torches were lit, and a crowd was beginning to gather around the poolside bar. As we eased to the slip, Francisco jumped onto the decking and tied off the boat.

"Grab your gear and follow me," Leonardo said. Bob and I complied, looked at each other but said nothing. We were following the mesh bag, and wondering when Leonardo would release the object for us to inspect.

"Come on," Leonardo said, motioning us toward the restaurant at the Victoria as he and Francisco entered the back of the kitchen. "Let's go in the kitchen and look at what you found. I think it's a valuable piece," he said.

We scurried through the doorway leading back to the storage area. We were among familiar faces, and the curiosity was high among those who were working, all of whom knew us. Leonardo reached a small table in the back of the kitchen, where the seafood and oysters are prepared for the guests. He stopped, looked at Bob and me, and then over to Francisco. Without saying a word, he took the mesh bag, pulled the draw string open, and gently emptied the contents onto a towel he'd spread across the metal table. Using one hand to hold the large shiny object, and the other to pull the bag from around it, Leonardo soon had it free and laid it flat on the table. We were stunned. A huge smile came across Leonardo's face. It soon became contagious as we each repeated the gesture. We looked at each other, enthralled with what we had found.

"Is it real?" Bob asked. "Is this the real deal?" he said.

Leonardo picked up the item, held it to his mouth and bit down on the edge of one end, and then handed it to Bob. "It's the real deal, my friend," Leonardo said.

"Damn! It's beautiful," Bob said, mesmerized by the piece. He handed it to me next. Holding it was electrifying. It was heavier than I had expected. It hadn't seemed that heavy in the water, but everything has a certain level of buoyancy in the ocean.

"Leonardo," I said, "it's beautiful. What year do you think..."

Leonardo didn't let me finish.

"About the 1760's maybe," he said. "We will need to look this piece up, along with the location. I have the coordinates, but first we must put this in a safe place. There is a curse that sometimes comes with finding ancient pieces like this," he said. "It's like waking the dead and disturbing the evil spirits. People will know that we found something, and they will come. We will have to work fast to file the claim for the area, but the actual location will have to remain a secret. If any of the evil ones find out where we were, they will plunder the site and take what they can find exactly like the pirates and privateers did in the old days," he said.

"The old man at Rocky Point was right then," Bob said, looking to Leonardo for confirmation. The old man had told us of a wreck site that perhaps dated back to the 1700s. Maybe it was an English privateer's ship or one of Captain Morgan's infamous legions of pirate ships he used for looting boats traveling from Jamaica to Panama. The heavy piece of gold bar may have been from one of those ships.

"Whatever you do, do not speak of this piece. It is yours, Ethan, but with it comes many dangers on the way to the fortune," Leonardo said.

"How much more could there be," Bob asked, using a low voice.

"Much more," Leonardo said. "Mucho!" he said. "But first we must hide this piece. You must trust me," he said. "Stay together, and do not walk around alone. We must tell Julie and Lindsey, too. They do not need to be alone, not now," he said.

Leonardo told us where he would hide it. Francisco knew as well. We were all sworn to secrecy. An official claim had to be filed and the piece registered. This would attract the attention of the Belizean government. Things were about to get complicated.

Chapter

27

Leonardo left us standing at the table. We stood in awe of what we had experienced. We were absorbing what Leonardo had said and his new sense of caution. Thoughts of the discovery of one of the most valuable treasure finds in fifty years were racing through our minds. We were astounded! Julie and Lindsey had arrived back from their shopping trip. We met at an outside table and told them what had happened. They were shocked, as well. We all had so many questions. At first, it was hard to get our heads around the fact that we might be on the verge of discovering the largest ancient sunken treasure since Mel Fisher's discoveries in the 1970's.

"What do you make of what Leonardo told us?" Bob finally asked in a low voice.

"I'm not sure, Bob," I said. "I trust Leonardo. So, I have to take him at his word. He knows how these things work, I suppose."

"How valuable do you think the piece is, Ethan?" Julie asked, finally. Lindsey was looking with intent eyes, although she hadn't said anything.

"If it is as pure as I think it is, that piece alone could be worth tens of thousands of dollars, maybe even hundreds of thousands," I said.

"How much more do you think is down there?" Lindsey asked, finally joining the conversation.

"Honey, if this is one of the wrecks that we think it is, it could be worth millions, maybe even billions. The only problem is figuring out how to get it off the seabed," Bob said.

"My God," Lindsey said, putting her hand over her mouth in disbelief. Her eyes were as big as half dollars. We were all in shock.

"Ethan, will it be possible for us to successfully secure our claim on this item?" Julie asked, purposely not using the word "treasure" for fear of someone overhearing her.

"I don't know. That's one of the main things that Leonardo is checking out for us," I said.

"Don't you have a friend back in Georgia who is a nautical expert of some kind?" Bob asked.

"Yes, I do in fact," I said. Julie perked up and looked straight at me.

"Yes, you do. We do. Don!" Julie said with enthusiasm. Now she was perky. She was thinking about how we could secure the treasure and reap the benefits. Don could play a key role.

"His name is Don Sullivan," I began. "He's an expert in nautical archaeology and is well-read in the area of ancient sunken ships. He lives in St. Simons, Georgia."

"Can you get him down here?" Bob asked. Everyone suddenly was looking at me. I looked at Julie.

"I can call. I'm sure he'll be interested, but I guess it would depend on his schedule."

"Is he married?" Lindsey asked. "I mean, I was only curious," she added.

"Yes, he is. In fact, we go way back," I said, glancing at Julie. "I've known them both for years, and once worked with his wife," I said.

"What does she do?" Lindsey asked.

"She works as a consultant for a company that provides training assistance to schools and teachers in the rural south," I answered.

"And her name is..." Lindsey said, showing a curious look.

"Myra Jean Hutchinson," I said. "She carries her maiden name since she has been known by that name in the professional circles of education and state politics," I said. Bob looked curious now, arching one eyebrow.

"Hutchinson. That name sounds familiar," he said.

"Well, she is from Atlanta. The Hutchinson name is a prominent name in the Atlanta area," I said.

"I think I knew an art dealer in Atlanta with the last name Hutchinson," he said.

"Could be related. The Hutchinsons are all over the place," I said.

"Will she come down here with him?" Lindsey asked.

"I suppose. I'll know more after I talk with Don," I said.

"Ethan, should we call him and see if he is even interested in this new twist?" Julie asked.

"Yes, I can do that. And he will be interested; I can almost guarantee that," I said. "Excuse me for a minute while I go call Don. Then we'll know where we stand. He is the best expert in this area. That I know!" I said.

"Do you know anyone who specializes in this sort of thing," I said, looking at Bob.

"No, not a soul. Your friend Don will have to be our ticket. I hope he'll agree to come down," Bob said. I left the table to make the call. After only a few rings, Don answered. We had a lively conversation that I had to cut short. After I explained why I was calling, Don immediately agreed. He was on the way.

I returned to the dining area where the others were waiting with anticipation.

"What'd he say?" Julie asked, as Bob and Lindsey looked but were saying nothing.

"He's packing as we speak," I said. "He'll be here on the next flight."

"We'll need to tell Leonardo, so he can arrange someone to meet him at the airport in Belize City, and then arrange a flight over here to the island for him," Julie said.

"What about his wife, Myra...isn't that her name?" Lindsey asked.

"He said he would call her, and that she'll probably call us. I'm sure she won't miss this, even if she has to make some changes in her schedule. This is right up her alley."

"What kind of person is she?" Lindsey asked.

"She's all southern," I said. "Seriously, she's as close to southern blue-blood as you'll get. She's a hoot, though. She'll love this situation down here.

"Ethan," Julie said, "You and Myra have been friends for a number of years. Don't give Bob and Linds' the wrong impression."

"Oh, no, no, no," I said, now a bit embarrassed. "I meant that she is... oh, forget it. She's a very delightful and colorful person. You guys will love her," I said, trying to recover.

At that moment, my cell phone rang. It was Myra Jean. I motioned and pointed to the phone. "Hey, Myra, how are you?" I said. "Yes, it's big, very big. Are you coming down? Great! When? Great! I'll arrange for someone to pick you up at the airport in Belize City. Good. Okay. See you then," I said, as the conversation ended. "She may beat Don down here," I said, chuckling.

"Anybody hungry?" Julie asked. With that, we turned our attention toward our table of food. We all suddenly felt the hunger pangs in our stomachs. It was like an adrenaline collision. We were famished.

Chapter

28

Myra and Don arrived late the next morning. Luckily, they had arranged their flights to arrive within an hour of each other. Leonardo met them at the airport. Once their luggage was cleared, they boarded the small Cessna 165, and flew the 45-minute flight out to Ambergris Caye. We had lunch and mimosas waiting for them when they arrived.

"My God, it's so great see you two," Myra said, as she made her way into the house. She immediately embraced Julie and me. Don looked on and smiled sheepishly.

I introduced Myra and Don to Bob and Lindsey. The conversation was on a roll. I shook hands with Don, and we each made some comment about the fact that things would not be dull now that Myra had arrived.

"Oh, hell no," Don said. "I'm not sure you know what you've started," he said laughingly. "Seriously," he said, "I can't wait to hear all the details."

"Let's have some brunch and drinks first," I said, "then, we will show you what we found."

"What?" Don asked in shock. "You have a piece from the wreck site?"

"Shhhh." I said and gestured with my hand. "Yes, we have one piece. It's about this long, this wide, and this thick," I continued, measuring out the size with my hands. "And it's the shiniest yellow-gold you've ever seen." Don's mouth fell open in disbelief.

"I can't believe it," he said. "How did you find it? Better yet, how did you bring it up?" he said.

"It's a long story," I said, "so, let's have some lunch first."

With that, we took their luggage upstairs to the spare bedroom where William and Elizabeth had been. They took a few minutes to change clothes and freshen up while Julie and Lindsey finished preparing the brunch. Bob and I were making room on the screened porch for the six of us to sit around our small table. It consisted of smoked mahi-mahi, fresh shrimp, mussels, fruit, strawberry jam, and freshly squeezed orange and mango juice. Drinks included freshly made mimosas, bloody Marys, bottled water, and for those who liked a hot drink afterwards, black coffee.

It wasn't long before Don and Myra made their way down to the porch. It was obvious they felt relaxed.

"This is fabulous, ya'll," Myra said. "How'd you guys find this place?" she asked.

"We vacationed here some years ago," I said. "When we began talking about coming down here, we immediately thought about trying to acquire this place as our accommodation. It's owned by an attorney in Nashville, Tennessee and his law partner who now lives in Canada," Julie explained.

"Yes, and while I was attending Vanderbilt, one of the professors there was friends with the guy. In fact, as a practicing attorney, he would teach a class from time to time as an adjunct professor. He was friends with several of the profs there," I said. "At any rate, once we made the commitment to come here on this little adventure, I contacted one of my old professors and asked him to arrange a meeting. I wanted us to meet face-to-face, since we were going to ask to lease it for a year. He would have to forgo any personal trips down here. We didn't know how he would react to our offer, or even if he would consider it," I said.

"Well it certainly looks like things worked out for you, Ethan," Myra Jean said.

"Yes, and I'm glad that Bob and Lindsey could join us, too. It has been a very eventful trip. We'll fill you in on the details later," I said.

"Ethan, Bob, do you know what ship your artifact came from," Don asked, taking a long sip of his mimosa.

"We're not exactly sure at this point, Don. There are several ships that reportedly went down near the area where we made our discovery," I said, speaking in code.

"I printed off a copy of the known and suspected shipwrecks dating back to the early 1700's. When you're ready, we can look over it and see if there are any clues," Don said.

"When we finish here, I'll call Leonardo and arrange for a viewing," I said.

"A viewing? What the heck do you mean?" Myra asked.

"Our friend and partner in this venture, Leonardo, the same guy who arranged to pick you up at the airport, has stored the item in a safe place," I said.

"Where did he hide the thing?" Don asked with a slight chuckle. "Can you really trust this guy?" he said.

"Yes, we trust him. I've known him since the last time we were here," I said.

"Besides, Don, we really don't have a choice," Bob said. "He's also the one who led us to the site. And prior to that, he took us to talk with an old man who remembered stories about shipwrecks as a child. That was really the key piece," Bob explained.

"Oh, I hear you. I didn't mean to imply anything negative, guys," Don said, retreating from his line of suspicious questioning.

"Oh, come on Don, they know what they're doing!" Myra said in our defense. "And you ought to be just the person they need to provide some validity to the identification process. Heck, that's why you're…or we are down here."

"I know, Honey," he said. "You know it's my nature to question things, especially something this big. Do you realize what all of this could mean?" he asked exasperatingly.

"Of course, I do," she said incredulously.

"Time out!" I said, holding up my hands in a "T" formation. "Myra, we are not offended by Don's questioning. He's really trying to make sure we're doing the right things to protect ourselves."

"Exactly," he said.

"Besides, that's also why we called and asked him, and you, to join us down here. We need his expertise, and you need to relax and unwind. You're not in Arkansas anymore, Dorothy," I said, trying to inject some humor. Myra was the type to work 24/7 until she could go no more. She would crash for a few days, or even a week, and then ignite her jet engines again. Don, on the other hand, was as laid back as a salamander. He was very knowledgeable about history in general, but nautical archeological history specifically. Although his degrees were in history, he had turned his hobby of researching ancient sunken ships into a profitable consulting business. He was often contracted to meet and work with scientists from NOAA, the National Oceanographic and Atmospheric Agency. He had also worked with research institutes such as Woods Hole Exploration and Research Institute. Most recently, Don had worked on a team from the University of North Carolina who confirmed that an anchor taken from a site located south of Ocracoke Island, North Carolina, was from Blackbeard's Ship, the Queen Anne's Revenge. We had heard the whole story from Don several times.

Originally called La Concorde, the boat was renamed Queen Anne's Revenge after being captured by Edward Teach, better known as Blackbeard. Stories and folklore surrounding the exact location of Blackbeard's hideouts have been sprinkled throughout history. Ocracoke Island, North Carolina, located approximately 40 miles due south of Cape Hatteras, was one of the best known of Blackbeard's hideouts. The area contains two well-hidden inlets where Blackbeard and his pirate crew anchored for respite. The exact location of the shipwreck that produced the anchor, however, is a highly guarded secret.

"We think the gold ingot we recovered from the site is the real thing," Bob said to Don. The girls had moved into the kitchen to retrieve more fruit and drinks. Myra was laughing hysterically at whatever Julie and Lindsey were saying, probably one of the many funny stories about either Bob or me.

"How much does the piece weigh, you think?" Don asked.

"If I had to guess, I'd say it weighs 12 to 15 pounds, maybe more," I said.

"Yep, I agree," Bob said quickly.

"You gotta be kidding me," Don said, flabbergasted at what he had heard. "Do you know what that could be worth, guys?" he asked.

"Well, I haven't actually calculated it, Don," I said, looking at Bob. "Have you?" I asked.

"No, but we can do a rough calculation," Bob said. "Let's see, if gold is going for $1800 per ounce, and if we have, say, 10 pounds of pure gold, then..."

"Hold on, Bob, let's do it the quick way," I said, grabbing a calculator. I did the calculation: 10 times 16 equaled 160, times 1800. "Assuming a mere 10 pounds and not 12 or 15, we're looking at a piece worth about $563,000," I said.

"No way," Bob said, shocked at the size of the figure. He called for Lindsey, and the girls returned to the porch, drinks and food in hand.

"We were doing some calculations. This one piece, based on some conservative approximations, could be worth about $550,000," Bob said. They froze. They were motionless.

"Are you serious?" Myra said. She took a long sip of her drink.

"Yes, we're serious. This could be the mega deal," Don said. "When is your next dive?" he asked.

Bob and I looked at each other. "We need to call Leonardo and find out when he and his brother can take us out there again," I said. "In fact, I need to bring you up to date on something else," I said.

"According to Leonardo, when an ancient sunken shipwreck is disturbed, there is the belief that it can release the spirits of those who inhabited the ship when it went down, or even those who were perhaps killed on board the ship before it sank," I said.

"What did he say about the piece that you found?" Don said.

"He warned us about the possibility of danger," Bob said.

"Yes, he warned us that we shouldn't travel alone, or late at night," I said. "He also said that we should be very wary of people following us or lurking around."

"He told us something else," Bob said. By this time, Myra, Julie and Lindsey were listening with eager ears, their eyes focused on what Bob and I were explaining. "He told us there are two inherent dangers to removing pieces from the wreck site. First, there are locals who will try to prevent us from claiming the site or would loot the site ahead of us. Also, according to Leonardo, removing the artifacts might anger the spirits," I said, "putting us in danger, as well."

"Don, think about it. The men who manned these gunrunning ships were pirates and privateers who were paid by the employing King or Queen. Take Henry Morgan," Bob said, "he was under the authority of the English Crown, at least until he went rogue. But according to historical records and folklore, people may not have really known that he had converted to life as a ruthless plunderer," Bob said further.

"So, do you have any idea what ship you've discovered? And, has it ever been excavated before? Was there any evidence of anyone previously at the wreck site?" Don asked.

"No, there wasn't any evidence that I saw. What about you, Bob," I said.

"Nope, I didn't see anything. But, Ethan, remember, we were only down there for about 30 minutes or so," Bob said.

"Yeah, that's true; but Leonardo didn't mention it either. We should ask him about that when we see him again," I said.

I had called Leonardo in between some of the conversation. He had promised to call back or to come by the house. We would make plans for the next dive trip out to the site, as well as for Don to have a chance to examine the piece. We would also compare notes on the research Bob and I had compiled to that point, in consultation with Don. We were glad to have Don and his expertise, and would tap into his knowledge base for additional pointers as we reached further into our exploration.

Chapter

29

The next morning, we awakened early. Julie, Myra and Lindsey had breakfast ready for all of us by 7:30. The air was cool and crisp. The breeze was slight as it eased its way through the palm leaves and branches of the hibiscus plants. The smell of the bacon and eggs, and the strong, black Central American coffee was magical. It gave us energy, both physically and imaginatively. We all ate hurriedly, and packed for the day. This was to be the day for our second dive. Leonardo had made the arrangements. We were to meet him at the café around 10:00 A.M. We would then drive to the point, transfer everything to the boat and, we'd be off. Leonardo would have our air tanks and other equipment. This trip would require a slightly bigger boat, since we had extra people going. We had decided we would all dive.

When we arrived at the dock, Francisco was there waiting. He had the boat secured and ready. He had twice the number of tanks for each person, wet suits, mesh bags for gathering artifacts, dive knives, and several spear guns.

"What are the spear guns for, Leonardo," I asked, as we began boarding the boat. Don and Myra were eagerly getting on board. Don was like a kid in a candy store.

"The spear guns are for our protection, Ethan," he said. "Remember, I told you that sometimes bad things happen when ancient sites are disturbed."

"Have you heard anyone speak about our last dive?" I asked.

"No. No one has said anything. No one has asked any questions," he said.

"That's good, isn't it?" I said.

"No, not always," Leonardo said.

"Why is that?" I asked. Don and Bob were standing near me now, and were looking on with the utmost curiosity.

"Because some news should have leaked out; I expected somebody to say something. Instead, there has been nothing, and that makes me very nervous," Leo said.

"How many people knew about the last dive?" Don asked.

"Not many. Francisco, the old man, myself, and of course Ethan and Bob," he answered.

"So maybe nobody knows," Don quipped with a chuckle.

"I doubt this," Leonardo said.

"So, who will have the spear guns?" Bob asked.

"Francisco and I will carry two each. You guys will swim between Francisco and me. We have to be very alert on this dive," Leonardo said.

"Did you get the permits in place?" I asked.

"Yes. All the permits are in place. I have filed a temporary claim with the Belizean government in Belize City. You will need to file the official claim once we return. The government requires two verification dives, along with some pictures of the wreck site, any artifacts that are undisturbed, and the coordinates," he said.

"Do they know the exact location now?" Don asked, sounding concerned.

"No. That will come later, much later," Leonardo said.

Leonardo directed each of us to a task, which we began working in earnest. Francisco launched the boat and we pulled away from the dock. The sky was clear and blue, and the surf was minimal. There was a slight breeze coming in from the southeast. This looked like a good day to be diving. We were at the dive site after about 45 minutes. Once we had gotten beyond the barrier reef, the waves were much bigger, but not like when a storm is approaching the coastline. The waves were big, but not rough and choppy.

"What next, Leonardo?" I asked. He was more tense this trip. It was apparent that he was more concerned with this dive than the last time. He had hardly said anything on the way out.

"Is everything okay, Leonardo?" I asked, turning away from the others to ask. "You tell us what we need to know. Do we need to postpone this dive?"

"No, no, Ethan. I am a little nervous because of what we spoke about before," he said. "I will say a Mayan prayer before we dive. I will ask the Gods to keep us safe," he said, as he glanced around in all directions.

The boat slowed as Francisco began to position it in the right spot.

"Throw the anchor," he said. Bob was the closest to it, so he grabbed it and tossed it overboard. The rope quickly became taut.

"Is that good, Francisco?" Bob shouted from the bow of the boat.

"Yes, Mr. Bob. Perfect," said Francisco.

"Okay, here's the plan. Everybody listen for a moment," Leonardo said, as he motioned for everyone to gather around him. "It is important that we pair up when we're down at the site. As we descend, everyone needs to stay together. Keep your eye on the group. As we get to the site, I will direct you. I want you to work in pairs. If you find an artifact that is partially showing, but you can't move it, you can only take a picture. You each have an underwater camera. Moving an object that is buried deep in the ocean floor will cause a sand cloud, and you will become disoriented. You will feel the current swaying back and forth across the bottom. It will seem to you that it isn't moving you, but it will. It will carry you away from the site and out to sea. You must be very aware of where you are. You will have two tanks, but," he said, looking at me, "conserve your air. Control your breathing. You will need 10% minimum to resurface. Francisco will be our lookout. He will watch for intruders and will watch you. Pablo will stay with the boat," Leonardo said.

"How deep are we going?" Don asked.

"About 90 feet, I think," he said. Don looked at me, and then at Bob with approval. We were all serious, but a little apprehensive. This dive was different from the first. We had a greater sense of mission. The first dive was a more spontaneous adventure. We had no idea what we would find on the first dive.

"Okay, is everybody ready? Are there any questions?" he asked.

"We're all ready," Bob replied.

"Okay, everyone follow me and do as I do," Leonardo said. With that, he stepped to the edge of the boat and said his Mayan prayer before falling backwards into the water. One by one, we followed with the same entry. The water was tepid and clear. Leonardo motioned for the group to dive. As we launched ourselves under water, the world changed. It was magnificent. Like before, it was like flying over the vastness of an underwater world. Once again, I was in awe of the mere site of it all. I looked over at Julie. She, too, was excited by the vastness of the ocean floor that lay beneath us some 90 feet below.

Our descent was slow and deliberate. Bob and Lindsey swam to my left, while Don and Myra were to my right. Leonardo was leading the descent, while Francisco brought up the rear. Both Leonardo and Francisco had two spear guns, one strapped to a shoulder, and the other in one hand. I watched Leonardo and Francisco as we made our way closer to the site. Francisco was like the centurion, guarding the gate. I felt strangely nervous, but the excitement of returning to the wreck site out-weighed any fear at the moment.

Leonardo motioned for us to gather around him as we reached the floor of the ocean and the wreck site. This was like a field trip, I thought, as he motioned and directed; then, pulled out what looked like a small dry-erase board and a marker. He began writing short instructions. This was too cool, I thought. Then, he held up the board. It read, "Be very aware of where you and your partner are!" This changed the tone. It was a stark reminder of what he had told us about the currents. I also thought about Francisco and his primary role, as the centurion.

Leonardo directed us as we swam in different directions, but we kept site of each other. My breathing was much better this time, much more controlled. I looked at Bob, pointed to the O2 gauge, gave a thumbs-up for myself, and then motioned with my hands. Bob gave me a thumbs-up as well. I glanced at Julie. Her breathing was much more controlled than mine.

As we approached the dig, I could see the spot where the first piece had been located. It was near an outcropping that looked like a rock, but was actually part of the ship. As we approached the huge mound of sand and plant life, I knew that we were about to descend another 15 feet or so. This would be the honey hole, I thought as we swam closer. The shade of the water changed slightly like a warning sign that the depth was about to change. It did. We all paused as Leonardo signaled us to wait. He instructed us to check the air gauges. We all were at or near 80%, which was good, and certainly better than last time. A smile came across Leonardo's face. He looked back behind us, and motioned for a sign from Francisco. He gave a thumbs-up as well.

Leonardo gave the signal and we followed. Down into the deep we descended. It seemed to take forever, but was probably only a few seconds, I thought. We divided into pairs, as we had discussed. With our mesh bags in one hand, and dive knives in the other, we began combing through the sand, looking at every odd colored object or rock we came across. Don drifted toward Julie and me. Myra remained on course, and was deep into the dive now. She has a tenacious spirit when it comes to a challenge, and she had locked in on this dive. I motioned to Julie to keep an eye on her. Don had seen something that caught his eye, and looking at me, he pointed toward it. We both went to the object.

Bob and Lindsey were nearby. In fact, I estimated that we were all working within a twenty square foot area. Leonardo was on one side of us, and Francisco lingered above us and to the other side of the imaginary square. Don gave a signal. He looked at both Bob and me, and then to Leonardo. He had something. Don, being the expert, began gently fanning around the object. A small cloud of sand dust swirled around. He pointed for Leonardo to examine the object. It had an odd shape, and its surface was crusted over. What had he found, I wondered. About that same time, I heard the muffled sound of Myra's voice. I looked over, and she, too, had found an object of interest. Glancing up to Francisco, I thought he might swim down to assist Myra. He didn't. He maintained his station.

Leonardo had provided us with marking flags, which were very similar to the marking flags back home that the utility company uses to mark a water or gas line underground. He signaled for her to mark the find. She complied. As soon as he had everybody's attention, he and Don began to uncover the object. At first, it looked like a rock covered in sea urchins. Then, Don pulled it up and gently peeled off some of the muck that surrounded the piece. With as big a smile as he could emit with a breather in his mouth, he presented it to the group. It was a silver wine goblet. The adrenaline rushed through all of us. Don placed the object in the bag. Leonardo swam over to where Myra had placed the flag. He began to fan the spot where another object was protruding from the sand. After a few minutes, he lifted the piece. It was a hook; the type that would ordinarily be attached to a long pole. It could have been used for pulling catches aboard the vessel. It also was probably used to pull objects, like nets or people onto the ship as they attacked the various merchant ships that traveled the route. Leonardo was pleased, but worked intently. Myra was obviously excited. Don motioned for her to check her air. In fact, we all did at that point. She held up four fingers, which meant 40%, which was good. We all seemed to be between 40 and 50 percent. That meant that we had about 20 minutes, I thought, as we swam to the next spot.

Bob and Lindsey were back at a spot they had been meticulously exploring. Leonardo approached slowly and deliberately. He held back for a moment, and then moved closer to Bob. I could tell he was assessing whatever it was that Bob and Lindsey had found. Then, his motions changed. He pointed to Bob and Lindsey, and instructed them to dig and pull. What was it they had found, I thought, as the rest of us looked on with excitement. Then, with a unity of motion, they pulled, lunging backwards. It was a big object, I thought. A huge cloud of sand dust engulfed them for a few seconds. We waited with tenseness. Francisco was watching the perimeter. Leonardo, Bob and Lindsey turned and held up the object. It was a small brass bell. This was fantastic! There would be a name on the bell, I thought, as he placed it in the bag. I patted Bob and Lindsey on the shoulder congratulating them on their find. Leonardo signaled again for us to check our air. It was time to ascend. Leonardo motioned to Francisco, who waved his hand for us to follow him. Leonardo took out his board and wrote, "Go up slowly!" Leonardo would bring up the rear, while Francisco would lead our ascent.

Once we were at the surface, the elation was incredible. One by one, we boarded the boat and removed our tanks and belts. We were all anxious to have a look at the objects. Leonardo bent down as if to work on a tank and said without looking at us, "We will wait until later to look at the objects. Pablo said that a strange boat has been moving around the area. He said that there were three men on the boat and that they pretended to be fishing. Pablo said that they kept their eye on him and this boat more than their own fishing lines. One fish got away while they were looking at our boat through a pair of binoculars," he said.

"What's the plan?" I asked. The others hadn't noticed yet what was happening.

Leonardo continued to explain. "We will take our time getting back in. We will offload normally and secure the boat. Francisco and Pablo will take care of the equipment, and I will put the objects in that black bag. We'll go to my place and look these over. Francisco will come back out with some other guys and guard the area while pretending to be fishing. We have to hurry though. If these guys are poachers, we have to act fast," he said.

"I'll explain it to the others," I said.

****

The approach to the docks was uneventful. It was like any other normal approach and docking. We off loaded the equipment, said hello to a few of the other dive groups, commented about how clear the water was, and how great the water felt with the midday sun beaming down. Soon, we were loaded and headed toward Leonardo's house where we entered through the kitchen door. There, he had a large wooden table used to prepare the meals and prep the food. This time; however, we would use it as an examination table. Leonardo pulled each item from the bags as we stood around the table and watched in awe. Leonardo had placed three rectangular shaped plastic containers filled with water onto the worktable. As he pulled each item from the mesh bag, he placed it into one of the plastic containers. It was important to preserve the artifacts and take the necessary steps to avoid any deterioration caused by the open air. The objects had been submerged beneath the surface for hundreds of years. Don stood next to Leonardo, and he assumed a leading role in handling the objects. We all were amazed and felt exuberant. Then, Leonardo's radio called for him. "Leonardo, it's Francisco," the voice said. "The boat, it's back, and there are six men this time," he said. "I think they are going to approach us. They have been moving closer," he said, his voice more alarmed.

"Okay, Francisco, don't endanger yourself. I will call Juan and the others, and have them launch immediately," Leonardo said.

"Okay. I'll hold them off as much as I can. Do you want me to use the big gun?" Francisco asked. This came as a shock to us. What big gun? We looked at each other but said nothing.

"Leonardo, what's going on?" I asked.

"I told you that bad things might happen. Well, it's started," he said.

"What big gun is Francisco talking about?" I asked.

"We have an old WWII bazooka. I didn't tell you about it because I didn't want to worry you," he said.

"Does he know how to use it?" I asked. Don was almost laughing out loud, while Myra was elbowing him in the ribs.

"Yes, he knows," Leonardo said. He turned back to the artifacts, and began gently pulling some of the loose crusty material away from each object. "Look, Ethan, there's a name on this bell, but I cannot read it."

"Let me take a look," I said, as Don and Bob leaned in to examine the bell, as well.

"Leonardo, they are approaching with much speed now. I am going to fire the big gun," Francisco said, as the sound of his voice broke the concentration of our examination.

"How close are they?" Leonardo asked in the radio mic.

"About 100 yards and closing in fast now," he said.

"Fire one over the bow, Francisco," Leonardo said. "And hold open the mic."

"Okay," he replied. The sounds that came from the speaker were of Francisco and the others scurrying around the deck of the boat. They were speaking in Spanish. Then, we heard a loud boom.

"He fired the 'zooka," Leonardo said. We stood in shock of what was happening.

"Leonardo, what does this mean?" I asked.

"It means that we now have competition," Leonardo said and smiled.

Chapter

30

Back at the house, we all changed our clothes, made drinks, and sat down to discuss the events we had witnessed. What we had experienced was mind-boggling. With the help of Leonardo, Francisco, and the others, we had successfully verified the wreckage site, had the information and pictures of the wreckage to file the official claim, and had been threatened by modern day "wanna-be" pirates of a local flavor.

"I cannot believe what happened," Don said. He was both excited and astounded at the same time. "My God, you guys, this could be the mother-load."

"I know, I know," I said. "Leonardo, what do we need to do next?"

"Sit tight for now Ethan. We now have competition, but Francisco and his buddies will protect the site," he said. "We will need to complete the claim tomorrow morning. You and Don, I guess, will need to accompany me to Belize City."

"I think there's something else we need to talk about, Leonardo," I said.

"Sure, Ethan, what is it?" Leonardo looked curiously.

"Leonardo," I began, "Bob, Lindsey, Julie, and now Don and Myra Jean, and I have discussed how to protect the assets as well as the interests in the wreck site. We have also discussed one other aspect." Leonardo shook his head, but clearly didn't know where this was going.

The six of us had researched and discussed the formation of a corporation for the purpose of protecting our interests and assets in the wreckage. After the events of the last dive, we were all even more determined to do whatever was necessary. We also wanted to take care of Leonardo and Francisco and their families.

"Leonardo, we want to set-up an international corporation that will protect the artifacts at the site, as well as us....including you and Francisco and your families," I said. Leonardo looked surprised, even confused.

"Do you know what this will do or how it will benefit you and your family, Leonardo?" Bob asked.

"No, not really. I mean, I understand what a corporation is, but how do I play into this?" he asked. Bob and I looked at each other, and then over to Myra Jean and Don.

"Let me explain, Leonardo," Bob said, glancing at the rest of us for a non-verbal cue to continue.

"It's like this," Bob said. "We'll get Mike, our friend in Atlanta, to set up the corporation and base it in the Bahamas. You will be part of that corporation, and will benefit the same as us."

"What do you mean, benefit?" he asked.

"Well," Bob continued slowly, now realizing that Leonardo may not have a clue about the value of the sunken treasures. "Leonardo, the wreck site is littered with valuable artifacts. We have to protect it or it will be plundered."

"Yes, I know, Bob. But, why the off-shore corporation?" he asked.

"Good question," Bob said. "Let me explain. In order to be able to get some of the artifacts out and into the hands of those who can best evaluate them and protect them from decay, we have to take possession of them."

"Yes, I understand that part."

"Once we are able to bring some of the artifacts to the surface, we will be able to sell some of them in order to finance the operation, kind of like Mel Fisher," Bob said. "Leonardo, this could...no, this *will* change your family's life. We want you and Francisco to benefit financially from this venture," Bob said.

"Is it really that valuable?" Leonardo asked.

"Hell, it could be worth millions, Leonardo," Don said. Myra punched him with her elbow. She didn't want him to derail the conversation.

"I don't know, Bob. I'll have to think about this. I told you and Ethan about the evil spirits and the ghost spirits from the deep. I don't know. I will speak to Francisco and we can talk about it tomorrow morning on the flight over to Belize City," Leonardo said.

"Leonardo," Julie said, looking at him in a tender manner. "We don't want to plunder like the guys who seemed to be after us today, but we do want to benefit from what we've found. Otherwise, it would be left to whoever could take it and sell it cheaply to the tourists without it benefiting the people of Ambergris Caye," she said.

"I know," Leonardo said, "that's my worry."

"Part of what we want to do is to set-up a fund for the people of Ambergris Caye, Leonardo," Bob said.

"And Myra Jean here will help set-up a new school for the kids here on the island," Don said, looking over to Myra Jean who was now fighting back tears.

"Leonardo, why don't you and Francisco join us for breakfast in the morning before flying to Belize City?" Lindsey said finally. "Come early. I'll have a full breakfast ready with piping hot coffee," she said. Leonardo smiled, shook his head, and I think finally realized that we were serious about helping him and Francisco and their families, as well as the people of Ambergris Caye.

The Belizean government would take about 40% of the find, but we had a plan for setting up a nautical museum highlighting the history of Ambergris Caye and Belize. We also wanted to take care of the people and children on the island. Our plans included a new school and community center. We also wanted to set-up a program with some of the locals and some college students back in the states to help rebuild the homes that had been damaged or destroyed by the recent storm.

Leonardo left with a curious look on his face and without saying much. We looked at each other, and then Don said, "Heck, let's eat. I'm hungry. All this excitement and being chased by would-be robbers and murderers has me famished!"

"Oh, Don, you're always hungry," Myra Jean said, rolling her eyes and walking toward the kitchen door. "Come on girls, let's fix the guys something to eat before they dry up and blow away," she said. Lindsey and Julie looked at each other and giggled as they moved toward the kitchen.

"Gosh darn, see what I have to put up with," Don said. "I don't get any respect from her. She gives me grief all the time. Heck, if I only ate when she ate, I'd die of starvation. Look how skinny she is. She eats like a dang bird," Don said. Bob and I sat there. I glanced at Bob and he raised his eyebrows as if to say 'don't say a word.' Don kept on complaining for a while, until Bob got him refocused on the wreckage.

"Don," Bob said, breaking the trance of the moment, "how much do you think is down there?"

"Depends on what ship it is," he said. "We need to try to make a determination on the identification of the wreckage. Do you guys have any ideas?" he asked.

"It could be the Mary Oxford which was lost in 1764. She was sailing in from Jamaica, and reportedly had quite a bounty of silver and jewels, but there's no record of gold pieces," Bob said.

"Or, it could be the Cour Volant which was seized by Captain Morgan himself. It had been the flagship of a French pirate. This was after Morgan had been commissioned by his uncle, the Lieutenant Governor of Jamaica, and had been directed to plunder the coast of Central America. His ship, the Cour Volant, along with the Oxford, was attacked by Spanish pirates," I said.

"Where was it attacked?" Don asked.

"It supposedly went down near the area where we found the wreckage," Bob said. "There's evidence from the logs of other ships that were in the area when the cannon blasts erupted," he said.

"Then we need to find something that identifies the wreckage as the Cour Volant or the Oxford," Don said.

"Right," I said. "In fact, the Cour Volant was the ship that reportedly, according to records, was carrying $750,000 worth of silver and jewels. It was also supposed to be carrying part of Morgan's bounty of 250 thousand pieces of gold," I said.

"How much?" Don asked. "No, don't answer that. I heard it the first time," he said. "Are you serious? My God, Ethan, this is unbelievable!"

"This is why it's important to set up the off-shore corporation," Bob said.

"Right," I said. "If we can secure the claim to the wreck site, and have the assurances from the Belizean government, then we can protect the site. Also, the international corporation will provide us an avenue through which we can channel the artifacts," I said.

"We also need to get a team of divers down here from North Carolina," Don said. "As much as I hate to call them instead of the UGA guys," he said with a mutter, "The North Carolina Underwater Archeological Team is the best in the business."

"Unless you want to get Bob Baler," Bob said.

"Who?" Don said as quickly.

"You know, the guy who first found the Titanic," Bob said.

"Oh yes, I know who you're talking about," Don said. "I think the boys from UNC will do fine. They'll be a lot less expensive, too," he added.

"Can you call them, Don?" I asked.

"Yeah, sure. I think I have the head guy's number in my briefcase. Let me go see," he said, and left to go upstairs.

"Dinner is ready," one of the girls yelled. Bob and I looked at each other. We were hungry but had not even thought about eating until the dinner bell was sounded.

"I'll get Don," I said.

"Good, meet you in the kitchen then," Bob said. The dinner that night consisted of grilled blue fish, scallops sautéed in white wine sauce, new potatoes and greens, and fruit custard to top things off. Maria, Francisco's wife, had dropped by the house earlier in the day with the assorted vegetables, fruits, and fish. The meal was delicious. After such a long day, we were all exhausted. The meal was a great ending to a most adventurous day, but more had to be planned. Don would call his colleagues in North Carolina, who would be on the next plane to Belize. Their research vessel would arrive a few days later on the Caye. The next morning, we would fly over to Belize City to file an updated claim for the wreck site.

Chapter

31

The flight over to the mainland the next day was uneventful. We landed at the far end of the airfield and taxied our way up to the hanger area where the smaller planes were located. As soon as we came to a stop, an armed guard rolled up in a military jeep. It was a stark reminder that we were in a third world country where the military played a significant role in maintaining security. Leonardo stepped out of the plane and exchanged conversation with the guard, all in Spanish. The guard looked at Bob, Don, and me, as if we might be suspects of some heinous crime.

"What the heck do you think they're talking about?" Don said.

"I don't know, but this all makes me a bit nervous," I said.

"Yeah, same here, but don't look at him. Don't make eye contact. Act like everything is normal," Bob said.

"You think he knows why we're here?" Don asked.

"Don't know, Don. I have been expecting something else strange to happen ever since the situation at the dive site," Bob said.

"I agree," I said. "We need to get this claim filed as soon as possible, and then Mike can do his thing."

"So, how exactly will that work, Ethan?" Don asked. We were all sweating profusely. We were stuck sitting in the cabin of the Cessna, which was now like a hot-box. It wasn't like you could roll the windows down. We tried to busy ourselves with conversation while Leonardo continued to negotiate with the military guard.

"International law permits a person to set-up what is, in effect, an off-shore corporation. The advantages are numerous. It will provide us a conduit through which to channel the artifacts, whether we keep some, sell some, or arrange to have some of them displayed," I said.

"How much will that cost?" Don asked. He was always worried about the cost of everything, except when it came to scotch whiskey and cigars. Don once flew to Ireland to purchase a bottle of hundred-year-old scotch. While he was in the area, he traveled to London and picked up some Cuban cigars, albeit illegal, and somehow got them back to the states.

"It'll only cost you a bottle of your good scotch," I told him. He began laughing.

"Okay, Okay, I won't ask again," Don chuckled.

"Seriously, Mike will take care of everything. He has attorneys on staff that specialize in this kind of thing," I said.

"What do you suppose is taking so long?" Bob asked in a low voice, making sure not to look directly at them.

"I'm guessing we'll have to grease a palm," I said. "After all, you gotta remember where we are."

"You have some cash on you, Ethan?" Bob asked.

"Yeah, I have some, but not a lot. Since I was thrown overboard, I don't travel with a lot usually, but I did bring extra for this trip, to pay the guy for the services," I said.

"Oh yeah, what'd you ever figure out about that situation?" Don asked.

"We have some ideas. Julie and I saw the captain of the vessel we sailed down here on, and he and his buddies were acting weird," I said.

"Did you go to the authorities?" Don asked.

"Nope. We decided to act like nothing ever happened in hopes that it would flush the guilty parties out of hiding," I said.

"So you think they are on the Caye?" he asked.

"Yes, we do. In fact, we think we know who they are and where they are staying. We can't prove the connection, though," I said.

"And no cards or travelers' checks have surfaced?" he asked.

"Nada. We think they were sold to someone who would send them to another country, like Guatemala." I said.

"Wow, I would have never thought that!" Don said.

"Well, you have to remember that down here, Guatemala is kind of like the state next door back home. People here go back and forth all the time. The only difference is that you're more likely to get shot," Bob said.

"Really?" Don said, astounded at the stories Bob was recounting from his days of travel in the countries of Guatemala, Nicaragua, Honduras, and Costa Rica.

"Here he comes," I said. "Let's see what the dude said."

"Okay, you guys, we can disembark now," Leonardo said.

"What happened back there?" I asked.

"Don't ask me now, Ethan. I'll explain later. You will have to pay him a fee to fly out," he said. We walked in silence past the baggage area, where other guards were stationed. The guard who had conversed with Leonardo was now talking to some buddies, other guards. They were laughing as one of the other guards gave the dude a light for his cigarette. He glanced toward us, moved his head in an upward motion, as if to convey a conversation later before exiting. Each guard was equipped with a military style automatic machine gun. They also had handguns strapped to their waists, and a military combat knife strapped to their ankles.

"My God, we're in the middle of a freakin' war zone," Don said in a low voice.

"I wouldn't say that out loud," Leonardo admonished. "Walk with confidence and subtle determination," he said. I was astonished at Leonardo's level of understanding of the complexities involved in managing impressions and perceptions. Bob and I looked at each other and smiled. We both felt a bit more confident. Leonardo was in charge.

Filing the claim took about an hour. Leonardo had arranged for a Belizean attorney to meet us at a small café, where we solidified our arrangement for his services. It cost us $1500 American dollars for the attorney. It would costs more to control the artifacts. Leonardo had warned us that it would take some cash to get things expedited and approved quickly. Once the attorney's services were secured, we were ushered in ahead of the line. We listened intently, trying to pick up the meaning of the conversation, all of which was in Spanish. After several minutes, orders were given, and a secretary produced some forms for us to sign.

"What do these forms say, Leonardo?" I asked.

"These are your official claim forms," he said. "The first set will mark the claim in your name. You may also want to include the name of the corporation," he said.

"How much will all this cost?" I asked.

"We'll get to that in a few minutes," he said. "Now, this second set of papers is your agreement to surrender 40% of your findings, either in actual artifacts or in currency to the Belizean government. It's from the Tourism Bureau. They will have a person on site to monitor the activities, and to ensure they get their share," he said.

"Will they interfere with what we want to do?" I asked in a low voice, not knowing if they spoke or understood English.

"Only if you don't pay them their fee," he said, smiling.

"Forty percent," I heard Bob say. I signed the paperwork as the secretary presented more forms for more signatures. I looked up at Leonardo, who seemed to sense my concern.

"Everything is in good order, Ethan," he said. "Francisco and I are in agreement with your plan...as you explained it last night," he said. A huge feeling of relief came over me. We had not discussed the details of the conversation, and I had been trying to figure out when and how to bring it up again. Now that I knew Leonardo and Francisco were on board, I knew things would go more smoothly. They would have a stake in how all this worked out. I glanced at Bob and Don, who were smiling slightly. We felt awkward. We were surrounded by armed military guards. It was a way of life for the people here.

The flight back was exhilarating. With the claim in place, we would now have protection provided by the Belizean government, although it would cost us 40% of whatever we found. Mike and his team had gotten the corporation set up through a Swiss bank located in Freeport, Bahamas. We would now position ourselves for the reclamation dives. This is where Don's research buddies would come into play.

"As soon as we land," Leonardo said, "we need to ready ourselves for the next dive...today."

"Okay. Will Francisco have everything ready to go?" I asked.

"Yes. I instructed him to get with your wives, and get all the equipment ready to go."

"What about the government dudes?" Bob asked. "Don't we have to wait on them?"

"No. No. They will be there when we get there," he said.

"What about the guys that tried to nail us on the last dive?" Don asked.

"We will take our spear guns again, Señor Don. It is the best way to ensure our safety," Leonardo answered.

"What about the Belizean government guys? Won't they help defend or protect us?" I asked.

"They are only interested in their share of the treasure. If we were to encounter danger, they would only protect the wreck site, not us," he explained.

"Should we all have a spear gun, then?" Don asked.

"No, Francisco and I will maintain surveillance once we are in the water. We have also asked Juan, our cousin, to accompany us. He is an experienced diver, and will be an extra set of eyes," Leonardo said.

The touchdown was flawless. To our surprise, Francisco, Juan, and the girls met us at the airfield. We loaded our gear in the truck, and were off to the docks. Within 20 minutes, we were on our way to the dive site. Introductions were made, but the focus was on the water as Francisco and Juan scanned in all directions. Leonardo and Francisco talked among themselves. I couldn't hear what they were saying, but I nudged Bob and subtly motioned toward Leonardo. Bob glanced back at me as if to say that we needed to have a conversation later. I nodded my head in affirmation, as did Don. From my peripheral vision, I noticed that Myra and Lindsey had been watching the exchange between Bob, Don, and I with intensity. Julie had been focused on Leonardo and Francisco, and Juan seemed to be playing a minor support role. Julie was gifted at reading body language, which always gave her the upper hand or advantage whenever we had a disagreement. It was like she had X-ray vision.

The sun was beating down on us. It was a hot day in western edge of the Caribbean Sea. "Okay, we are here," Leonardo sounded as the boat came to a slow idle. "Drop an anchor, Juan," he said. Juan jumped into action, and anchors were dropped and secured on both ends of the boat. "Suit up everybody," he said. We all eagerly complied, saying very little.

"Same procedure as last time, Leonardo?" I asked.

"Yes sir, Ethan. You guys get into pairs, and stay between Francisco and me, no matter what," he said.

"Oh hell, no matter what...what does that mean?" Don asked.

"That means we may have company this time," Leonardo said.

The comment had been rhetorical and not actually meant for a response. "Don, would you get your butt in the water and shut up?" Myra Jean said in a low but demonstrative voice. "Hell, this is supposed to be your specialty, so shut up and get in the water," she said.

"I love you, too, honey," Don said, somewhat laughingly.

"I do expect that the looters will visit us again; so, we need to be very expeditious with this dive," Leonardo reminded us.

"What is our main objective today?" Don asked.

"I think you need to bring up as much as possible in the mesh bags," Leonardo said.

"I can do that," Bob said.

"I will help point in the direction of the most accessible artifacts. Señor Don, I need you to help me with that part," Leonardo said.

"Sure." Don said.

"Ms. Julie, if you and the others...meaning the other women, could follow the same steps with picking up the most notable items, that will be great," he said.

"Got it. No problem," Julie said, her heavy British accent slipping out. Leonardo paused and smiled before giving Juan instructions about assisting us with lifting the objects in such a way to cause as little sand dust as possible.

With everyone in the water, Leonardo gave the signal, and we all plunged down into the clear water on the western edge of the Caribbean Sea. The wreckage was in 90 to 110 feet of water, and debris seemed to stretch about a 100 yards.

Leonardo stopped us all when we reached a sandy ledge, a few yards from the part of the wreck site where we had lifted the gold bar. Leonardo guided each pair of divers to a different area, but all within the same direction. We had to stay in close proximity in order to have the advantage if we were attacked again by the looters.

"Go this way," Leonardo mumbled, and pointed Bob and me to an area where we had dug previously. "You go this way," he pointed and mumbled to Julie, Myra and Lindsey to work in a different location. Their spot seemed to have smaller items like goblets, plates, pots, and other items that would be associated with a ship's galley. In an underwater wreck site like this, however, one never knows what might be found right under the surface of the sandy ocean floor.

Leonardo motioned for Don to follow him, as Francisco hovered above us and scanned the area in a 360 degree motion. Soon, we were all in the midst of sifting through the sand, occasionally finding an interesting piece that made it to the mesh bag. We only had about 20 minutes, since Leonardo wanted to play it safe on this dive.

Leonardo signaled to us to check our gauges. I had 60% of my air left. The others were about the same. He gave a thumbs-up, and motioned for us to keep digging. Francisco was on his post, but looking steadily in one direction. Don had moved over near Bob and me, and we had found what looked like some type of chest or box. It was obviously made of metal, since a wooden chest would have disintegrated. If it was a metal box or chest of some kind, it would be hard to get up to the surface.

Leonardo pointed to the same area where Bob and I had been sifting the sand, and Don joined the action. Myra Jean, Julie and Lindsey had also uncovered a treasure trove of jewels that seemed to be located in clumps as big as basketballs, all melted together by the crusted surfaces. As Don and I were digging out the metal box, which measured about two feet by 20 inches wide, by about 18 inches high, we noticed gold pieces all around the bottom of the box. Don motioned and pointed to the hole in the sand next to the box that was filled with gold coins. I wondered if the box had a hole in the bottom, or if the box itself might be filled with gold coins.

As we were separating the box from the suction of the seabed, Leonardo abruptly looked over his right shoulder. Francisco was motioning to him and pointing out in the direction behind us. Juan was assisting the girls as they were filling their mesh bags with jewels and other pieces fortuitously scattered around the tail end of the debris field.

At that moment, Don and I tugged one last time, and the chest gave way from the clutches of the seabed, and a cloud of silt enveloped us. As we began to maneuver away from the silt, Don pointed toward the surface. Almost instantaneously, Juan was at our side and began securing a line around the chest. Then, a commotion to my left caught my eye. It was Francisco diving downward toward an outcropping of rocks and crusty formations, as a spear narrowly missed him. I looked beyond Francisco and saw two divers racing toward us. They each had double tanks, which meant they had come in from a distance. Don nudged me toward the girls. They hadn't yet seen the oncoming intruders.

Don looked around, almost in a panic state, and motioned to me. He was looking for Bob who had been right beside us, but was now nowhere to be seen. Leonardo and Francisco were bracing themselves to fend off the intruding divers, when I saw Bob coming up behind the two intruders. He had his dive knife in one hand and a bar of some sort in the other. I motioned for the girls to stay behind the rocks, and asked in hand-signal fashion if Juan would stay, as well. He gladly agreed.

I nudged Don to follow me, as Francisco and Leonardo began to struggle with the two invaders. Suddenly, another spear zipped through the water. The water bubble trail was only about 10 feet from us. Don grabbed my arm. I thought he was going to want to retreat, but nothing was further from the truth. Shaking his fist, he motioned for me to follow as he swam toward the assailants. Bob was closing in from behind and pounced on the two divers. He was trying to cut their air hoses, which would force them to the surface. They began to roll and tumble. Leonardo and Francisco closed in with their knives and spear guns, and Don and I held our positions within reach of the skirmish and were ready to jump in at any second. Bob and one of the intruders began spinning downward. I motioned Don toward them, and he was suddenly spinning downward, entangled with the two of them. When they hit the sea floor, silt fanned out like a mushroom cloud. I could see air bubbles streaming upward toward the surface, which seemed miles away.

The skirmish continued for what felt like an eternity, and spread out twenty or thirty feet beyond our dig site. It was difficult to discern where anybody was, and then it happened. The sound of the spear guns could be heard clearly, even under water. One spear sailed upward toward the surface at about a fifty-degree angle. The next spear came sputtering out of the silt cloud, followed by bubbles and blood that began to drift upward and around the silt.

Like the end of a one-act play, one of the intruders began a panic ascent to the surface. His air hose had been severed, and he was holding his arm as blood trailed from the upper bicep. The dust cloud began to thin, and Don came darting from the tangle of mayhem. The girls were huddled behind the outcroppings, waiting with concern for the cloud to clear. Then, Bob tumbled out of the dust cloud with blood spewing from his upper body. The lower half of a spear was protruding from his right shoulder. He had several knife cuts on his arm. Francisco emerged from the silt and motioned us to the surface. He looked over to the girls, and motioned to them as well. He pointed to Bob and the blood flowing from his shoulder, and made a shark motion with his hands. Oddly, I had not felt panic until that point. We were 90 feet from safety with a bleeding man, in the middle of the Caribbean Sea. Sharks can smell blood miles away. We had to act quickly, but where was the other guy...and Leonardo?

We were about half way to the surface when Leonardo and the other intruder came floating up. Leonardo had tied the hands of the diver and was bringing him toward the boat. As we ascended in a deliberate but steady manner, I saw a shadowy shape in the distance that made my heart stop. The silhouette of a shark was about 75 yards out, and it appeared to be making its way toward Bob and me. I motioned toward the shadowy creature, hastening the ascent. Once on the surface, we hurriedly got everyone into the boat, including the injured Bob and the now bound and captured intruder diver. Leonardo barked orders to

Francisco, "El apuro, el apuro, salga de aquí [Hurry, hurry, let's get out of here, Francisco]."

"Por favor, Si!" he replied. Francisco swung the boat around starboard and gunned the engines. In a split second, the boat had planed out and was skipping across the surface of the water.

"What do we do now?" Don asked, looking at both Bob and me. "I mean, we have the loot, but we also have a looter," he said with a chuckle.

"We will hand him over to the authorities once we reach the shore," Leonardo said.

"Do you know him Leonardo?" I asked.

"Yes, he is one of the goons who worked for the Captain you suspected of throwing you overboard when you first arrived on the island," he said.

I felt my stomach hit my throat. I felt myself becoming angry, and then felt Don's hand on my shoulder. "Not now, Ethan. Save it. We know now, and now he knows we know," he said.

I looked over at Bob, who looked a bit pale. "How you holding up, my friend?" I asked.

"Couldn't be better," Bob said. "But don't let this goon out of your sight. I'm not finished with him or his buddy yet," he added, looking the guy squarely in the eyes. It was clear that Bob was pissed. His spunky attitude might cause one to forget he had a spear sticking out of his shoulder.

"What about Bob's shoulder?" Don asked.

"We'll take care of it at the house," Lindsey said. She had a calm demeanor, and didn't seem panicky or overly concerned.

"Hasn't he lost a lot of blood?" I asked Lindsey.

"No, not as much as you might think. The spear went through the fatty tissue on the outside edge of his ribcage," she said. "He's lucky, though."

"Hell, I'll be fine, Ethan. It's this guy you need to worry about," Bob said.

I looked down at the mesh bags. They were filled with gold coins and jewels as well as some odd items. Then there was the chest. It looked smaller than it had under water. The surface was crusty and slimy. The lock on the front was encrusted from being under water more than three hundred years. It would be difficult to open.

The Belizean authorities met us at the dock. Four armed and fully uniformed military guards boarded the boat and took custody of the intruder diver. There was an exchange between Leonardo and the head officer, who looked at the mesh bags and the chest. "Bueno, regresaremos a reunir nuestra porción," the officer said, then saluted Leonardo and tipped his hat toward us as he departed with the now handcuffed prisoner.

"So, Leonardo, what did he say?" I asked.

"You are safe, Ethan. They will be back later tonight or tomorrow to get the government's portion of the treasure, as you agreed."

"How will we divide all this, Leonardo?" I asked.

"We need to get everything to your place since it's outside of town. Juan and some of his buddies will form a guard line around the perimeter of your house. Word will surely have gotten out about this find," he said.

"We need to get Bob to the house so Lindsey can tend to his wounds," Don said.

"Yes, let's load and go," said Leonardo. "Francisco will join us later after he has secured the boat and diving equipment."

Bob grunted as we sped down the bumpy gravel road leading to the house. Once we arrived, we helped Bob to the study on the first floor, while Lindsey gathered the various make-shift instruments she would need to extract the spear from Bob's shoulder.

"I'll need some of your scotch, Don," Lindsey ordered.

"I'm on it," Don said, hurrying to the liquor cabinet and grabbing the bottle of 100-year-old scotch. "Are you going to pour it on him or in him?" Don asked.

"Both!" Lindsey said.

Once towels and pillows had been gathered and positioned, Lindsey made Bob drink a full glass of the scotch whiskey. He coughed and gagged a little, but got it down.

"Dang it, Lindsey, don't drown me in this stuff," he said.

"Hell, it'll be the best way to go if you have to go," Don quipped with a chuckle.

"Yeah, but you don't have a dadgum spear sticking in your shoulder," Bob said.

"When's that liquor going to take effect?" Julie asked, as she eased up to Bob's side and wiped his forehead.

"Hell, I've not had this much attention from you girls since Linds' and I got married," Bob said, his eyes now appearing a little heavy.

"Yeah, don't get used to it bud," Lindsey said. "Okay, here's what we're going to do. Julie and Myra, will you be my assistants?" Lindsey asked. They quickly moved into position, nudging Don and me out of the way.

"That's okay with me," Don said, pouring himself a drink from the same bottle.

"When I start to pull this thing out, pour some of the scotch over the opening of the wound," she said.

"Oh God, there's goes my 100-year-old scotch," Don murmured.

"Don, don't you have something you can do before I take this spear and poke you with it," Myra Jean said, grabbing the bottle from Don's hand.

"Here you go, Lindsey, I'll do the pouring," Myra Jean said.

"Okay, Julie, will you stuff these strips of cloth into the wound as soon as I pull the spear out and as soon as Myra has poured the scotch into it. It can be almost at the same time," she said.

"Got it," Julie said.

"I'm ready," Myra Jean said.

"I'm not," Bob said.

"I love you darling, but grit your teeth NOW!" Lindsey said firmly. With a coordinated motion, she pulled the spear from Bob's shoulder, as Myra doused it with the scotch and Julie applied the strips of cloth as compression against the spewing blood. Bob groaned as he bit down on the towel Lindsey had given him. It was over in 10 seconds or less, and the bleeding stopped within minutes.

"Jesus, honey, that hurt like hell," Bob finally said. "I'll have another drink if you don't mind. Geezze!" he said.

"Hell, I'll have one with you," Don said. Myra Jean rolled her eyes.

Chapter

32

With Bob resting, his shoulder wound patched up for now, we turned our attention to the items brought up in the mesh bag. While we were tending to Bob, Juan had filled a large metal tub with water from the ocean. He had also sent Maria to get some antibiotics. We had by now become accustomed to the islanders helping us out whenever we needed medicines of any kind. In third world countries, if you have money, you can purchase whatever you need medically. The antibiotic was probably a derivative of amoxicillin. Maria also had a small bottle of morphine in liquid form, for pain. We would add a few drops of it to Bob's orange juice to help him sleep.

Leonardo soon returned, and told us that he had some of his cousins guarding the perimeter of the house.

"How many cousins do you have, Leonardo?" Don asked, seeming genuinely curious.

"I'm related to half the island, Señor Don," he said. Myra Jean cleared her throat as a signal to Don not to go down that road of questioning.

"Let's see what we have in the chest," Leonardo said, motioning for us to follow him. "How is Señor' Bob, Ethan?" he asked.

"He's resting now that the spear is out," I said.

"What? The spear is out of his shoulder?" Leonardo asked, stunned at how quickly it had been removed. "Who pulled it out?" he asked.

"Lindsey did, actually," I said.

"Whew," he said with a whistle. "She must be some tough lady, Ethan."

"Yes, she is, Leonardo," I said.

We continued following Leonardo toward the metal chest. "Leonardo, let me ask you something," I said.

"Sure, what is it?" he said.

"Leonardo, I want to make sure we're okay here. I mean... you and me, with this sunken treasure thing," I said.

"What do you mean, Ethan?" he asked.

"Leonardo, we had no idea that we would find what we have now stumbled into. It's all because of you that we found this treasure," I said.

"Maybe, but it was you guys who were inquisitive enough to explore the myths and dive the deep water. Most people aren't as determined," he said.

"It's important for you to know that we want to help the people of Ambergris Caye. We want them to benefit from the wealth that comes from these artifacts, as well as you and Francisco, and your families," I said.

"Yes, I know, Ethan. I have no doubt. I trust you. We have known each other for a long time. Besides, I can read the true intent of a person. It part of the Shaman way," he said.

"Really? Good. So, we're okay?" I said.

"Yes, Ethan. No problem with us. But, those guys who jumped us today. There will be more. And you cannot trust the government either. They are greedy," he said.

"What do you suggest?" I asked.

"I think you should secure the dive site as soon as you can. Pull and secure whatever you want to excavate, and then hand over the area to the government, with the agreement that you can return to explore again. That will get you the most protection from looters, I think," he said.

"Sounds like a good plan, Leonardo. I'll discuss it with the others," I said.

"Let's get this chest open and see what we have," he said, changing the focus of the conversation.

We gathered around the table. The tub of artifacts we had recovered from the bottom shimmered. The gold pieces were a shiny yellowish gold. Some of the other pieces, the silver ones, would have to be treated. Then, there was the chest.

"Let's get this thing open," Don said.

"I think it might require a little persuasion," Leonardo said. He picked up a hammer and small steel bar, and began to pound away at the lock on the chest. Within minutes the locked popped off and landed in the water in two pieces.

"Now, let's see what's inside," Leonardo said. He again hammered away at the chest. Francisco joined in the effort with a hammer and large screwdriver. Finally, with a unified effort, the top of the chest gave way. We all stood there, not moving a muscle.

"Hell, open it," Don said.

"What's in the damn thing?" Bob yelled from inside. "I'm not too drugged to want to know what's happening in there," he yelled.

"Stay in bed, Bob," Lindsey yelled back. "I'll come get you in a minute."

Leonardo and Francisco reached down and forced the box open. We were all amazed. We stood there and stared.

"Well, what's in it.....helloooo out there," Bob said. "Did you guys get kidnapped by aliens or what?" he said.

"Or what, that's for damn sure," Don said.

"Oh my God, look at that," Myra Jean said. Julie and I stood there, staring at it, taking it all in. What lay before us was a chest filled with gold coins that were about one half inch thick by three inches wide, silver pieces, and an assorted mix of jewels... emeralds, rubies and other colorful stones. This was like a treasure chest right out of the old Sir Francis Drake movies I watched as a kid. It was unbelievable.

"Holy moly, how much do you think this is worth?" I asked. "Don, you're the expert. What do you think?"

"I think it's worth a lot, and I mean a LOT," he said. Don's mood had now shifted. He was serious. "Let me see, guys," he said. He ran his hands through the coins, examined some and counted some, looked at the silver coins and then the jewels. He looked up at each one of us including Leonardo and Francisco. "This could be worth five to ten million, or more. It could be *much* more! I can't say until we get everything out and get an accurate count. And we need to do that tonight," he added.

"I agree, Señor Don," Leonardo said. "The Belizean government will be here tomorrow morning to collect their share. They may even come during the night," he said.

"Let's do it," I said. All agreed, and the process of cleaning and sorting the items began. Lindsey and Julie would check on Bob from time to time, and give him more drugs and scotch.

By 2:00 A.M., we had sorted, cleaned, categorized, and logged into an inventory each piece of artifact we had brought from the wreck site. The inventory included 310 gold coins of various sizes and weights, 152 gold bars or ingots, 214 pieces of silver, the equivalent of four gallons of jewels and precious stones of various sizes and cuts, from rubies to emeralds, and fifty pieces of various other items such as plates, goblets, and pots.

"Now, Don, what do you think the value might be?" I asked.

"If my calculations are even remotely close, Ethan, this all could have a value of between 5 and 15 million, maybe more, considering the majority is still on the ocean floor. It's hard to ascertain the complete and accurate value. I'd have to make some calls," he said.

"Holy moly," I said.

"Let me say this, though. I was being conservative. If my hunch is correct, you can double or even triple the value," he said.

"How do we handle the Belizean government, Leo?" I asked.

"Let me handle that. I will give them a sample to take with them, and a promise that by the end of the week, we will hand over their share," he said.

"End of the week? Are you serious, Leonardo?" Don asked, exasperatedly.

"If you want to keep any of it, that's the way you have to play it. Also, we need their help in protecting all of us at this point. And, I tell you, we must do another dive tomorrow. We need to find something that identifies the ship," he said.

"Like what?" I asked.

"Well, like a bell, an anchor, anything with the ship's insignia on it. In fact, if you can find the Captain's quarters, you might be lucky enough to find the ship's seal," Don said.

"He is right, Ethan. But for now, we need to contact the authorities and invite them out tonight," he said.

"Okay, I'm game, but how will that help us," I asked.

"For one thing, Ethan, we can give them some of these gold coins and gold bars as a token of our word," Leonardo said.

"Yeah, I can see that working, but what about the goons?" Don asked.

"That's why we contact them now. If they know they will get more tomorrow or by the end of the week, they will protect us," Leonardo said.

"I hope they do better than they have so far," I said.

"They will, I predict," Leonardo said. "They don't need to see the whole thing, give them a small bag full. This will get them excited and they will protect us," he said.

"The guys from UNC should be here tomorrow. They can help us on the dive, and assist in coming up with a more accurate value of what we have," Don said.

"Hey, that's a good thought," I said. "Can you call them and see what their ETA is?" I asked.

"Yep, I'll call them now. They will wet their britches when I tell them what we have found so far," Don said, as he got up to go toward the house.

"You gonna use your cell phone for the call, Don?" I asked.

"Yeah, why?" he asked.

"Security, that's all," I said.

"Yep, right again. I'll speak in code. They'll understand it."

The amount of gold and silver was mind-blowing. We would have to come up with a plan to pack this stuff and get it out, all without getting bogged down with the Belizean government.

Leonardo had made the call to the authorities about their sampling of the gold. They arrived within an hour. It was now a little after 3:00 A.M. Leonardo and Francisco took a small box of gold and silver coins, along with some of the ingots and jewels, and led the officers to the side of the property. An involved conversation ensued, and they finally shook hands. They turned and began walking back to their jeep, and then turned and waved to all of us. We were on the front porch of the Big House watching and waiting with great anticipation. We waved back, as Leonardo and Francisco walked toward the porch. Bob had fallen asleep, and was resting well.

"Well, fill us in on what transpired, Leo," I said.

He began laughing. Francisco was grinning from ear to ear, and began laughing too.

"What? What?" I said. "Tell us."

"When I explained to them what your plans were, as far as some of the money is concerned, they were delighted. At first, they did not believe it, but I told him about the conversation you and I had yesterday, Ethan," Leonardo said. "He said you had the full support and protection of the Belizean government and its military, including… the Belizean navy," he said. He was beaming!

"You got to be kidding me," Don said.

"No, it's true," he said. "In fact, tomorrow, we will have a military escort to the site. The navy ships will be posted within a 50 mile radius of the wreckage. They will also post a ship there after we leave in order to maintain the protection of the site," he said.

"I can't believe it," Julie said. "I'm blown away."

"What about the team coming down from the University of North Carolina? Will they be able to work on this project?" Don asked.

"Oh yes, they want all the help we can give to this project," Leonardo said.

"Do you know what this means to your families?" I said to Leonardo and Francisco, again.

"Yes, we do, and we are very grateful," Leonardo said. Francisco replied with a "Si, Señor Ethan."

Chapter

33

The next morning came early. Leonardo and Francisco were at the back door at 7:00 A.M. "We came for breakfast, Ms. Julie," they said. Julie and Lindsey had insisted they join us for breakfast. "How is Señor Bob," Leonardo asked.

"He's sore, but okay this morning," Julie said. "He's been complaining a little, which means he's feeling better," she said, laughing.

"Yeah, Leonardo, you should have been here this morning when Lindsey pulled the cloth out of his shoulder to change his bandage," Myra said. "You sure you didn't hear him down at the Victoria?" She busied herself completing the fruit salad.

"No, we didn't hear him, but I know that must have hurt very badly," Leonardo said. "Did he want another shot of the scotch?" Leonardo said laughingly.

"Yes, he did," Don said, as he entered the kitchen. "I had to hide my good scotch!"

"He did not, Don. You're so full of it," Myra snarled.

"She's right, Leonardo," Don said, "the scotch is safe. So what's on today's agenda, for dive number four?"

"We need to recover something that identifies the ship. There are several possibilities, Señor Don, but we have to make sure, if we can," Leonardo said.

"It could be from one of the Spanish treasure ships that came from Honduras or Guatemala in the mid 1500's," Julie said.

"Awh, I see you've been doing a little research," Don said.

"It could also be the Santa Yaga, which was lost off Three Brothers near the northern tip of Ambergris Caye. The location of our wreck site is in close proximity to where the Santa Yaga supposedly went down," Don said.

"But more than likely, it is one of the ships from Captain Morgan's fleet, perhaps the Oxford," I said.

"Yes, it could be," Don said, "especially since it went down in this same area, probably around 1650 or so and reportedly was carrying 250,000 pieces of silver and gold. Morgan had gone rogue once his brother became the Lt. Governor of Jamaica. It was at that time that he was commissioned to search for and secure assets from the pirates in the western Caribbean."

"That is correct," Leonardo said, which surprised us all. "In fact, Morgan ran the coast of South and Central America with much recklessness. The stories surrounding the lost treasure of Sir Henry Morgan have been floating around for many years, since I was a young boy," he said.

"This was when Spain and England were at war," Don added, "and each needed all the assets they could gather. Morgan was a scoundrel, and he set out to seek revenge on all those who had worked against him. It has been told that when Morgan lost his flagship, it was carrying 250 million pieces of gold and silver coins, quantities of jewels, casks of ale and rum, precious spices, silks, and enough weapons to outfit an entire army," Don said.

"So, if we look at what else is down there besides the gold and silver, we might be able to identify the wreckage through a process of elimination, right?" I asked.

"That's right," Don said.

"Well, get your butts to the table; breakfast is served," Myra Jean said.

We all sat down for another delicious and hearty breakfast. Soon after, we were on our way to the dock. The dive equipment had been serviced and loaded and was ready for our launch. This would be our fourth dive, the one that would define the discovery of our lives. We made our way to the dive site under the watchful eye of the Belizean government. The waves were cresting at six to eight feet and were white-capping. After a few minutes, we arrived at the site. A Belizean Navy Ship could be seen on the horizon. We scanned the area in a 360-degree fashion and saw nothing.

"Let's do this," I said. "You ready, Leonardo?"

"Yes, I'm ready," he said. There was dread in his voice. It made me nervous. We were all a little apprehensive, still getting over the shock of the day before.

"Leonardo, you nervous about something?" I asked. I had learned to ask. He would tell you if there was something bothering him.

"No, nothing, Ethan. I'll be glad when this is done. Those banditos will be back," he said.

"You don't feel safe with the Belizean navy being right off our starboard?" I asked.

"Remember, Ethan, I said do not trust the government. They are an evil necessity and have their own greedy agenda," he said.

"Hell, that doesn't sound too different from our government back home," I said.

"Get suited up," Leo said. We got ourselves ready to dive. There was a strange air over the boat. Nobody spoke, and no one emitted any excitement. The team from UNC was in an adjacent boat, and there wasn't much noise coming from their boat either. There was a strange feeling indeed, but none of us had a clue why.

"Everybody ready?" Leonardo asked. Everyone signaled that they were. One by one, we all flipped backwards into the water. We descended down through the 90 feet of water to the wreck site. There was an eerie feeling this time, and it showed on all our faces. Were we being greedy, I wondered? The mood was intense, but we also knew we had a job to do.

Three UNC guys swam over to Don. They greeted each other, and then swam over to me and Leonardo. Through a series of hand motions, we began our search. We had to find something to identify the ship, and we had about 30 minutes to do it.

Leonardo and I were on one side of the wreckage, and Don and his UNC boys were on the other. Sand silt mushroom clouds encircled us, but we kept low to the bottom and kept sifting through. During this process, we found more artifacts associated with the ship. There were forks, wine goblets, plates, and various pulleys and barrel rings. We were down to the 20-minute mark when Don and one of the UNC guys flagged for Leonardo and me to join them. We swam over, and Don was pointing to an object buried deep in the sand.

It was round and long. Some of the other guys swam over, we all began to dig and remove the sand, which created one hell of a silt cloud. After a couple of minutes of feverish digging, we all stopped, and waited for the dust to settle. When it did, we all plunged down to examine the inscription. There it was, in plain view, the bronze cannon from the flagship of Sir Captain Henry Morgan. It read, "The *Cour Volant*, 1688." Leonardo tapped me on the shoulder, and gave me a thumbs-up. Don and his UNC boys were excited, as well. Then, we all suddenly realized that we had about seven minutes to get this thing to the surface. We fell in like two teams attacking an enemy. The UNC guys had ropes and clips. Leonardo signaled for Juan to come down with a huge net, one usually reserved for lifting heavy cargo from the big barge supply ships. Once it was down below, it was quickly maneuvered under the cannon. The ropes were fashioned on each end. Leonardo looked at me and tapped his gauge. I looked at mine. I held up 4 fingers. We had four minutes. Leonardo and I wouldn't have enough air to get to the surface. We had already sent the girls topside. The verification of the cannon for the wreck site would mean millions more than we all had anticipated, more than we had ever dreamed of.

I tapped Don and showed him my gauge. I also motioned to Leonardo. We had 3 minutes of air now. With the cannon now secured by both the ropes and the cargo net, it was time to ascend. Don immediately grabbed one of the UNC guys. He made some hand motions, pointed to the gauges, and the three of us, Leonardo, myself, and the UNC diver, began our ascent. We would buddy breathe on the way up. I had never had to do this for real, and it was a numbing feeling. When buddy breathing, you're sharing someone else's air, and you have to be very deliberate with the ascent.

Don and the other two UNC guys would stay down and accompany the cannon to the surface. After what seemed a hell of a long time, we broke the surface. We bobbed up and down in the water, but we could breathe. Julie and Myra extended a ladder, and we boarded the boat. Juan and Francisco had made ready the hoist for lifting the cannon. As Leonardo and I were climbing on board, the wench began to draw in the line. The cannon began its ascent to the surface after nearly 350 years under water. If this was indeed the cannon from the flagship, it would put us over the top with the value of the wreckage. There was no celebration, no excitement, only an intense focus on the hoist. Slowly, the line was wound in as the object made its way to the surface. We all affixed our focus on the surface of the water. The motor of the wench slowed. I glanced at Juan.

"It's near," he said. Without a sound on both decks, we watched as the cannon broke the surface. One by one, the UNC divers broke the surface, and then Don popped up.

"Pull it alongside," yelled one of the UNC guys.

"Now, Leonardo, can you get another rope around both ends of the piece?" another UNC diver asked.

"Good. Now we're ready for the lift. Will it hold?" the UNC diver asked.

"Yes, it will hold," said Leonardo.

"Then, let's lift it. Go slow, and when it clears the edge of the boat, swing it slowly over the deck," he said.

The lift began. We all held our breath. Slowly, the wench squeaked and moaned as the cannon cleared the water. I had one rope and Leonardo had the other. We were on each end of the boat. Julie and Myra were standing and watching with as much intensity. Lindsey had stayed behind with Bob.

"Lift it a little more," the UNC diver said. Juan continued the hoist.

The wench began to smell. It was over heating. We had to get the cannon aboard quickly before the wench burned through and released its grip.

"Now, pull it over," he yelled from the water. "Pull it hard. This has to be it," he yelled. With a final tug, we all pulled in unison. The cannon cleared the edge of the boat.

"Now, hold your position. Slowly release the wench. I mean very slowly," the UNC guy ordered. We all had to reach down deep, but we held our positions. Slowly, the cannon began to be lowered to deck of the boat. Within seconds, it was done. We all fell to our knees and looked at the cannon. We rubbed it with jubilation, looking for the inscription.

"There it is," Leonardo said. Don was making his way up the ladder and into the boat.

"I'll be damned. Isn't that a pretty sight!" he said.

One of the UNC guys took a wire brush and began to brush away some of the crustiness from the surface.

"I do believe it reads, *"The Cour Volant,"* he said.

"Let me see that darn thing," Don said. He rubbed his fingers across and along the shape of the letters. "Yep, by God, that's it, all right."

"I think this calls for a little celebration," said Leonardo. "Bring out the beer, Juan," he said. Juan disappeared into the captain's covey, and returned with a small cooler filled with cold bottles of beer.

"Myra Jean, what you drinkin', Honey?" Don asked.

"Hell, I'm gonna drink one of these cold beers. I'm celebrating with the rest of you," she said.

Juan passed around the beers, and we drank them. Francisco secured the cannon to the deck so it wouldn't roll around. The UNC guys boarded their boat, and stored their gear away. They, too, were celebrating with a round of cold beers. Both boats were cranked and we began our trip back to shore. We did all this under the watchful eye of the Belizean Navy. I looked through some binoculars and saw an officer looking through his binoculars. It was strange. We were being watched the entire time.

Once back at shore, we off-loaded the cannon and took it to the Big House where we rigged another tub and filled it with seawater. We placed the cannon into the tub. All of the items would need to be transferred to a different facility.

"Ethan, the UNC boys will have their oceanographic research vessel here for a couple of days. Are you okay with transferring these items to their ship?" Don asked.

"What would be the plan from there, Don?" I asked.

"You tell me. We need to take this stuff somewhere so the reclamation and desalination process can begin. The longer we wait, the more we'll lose," he said.

"Can we verify the cannon as being the one we believe it to be?" I asked.

"I think so. I'll talk to the guys and get them to examine it closely. Maybe we can officially confirm that it came from the *Cour Volant*," he said.

"Where will we need to send this stuff?" I asked.

"Well, how much longer do you guys plan to be here?" Don asked.

"Don't know. We need to get a value on this stuff, secure some assets, and get the things done we promised to do," I said.

"And then there's the Federales to deal with, right?" he said. "I think we should shoot for getting the critical items aboard the UNC research vessel. It's equipped for the desalination process that needs to begin immediately," Don said.

"I can live with that; sounds like a good idea," I said.

"Now, the other stuff, like the coins and jewels, can be treated on board and given back to you, if that's what you want," Don added.

"Don, a thought occurred to me. Do we need to get this stuff insured through Lloyds of London?" I asked.

"That might be a good idea. Let me make a call and asked someone who knows more about this than we do," he said.

"Sounds great! I'll go brief Bob and the others. I think he's up and around now," I said.

"Yes, I think I saw him walking through the kitchen. If he's hungry, he's almost back to normal," Don said.

"Yep, I would agree," I said.

Bob had indeed recovered, although he was sore from the spear passing through the fatty skin of the side of his rib cage. The main challenge was keeping the wound clean and disinfected. Other than that, he was as good as a clean fiddle.

"What do you guys think about transporting the critical items, like the cannon and some of the other pieces, to the UNC research vessel? They're equipped for the desalination process," I said.

"Is that what Don recommends?" Julie asked. Lindsey was in agreement with the question.

"Yes, that is exactly what he recommends," I said.

"Then, let's do it," Julie said. Lindsey agreed.

"Can we keep some of the coins?" Lindsey asked.

"Yes, once they're cleaned and recorded," I said.

"Then, let's make the arrangements," they agreed.

The next move was to secure the cannon and the other items, and load them aboard a small boat once again for the trip to the research vessel, which was now positioned near the dock in front of the Big House. But, for some reason, I had a bad feeling in my gut.

"Ethan, when will you be ready to load the cannon?" Don asked.

"Soon," I said. "I want to admire it for a bit."

"I know that's tempting, but we really need to get it into the desalination tank on board the research vessel," he said.

"Bob, what do you think? When do you think we should move the cannon?" I asked.

"Can we get the information recorded, and the cannon photographed before we move it to the research vessel?" Bob asked.

"I don't think that'll be a problem," Don said.

"Then, I think as soon as we can get those things done, we should move it," Bob said.

"Okay then, I agree. Let's get those things done, Don, and then we can move it," I said.

"What about Lloyd's of London? Have you made that arrangement yet?" Don asked.

"Oh yes, let me call Mike in Atlanta. He'll have to get out of bed and kick some butt to get this done this quickly, but he's the guy to get it done," I said.

I made the call to Mike in Atlanta. I told him about our situation and what I needed him to do. After a few choice words, he assured me that within the hour I would receive a faxed agreement of assurance from Lloyd's of London. We were to sign it and fax it back. He would authorize the funds electronically, and we would be insured. An hour later, the deal was done.

"Let's load'em," I said. It was now early evening. This was going to be late night...again, I thought to myself.

"I'll go get the girls. They won't want to miss this," Bob said.

It took all of us to load the pieces of silver and gold, the jewels and miscellaneous pieces, and finally, the cannon. We made our way to the research vessel. The items were loaded on board and placed in the proper containment tanks for desalination.

"When will this vessel start back to the states?" I asked.

"As soon as we can get clearance from the U.S. Coastguard," he said.

"Coastguard," I said, almost in shock.

"Yes, you didn't think they would take off without some protection, knowing what's on board and its value," Don said.

"Well, I have to admit, I was nervous about that notion. That's why I was reluctant to let it go," I said.

"That's my bad," Don said. "I should have explained it better to you. These guys never, and I mean, never, go anywhere without some layer of protection," he said.

"That makes me feel a hell of a lot better, I have to say," I said.

"Hell, when we were working on Blackbeard's ship and raising the anchor, we had the United States

Navy guarding us the entire time" he said. "Once they have clearance from the Navy, they'll move into international waters, where a U.S. Navy Frigate will pick them up as an escort all the way into Key West or wherever they're taking the stuff," he said.

"Where's the best place to take it?" I asked.

"Probably, *he thought*, Key West, Jacksonville, or Charleston will be their choices. If I had to decide, I'd take it to Charleston. A friend of mine is in charge of the Hunley up there, and they have a *First Class* facility," Don said. "They have the simulated dive tanks and everything. It's quite amazing."

"Let's get the rest of the stuff situated. I'm ready for some food and drinks. And I do mean some of your 100-year-old scotch or maybe even a Knob Creek," I said.

"I think you're spot on, my friend," he said. "Let's do this and get out of here."

We boarded the boat for the trip back to the shore. The lights from the Big House reflected on the water, like a reflection in a giant mirror of glass. The sun had set and the tides had reached a calm, placid stillness. There was something eerie about all this; but, I couldn't put my finger on it. Once inside, we poured drinks while the dinner table was set. Leonardo and Francisco declined our invitation to stay and eat. They, after all, had been away from their families a lot since this excursion began. What would the next day bring?

We toasted the day's events and finds, and began to eat. The food was good; the drinks were enough to take the edge off. The cool breeze off the water, blowing through the palm leaves, made this evening seem magical. Then... there was the next day...

Chapter

34

The Belizean authorities appeared at 8:00 A.M. the next morning. They wanted to see all the artifacts; and, of course, take their share. We scrambled around and delayed them for a few hours. So far, at that point, they were willing to wait. They left with a promise to return later in the day. Little did they know that all of the artifacts had been transported to the research vessel.

We were eating lunch when the authorities returned. This time there were two vehicles, and their blue lights were flashing. They approached the porch, where we were sitting, eating our lunch.

"Señor Ethan, may we come in please?" the officer asked.

"Sure, Officer, how may I help you?" I asked, not yet sure why the lights were flashing.

"There seems to be a problem," he said. Here it comes, I thought. They've learned that the artifacts are on the research ship. It wasn't that we wanted to deliberately hide them, but we needed to take necessary steps in order to preserve the artifacts without degradation.

"Señor," he began, "there is something that has come ashore," he said. "Rather, Señor, a body was found on the beach near the docks where you and your friends have been docking the boat. We have already spoken with Leonardo and Francisco."

"I need to ask you and the others some questions," he said.

"Sure, Officer, please come in. We want to cooperate as much as possible; but, may I ask why you think we might know anything about this body?" I asked.

"No problem, Señor. I will gladly tell you. The body, or what was left of it, was wearing diver clothes. There was a mask and snorkel on his head. And, he was wearing a wetsuit...on his upper torso anyway," the officer said.

"I see. What time was the body discovered?" I asked.

"Please. Señor, allow me to ask the questions," he said somewhat defensively.

The thought occurred to me that we might end up being suspects in this situation. This guy...or this body... might have been the diver whose air hose was cut during our underwater skirmish.

The officer began his questioning.

"Señor, we know that you all have been coming in and out of the area near the dock. Do you recall seeing anything suspicious?" he asked.

"No, not on the docks," I said.

"Not on the docks, Señor? Did something else happen?" he asked.

I looked at the others, and they all seemed to signal in agreement. "Well, yes," I said, "we were followed by some looters on the first dive, but we scared them off," I said. "Two of the same group came back and attacked us on our second dive, and we brought one of them back and turned him over to the authorities.

"How many were there?" he asked again.

"Three or four the first time, I think," I said.

"Can you describe any of them, Señor?" he asked.

"No sir, I'm sorry, but it was hard to make out their faces underwater," I said.

"Tell me about the situation that happened to you when you first arrived," he said.

"You mean when I found myself washed up on the beach?" I asked.

"Si Señor," he said. I recounted the story, as much as I could remember. I told him about how I woke up on the beach with waves slapping me in the face and salt water in my mouth; and, how I didn't know where Julie was. I told him how far I walked and how Julie and I found each other. I told him of my lack of memory of the events of that evening. I did tell him whom I thought it was, and how Julie and I had confronted him in the dive shop.

"That is all very interesting," he said. "Señor, I wonder if you and Ms. Julie could come with us?" he asked.

"Are we being arrested for any reason?" I asked.

"No, no, Señor. I want to see if you can identify the victim from the beach," he said.

"Sure," I said, and looked at Julie. "We can do that," I said. "Can we come down in our golf cart?" I asked.

"Si Señor," he said, "as long as you come now," he said with a tinge of authority.

"Let's go then," I said. With that, we loaded ourselves in the golf cart, and left for the docks. I took my cell phone, even though the coverage and signal strength was spotty at best. I wanted some way to communicate with the others if I needed to. I suddenly remembered what Leonardo had said about not trusting the Belizean government. After a few minutes, we reached the docks. Leonardo and Francisco were there, along with another police vehicle and two other officers.

"Leonardo, you okay?" I asked, as we walked up to the steps of the dock.

"Yes, Ethan, but this is a pretty gruesome sight. I think the guy was attacked by a shark," he said.

"Really," I said, a little shocked. A shark, I thought. My mind flashed back to the other day when Bob was hit with the spear gun. Again, I thought of the guy whose air hose Bob had cut. These guys had attacked us and were trying to kill us, or at least seriously injure us.

"Leonardo, do you recognize this guy?" I asked.

"I'm not sure, Ethan. It...he kind of looks like one of the guys who attacked us last Tuesday," he said.

"Señor," the officer called. "Could you please come over here? Ms. Julie can stay there for a minute," he said.

"Yes sir," I said. I was trying to comply as much as possible. If it was the guy whose hose Bob cut, then it might complicate things.

"Señor, do you recognize the victim," he asked. The body or what remained of the body was indeed a gruesome sight. He was missing half of the left side of his torso, his right leg was missing from the hip down, and a good chunk of his head was gone. Of course, as one might imagine, most of his insides were missing, as well. Dead bodies in the ocean become feed lots for all types of fish. This guy, once he was killed by the shark, became the victim of the feedlot.

"It's hard to identify him, Señor. He's missing half of his face," I said.

"Are there any marks you recognize?" he asked. Like shark teeth marks, I thought to myself. This guy was reaching, but I wanted to be cooperative. We were in a third world country, I reminded myself.

"Not that I can see, but can you have one of your guys pull the wetsuit off his remaining arm?" I asked.

"Si Señor, no problem," he said. Then he shouted orders in Spanish. His men hesitated, and he became angry and began shouting more intensely. His men moved with great haste, reached down and pulled off the sleeve of the wet suit. There it was. It was unmistakable.

"Señor," the officer called, "do you recognize the tattoo?" he asked, now with more suspicion in his intonation.

"Yes, officer, I do," I said.

"Where do you remember seeing the tattoo, Señor?" he asked.

"At the dive shop," I said. "But Señor, ask my wife if she recognizes it as well," I suggested.

"Tell me first about the dive shop. Is this where you first confronted the Captain, Señor?" he asked. Something struck me as odd. I didn't remember telling him about this incident. How did he know, I wondered. I decided to be bold.

"Did I tell you about that situation, Señor?" I asked.

"Señor," he said, "allow me." He paused for a moment, and continued, "no Señor, you did not."

"Then how do you know, and what did you hear?" I asked. I had decided at that I had leverage... the artifacts!

"I heard from many people, Señor," he said. "News on the island travels fast and without secrecy."

"Yes, I should have known that," I said.

"So, Señor', tell me what happened, if you please," he asked. So, I recounted the steps from the café, where Julie and I decided to investigate the docks and what ships had been moored there. I told him that we saw the ship from which I had been thrown overboard.

"So was this guy in the dive shop?" he asked.

"Yes, I would say so. It looks like the same tattoo," I said. "Can I take a closer look," I asked.

"Sure, Señor," he said.

"Are you assuming that the cause of death was a shark attack?" I asked.

"That's one scenario," he said. This gave me pause, but I didn't flinch. I knew he was probably testing the waters on a suspicious theory, one that included an American party.

"What other ideas do you have, officer?" I asked, looking at him square in the eyes.

"One never knows, Señor," he said, with a calculated demeanor.

"Look, Officer, someone either drugged me or knocked me out and pushed me overboard. I was lucky to wash up on the beach. My wife was also drugged with something in her wine that night," I said.

"Then you would have a motive to react, Señor?" he asked.

I smiled and looked directly at him, "Señor, with all due respect, I do not murder people," I said. "But, I will tell you, I do intend to find out who attempted to kill us and robbed us of our money and credit cards," I said.

"Then what will you do, Señor, once you learn who it was?" he asked. This was clearly not going in a desirable direction.

"Then, Señor, I will file charges against the person with the appropriate authorities, including the United States Government, since we boarded the ship in Galveston, Texas," I said. "In fact, if satisfaction wasn't achieved here, I'd work to bring down the full wrath of the United States government on any person connected," I said.

"Those are strong words, Señor," he said. They were meant to be, I thought to myself.

"Again, with all due respect, let's look at the facts," I said. The Officer said nothing. "We were attacked and robbed, yet nothing has surfaced. The Captain and crew of the ship we came in on have been here in Belize ever since we landed. We have had some contact, and yes, a confrontation. I believe that something unscrupulous happened, and that it involved those guys. Months have gone by, and nothing. Four weeks ago, we began our treasure dives; and, suddenly, we're attacked *again*. And one of the goons who tried to kill us by shooting spears at us at the dive sight *might be* this guy who happens to be half eaten by a shark. If this is one the guys who attacked us at the dive site, Officer, then he got what he deserved," I said.

"Leonardo confirms what you say," he said, a slight grin on his face.

"Then, is that it, Officer?" I asked.

"For now, Señor, but I have to ask you not to leave the island for a few days," he said.

"Hold it," I said. Now I was pissed off. "Are we being charged with anything?" I asked.

"No Señor, not at this point," he said.

"Are you saying that we are suspects, and if so, for what?" I demanded.

"Señor, you are a guest in our country. You are not a citizen here. I have a dead body. This dead body is connected to you. What would you think, Señor?" he asked.

"Look, Señor, I... we, want to be cooperative, but unless you're charging us with something, I must protest not being able to leave the island," I said.

"It cannot be helped, Señor," he said.

"Have you checked into this guy's past, Officer?" I asked.

"We are doing that now," he said. "If he turns out to be a criminal of sorts, this will play in your favor. Until then, you will remain on the island. I will need your passports, please," he said.

I was in shock. "They're back at the house," I said.

"I will have one of my men accompany you back to the house to retrieve the passports. Once this has been cleared up, if you have no connection to this man's death, you will get your passports returned," he said. I had the feeling that he was attempting to flex his muscles a bit.

"Come on, Julie, let's go," I said.

"What's going on, Ethan?" she asked with concern in her voice.

"I'll explain on the way back," I said, as we loaded in the cart and sped off toward to the house. The others were waiting with impatience and eagerness. The officer followed in our dust cloud. I became angrier as I explained to Julie our new predicament. When we arrived back at the house, I went to the safe, got the passports and gave them to the officer. He promptly left.

"What the hell happened?" Bob asked.

"Yeah," Don said, "why did you give them your passports?" Don asked.

"The body that washed up is one of the guys Julie and I saw in the dive shop. He was part of the confrontation, remember," I said.

"Are they charging you with anything?" Myra Jean asked.

"No, but we can't leave the island until they clear us from any connection with the dead body," I said.

"You got to be kidding me," Lindsey finally said.

"I wish I were," I said. Julie started crying.

"Ethan, what are we going to do," she cried. Myra and Lindsey went to her side to comfort her.

"I've gotta think, Darling. We didn't kill that guy, and there's no way to connect us to it," I said.

"Yeah, but he may be the guy whose hose I cut," Bob said.

"Yes, I know, Bob. But, the last I saw, he was swimming away," I said.

"Yeah, me too," he said.

"So what does all this mean, Ethan?" Don asked.

"I'm not sure. I think we need to talk with Leonardo," I said.

"I'll go find him," Don said. He left in the golf cart with a cloud of dust.

"I hope he can find him, and Francisco, too," I said. "They were both down at the dock, and the authorities had already questioned them."

"Did Leonardo say anything to you?" Bob asked.

"No, he looked at us as we walked over toward where the body was," I said. "The main officer was a real jewel. I think he was trying to exert his authority," I said.

"I thought the guy got away," Bob said.

"Yeah, so did I, so did I," I said.

Chapter 35

Myra Jean had fixed a glass of tea, and we all sat down at the table. Julie had calmed herself, but Lindsey was staying close.

"I think we need to lay everything out, so we are clear on all the details," I said.

"I agree," Bob said.

With that, we began to lay out every detail, every move, from the very first day when Leonardo took us to visit the old man at Rocky Point who told us the story of the old wreck that was supposedly out there… that no one had been able to find. We had found it. Leonardo had warned us.

"I don't see how they can hold you here," Lindsey said.

"Well, let me remind you, this is a third world country. They can do what they damn well please. We're here at their discretion," I said.

"Ethan," Julie said, "do you think they are going to charge us with that man's death?"

"I hope not," I said. "I can't see the connection. I think I need to call Mike and get him to make some calls. The Belizean government is about to lose several million dollars worth of assets if we're hassled or charged with this crime," I continued.

"So you don't think they realize where the stuff is?" Bob asked.

"Nope. I don't," I said. "In fact, has Don said anything about the status on getting the clearance from the Coast Guard and the Navy?" I asked.

"Not exactly," Myra Jean said. "He's been on the phone all morning to somebody. I know they've been trying to get it all arranged," she said.

"I think we need to expedite that as quickly as possible," I said. "It might be the trump card we have to play."

"What are you thinking, Ethan?" Bob asked.

"Well, if they try to stick this on us, the Belizean government isn't getting a damned thing, not one artifact, if I have anything to do with it," I said. "Remember, Mike set up the off-shore corporation. It's untouchable."

"I'll get Don to make a call when he gets back," Myra Jean said. She looked very worried. What had been a tropical paradise had turned into an island of castaways.

"Hey, I think I hear the cart," Bob said. We all looked toward the road. We could hear the hum of the little golf cart. Don was on a mission now, and he would be determined to solve this dilemma.

"What'd you find out?" I asked, as Don pulled up in the yard.

"Not much. I couldn't find Leonardo or Francisco. I went by the café, and their wives had not seen them either," he said.

"Did you ride down to the docks?" I asked.

"Well, I attempted to go down there, but one of the armed guards stopped me near the Catholic Church. Ethan, I think they have brought more militia on this island," he said.

"What about the arrangements for clearance from the coast guard?" Myra Jean asked.

"Let me call again. It should be about in order," Don said. "Wait, what are you guys thinking?"

"Don, those artifacts are our leverage. They may be our only trump card," I said.

"What do you mean?" he asked.

"I mean that we may have to use the artifacts and the Belizean government's access to them as barter to get us out of here," I said.

"Holy crap, I see what you mean. Hold that thought. I'll call right now by God," he said, and he was off to another room to make the call.

"I'm gonna call Mike and have him start the diplomatic pressure process," I said. "This is ridiculous."

"I agree," Bob said. "I wonder where Leonardo and Francisco are. Do they know that we transported the items to the research vessel?" Bob asked.

"Good question," I said. "I think we have to assume they do know. We don't have time to be concerned with that now. We need to prepare," I said.

"Okay, guys, good news," Don said. "They have received clearance, both state-side AND international maritime clearance. There's a United States Navy Cruiser that's positioned in the Gulf of Mexico near Pensacola, that's headed this way," he said.

"How long before the big guns get here?" I asked.

"They said about six hours. That'll put them here around 4:00 this afternoon."

"Okay then, we have six hours to deflect the authorities," I said.

"What about working on clearing yourselves?" Lindsey said.

"Yes, that too, but I have to figure out who to talk to about all this," I said.

"How about some of us going in and speaking with the police?" she asked.

"I don't want you guys to endanger yourselves," I said.

"Ethan, I was the one who cut his hose. I need to go," Bob said.

"No, not by yourself, you're not," Lindsey exclaimed.

"Honey, Ethan and Julie have nothing to do with this goon, I do," Bob said. He had been calculating all the details. "Let's go and lay out all the events as we have here on this table. Then, he'll see that we're playing our cards face up," he said.

"There's only one thing, Bob. Don't forget what Leonardo said to us when we first started this treasure hunt," I said.

"What did he say?" Myra Jean asked.

"For starters, he said not to trust the Belizean authorities, that they were all greedy, and that they would lie for personal gain, even if it meant sacrificing one of us," I said.

At that moment, two military police rode up in their jeep. The same officer that had questioned me so intensely led the way.

"Señor Ethan, may we come in?" he asked, standing at the screen door.

"Yes, come in Officer. How may we help?" I asked.

"I've come to asked you to accompany me to the station for further questioning," he said. My stomach dropped to my knees.

"May I ask why, Officer?" I asked.

"We need to ask you more questions about the day you and your wife went to the docks and had the confrontation," he said.

"Officer," Bob said, "May I show you something that might help with your investigation?"

"Yes, by all means. What do you have for me?" he said. Lindsey began to object, but Bob waved her off. Bob showed the line of continuum of events that we had written out. The officer was intrigued and asked Bob a few questions about the dives we had made.

"So, Señor, what happened when you cut the diver's hose?" he asked. Bob recounted the attack from the divers, and how he was shot in the upper chest. He told the officer how he had had to cut the diver's hose in order to defend himself, and explained that the diver then swam off in the opposite direction.

"What did you do then?" the officer asked.

"We went to the surface as quickly as possible. We loaded our equipment and made our way back to the shore. After all, I had a spear in my shoulder, and we had the other attacker whose hands were bound ascending with us," Bob explained.

"Did you see the guy again?" the Officer asked.

"No, I did not," Bob said. The Officer turned to me.

"Did you see him again, Señor?" he asked.

"No, Officer, I did not," I said. He stood there for a few seconds. He began to pace back and forth, and then stopped and looked at the two of us.

"Señor, I think you and your friend should come with me. And I will also need your notes as well," he said.

Lindsey and Julie objected. "No, you cannot come, Señoras. Please give me some time to sort this out. I will be back in touch," the officer said.

"In touch, what do you mean, in touch," Lindsey said, now demanding an answer.

"Señors, please follow me," he said, walking out the door. He directed two other officers to apply handcuffs.

"Wait a minute, Officer; I thought we weren't being charged?" I objected.

"This is for your protection," he said, as the handcuffs were snapped into place. He led Bob and me to the second jeep, and the officers helped us step into the back. They drove us into town and placed us in a holding cell.

"Don, where the hell are you?" Myra Jean yelled. He came running back into the room.

"Where are Ethan and Bob?" Don asked.

"They took them away," Myra Jean said. Julie was crying, and Lindsey was pacing angrily back and forth in front of the table.

"What the hell did I miss?" Don asked. "My God, did they arrest them?"

"We're not sure what they're doing," Lindsey said. "Julie, can you contact Mike in Atlanta?"

"Don, I think you need to alert the guys on the research ship that they might have to haul ass at any time, especially if they see a Belizean military boat approaching," Myra Jean said.

"I'm on it. I agree. In fact, they may want to go ahead and move into international waters. I'll tell them now," Don said. He picked up his cell and made the call.

"Hey, it's me. Go now, and contact the U.S. Navy. It's gone from bad to worse. So, it's only a matter of time," he said. Then he hung up.

"It's done," Don said. "Is Julie talking to Mike?"

"Yes, and I hope he can give her some good news. She's about to lose it," Lindsey said.

"We've got to get a handle on this situation," Don said.

"Well, if you have any bright ideas, Don, spit'em out. This has gone from bad to critical all in about 60 seconds," Myra Jean said.

"Where are Leonardo and Francisco? That's who we need to find," Don said.

"As soon as Julie gets off the phone with Mike, I think we need to go into town, and scope everything out. This is all bullshit," Lindsey said.

"Okay, thanks Mike," Julie said, and she hung up the phone.

"So...what did he say, Julie?" Lindsey asked.

"He's working on it. He's contacting the Senator's office as well as the Governor's office. He said he'll get back with us, but not to expect any miracles," she said. She didn't look very hopeful.

"Let's go into town and find Leonardo," Lindsey said. "We have to take charge of this situation ourselves. The research vessel is making its way into international waters, and the U.S. Navy has been notified," she said. "The thing we need to do is affect the situation on our end."

"I agree," said Myra Jean.

"Okay, let's go then," Julie said.

They left in the jeep that had been provided with the house. Once in town, they went directly to the café where Leonardo and Juan worked. They asked

Leonardo's wife if she knew Leonardo's whereabouts, but she hadn't heard from him since the early morning.

"Let's go to the docks," Julie said. But when they reached the docks, they found a military roadblock.

"Hold it, no one is allowed beyond this point," the young officer said.

"Go get your commanding officer, please. I must see him immediately," Julie said.

"That is not possible, Señora. You must leave the area," he said.

Ignoring his order, she said, "Go tell him that I want to see him, and that it will be in his best interest and his country's best interest to talk with me now!"

"That is not possible, Señora. You must turn and go now," he said.

"Look, Officer, I don't think you want an international incident caused by your stupidity. Now, go and get your commanding officer," Myra Jean said. "You know, this kind of thing is why I don't travel outside the United States much. People in some countries think they can run all over any American. Don't they realize we can smash them like ants if they back us in a corner?" she said.

"Myra Jean, keep your cool," Lindsey said, "I'll take him out if he gives us any more lip."

"Sir," Julie said, approaching the officer, who was armed to the hilt. "Please get your commanding officer, unless you want us to tell the United States Navy Cruiser that's almost at your shoreline that we have been illegally held by your government, and that you refused to assist us in finding a thug who attempted to kill us not once, but twice, and who robbed us, took our money, and has harassed us for almost a year," Julie said sharply.

"Señora...." he began.

"You also need to tell your commanding officer that the Belizean government will not get one item, not another piece of gold or silver from the artifacts we have recovered if he refuses to speak with me," Julie continued. "Tell him he doesn't really want to piss off the United States."

The guard hesitated, took a step away from the group, stopped again and stared at Julie. She stared back. "Tell him," she said. He left and hurriedly walked over to the dock and disappeared around some wooden crates.

Don's phone rang. "Yes. Okay, great. Keep me posted. It is. Super. That's good timing. You wouldn't believe me if I told you. Okay thanks." He closed the cell phone.

"And...." Myra Jean prodded.

"It's done and they're here. That's all I'm gonna say," Don said, grinning.

"What else, Don? Spill it, Honey," Myra Jean said.

"Well, apparently, Mike's calls reached the right people. Seems the Navy Commander got a call from his commanding officer, who had received a call from D.C. instructing them to send in a launch party to retrieve Ethan and Bob and anyone else that needed diplomatic protection," he said.

"Are you serious?" Julie screamed.

"Yep, and they'll be here in about 20 minutes," Don said, feeling rather proud of himself.

"What about these idiots?" Lindsey asked.

"Seems that's being addressed as well," Don said. "Seems we have ourselves a rogue officer, one who wants to corner the market on... shall we say... racketeering Belizean style."

"You gotta be shittin'," Lindsey said, obviously astounded.

"Nope! In fact, the Belizean Military Police has dispatched a unit from the mainland. They're coming to take custody of the idiot," he said.

"How did you make all this happen?" Myra Jean asked.

"I didn't. One thing created another. I guess the timing was right," he said.

Julie and Lindsey heard a commotion coming from the gate by the dock, and turned just in time to see several U.S. Navy military personnel, fully armed, marching toward the roadblock.

"WHERE IS YOUR COMMANDING OFFICER?" they demanded. "GET HIM NOW, SOLDIER," they ordered.

"Are you Julie Scott," the Navy Lieutenant asked.

"Yes sir, I am, and these are my friends," Julie said.

"Yes ma'am. We're here to get you and your party out of here. Where is your husband?"

"They're holding him, and they're holding Bob, Lindsey's husband, as well," she said.

"No problem, ma'am, we'll handle it," he said. When the Belizean officer rounded the corner, he became defensive, and ordered the U.S. Navy officers to produce their orders. He told them that he was holding the two Americans in connection with the death of an unidentified diver.

"Yes Sir. I am here under the authority of the United States Navy and the United States Government. You are to release these people immediately," he said.

"Under whose orders?" he quipped, laughing. "This is not U.S. soil, Lieutenant. I'd be very careful if I were you."

"Captain," the Navy Officer said, "Your government has granted the United States Navy complete authority in this matter," he said.

"I'll have to see proof, gentlemen," he said.

"How about this, Captain," came a voice from behind us. It was the Admiral of the Belizean Military, along with an entourage of about 50 men. They had come from the other side of the port. The Admiral gave an order in Spanish, and the soldiers drew their weapons, and pointed them at the Belizean officers that had been detaining Julie, Lindsey, and the others.

"Lieutenant, please take your people so we can handle our internal affairs problem before it becomes an international incident," the Admiral said.

"Yes Sir. There's another matter, sir. The officer here is holding two members of this party."

"Captain, release the two people immediately. NOW, CAPTAIN!" The Admiral ordered. Two men scurried away and brought Bob and me to the roadblock where the commotion had intensified. We were in handcuffs. "Release them," he ordered.

"Ms. Scott, you and the others follow me," said the Navy Lieutenant, "follow me; we must go now."

After we had moved away from the roadblock, I turned and glanced. The Admiral had apparently ordered that the Captain and his few men be taken into custody. They were being ushered off toward a military boat on the backside of the port.

"Where are we going?" I asked.

"We have orders to take you to the house where you've been staying for you to gather your belongings. Then, we are taking you aboard the U.S.S. Kearasage," he said.

"The Kearasage?" Don said, "Geeze, I can't believe it. Ethan, do you know what ship this is? Hell, those guys have been in the Med while they were flying sorties in the Middle East."

"Lieutenant," I said, "what happens after that?"

"We wait for further instructions from Washington," he said.

"Washington?" I said.

"Yes sir, Washington. Will it take you long to gather your belongings?"

"No, we can be fairly quick," I said.

"Good. Frankly, the quicker we get back on the ship the better," he said.

"What about the UNC research vessel, Lieutenant?" Don asked.

"She is anchored off our leeward side, completely within protective gunnery range," he said.

"Is the U.S. Navy aware of the type of cargo and artifacts the vessel is carrying?" Don asked.

"Yes, Sir," the Navy Lieutenant answered. "Please be expeditious with your packing. We need to move quickly."

With that order, we hurried inside, and gathered and packed our things. I could not help but wonder what had happened to Leonardo and Francisco. Perhaps we could find out. I was hoping, but I wasn't very optimistic.

"Okay, we're ready," Don and Myra Jean said, as they came running out of the house. "I tell you Ethan, this has been a hell of a ride."

"Still is, Don. Come on, let's go," Myra Jean said. Bob and Lindsey came out with their bags, as did Julie and I. The Navy Lieutenant ordered some of the sailors to assist us with the luggage, computers, and other equipment.

"Is that everything?" the Navy Lieutenant asked.

"Yes, Sir, that's it," I said.

"Very well, then. Let's go. Don't look back folks. This must be a high level situation for us to be extracting you like this. Belize is a friendly country, but I think there must be trouble brewing across the border in Guatemala.

"Over what?" Don asked.

"Your treasure," the Navy Lieutenant said. Within minutes, we were aboard a small navy skiff, headed for the U.S.S. Kearasage. As we got closer, we could see armed units stationed along the bow of the ship. The skiff pulled alongside, and a rope ladder dropped from the main deck.

"Okay folks, all aboard. Welcome to the U.S.S. Kearasage, compliments of the United States Navy. Welcome to Home soil," The Captain said.

"Thank you, Captain, what do we do now?" I asked.

"The insigne will see that you're comfortable. Let us know if you need anything. I will contact you later when we are in international waters. We'll need to debrief each of you in preparation for our arrival in Jacksonville at 0900 hours day after tomorrow."

"Thank you, Captain," I said, as he turned and disappeared down a gangway. We turned and looked at each other. What had happened? There had to be something more to this story, but what?

Chapter

36

We settled into the lounge area of the ship where we had been assigned. We were in an awkward situation. We had been plucked from a Central American country and had survived a close call with a rogue military officer who was apparently positioning himself for a coup. Word on the street was that he was in bed with the Guatemalan resistance group, who had been hiding out in the jungle along the border between Belize and Guatemala. They were apparently planning a military take over, and the acquisition of the artifacts seemed like a good way to finance their insurrection.

"What do you think is behind all this?" Bob said in a low voice. "Do you think it is really related to an insurrection?"

"I have no clue, but I think it's possible that we stumbled into a hornet's nest," I said.

"How do you figure?" Don said. The girls were listening intently, but not saying anything. We were all more relaxed now that we were aboard the U.S. Navy ship, but this situation only added more questions to the growing number we still had not answered.

"Well, if you go on the premise that we accidently fell into the sequence of events unbeknownst to us, and that "they" got wind of the treasure and its value, it would make sense that they would try to take it," I said.

"But that would be messy," Bob said, "which is why Ethan and I were whisked away as quickly as we were, and on such flimsy charges."

"What do we do now? What happens now?" Don asked.

"We wait to be debriefed for one thing," Bob said. "And I think there's more to this than a rescue, although I may be wrong."

"It's a mystery to me," I said. "Are the artifacts in any danger, Don?"

"I don't think so," he said. "I haven't been in contact with the vessel and the UNC boys since we were plucked from the island, so I'm *assuming* everything is OK."

"Yeah, you gotta watch that...you know what assuming does," Lindsey said, finally speaking.

"What do you think about all this, Linds'?" Bob said.

"I think I'm glad to be aboard the United States of America! That's what I think, boys," Lindsey responded without hesitation.

"Amen to that, Sister," Myra Jean said.

"Seriously, whatever the details, whether it was because of an impending insurrection or whatever, I think we had about played all our cards. We're damned lucky... *whatever* caused this intervention."

"I couldn't agree more, Lindsey," Julie said. "This was a tremendous dream from the beginning, and it almost turned into a horrific nightmare. I'm glad to be on this ship. I agree with Linds," she said looking around to all of us.

"Okay. Okay. I'm convinced. It's been a ride..." I said.

"Yeah, and the ride is over. Pour the drinks, light the candles, and start up the band; it's party time," Don said.

"Oh, shut up Don. You're crazy as hell. We're trying to figure out what is behind all of this," Myra Jean said. "We're trying to be serious, here."

"Hell, I'm not, by God. My country just rescued me. I'm celebrating. God Bless the United States Navy, and God Bless the United States of America!" he proclaimed.

About that time, a corporal came in the room, and announced that we were now in international waters, and that the Captain would like to have our company in the strategy planning room. He instructed us to follow him, and we did.

We entered the strategy room, which was a huge conference room with five hidden screens, and television or computer monitors mounted on every wall. I assumed this was the place where the Navy personnel formulated their strategic plans before launches or attacks were carried out.

"Come in, come in, and make yourselves confortable. We have lots to discuss," the Captain said as he directed us around the conference table. "Can we get you something to drink? We'll have chow call in about 45 minutes at 1800 hours. You'll be welcomed as our guests this evening. The chefs are preparing a special meal for the occasion," he said.

"Captain, Sir, we're all a bit confused. Can you explain what's happening? I mean, I think we know some of the pieces, but this thing mushroomed in front of us, and we lost control of it," I said.

"I'll be glad to explain, as much as I can. But I think when I finish with the part of the story I can tell you, you'll understand. First, let me say, welcome to the U.S.S. Kearasage, and back to the United States of America."

"Amen to that, Sir," Don quipped.

The Captain began to explain. "It appears that when you made your discovery of the sunken treasure, and its value became known... as well as the fact that you actually pulled up the cannon from the Cour Volant... it set a number of events in motion, most of which you were never aware," he said. "But WE, the U.S. military, were. We have been monitoring this group in Guatemala for over a year. We knew there was a connection in Belize, so when you guys applied for your visas, we began monitoring you, under the authority of the Patriot Act. We were also monitoring the communications between various parts of the Belizean military. So, when the call came in from your Governor's office, as well as Senator Isakson's office, we knew the time to act was now. In fact, your activity may have helped flush out the members of the insurrection. You see, the Belizean Captain who took you into custody, was one of the main organizers and could *not* be trusted. It was also a wise maneuver for you to transport the artifacts to the UNC research vessel. The UNC guys had already contacted us, and were keeping us abreast of every move from all angles.

"Unbelievable. Amazing," Don said.

"Captain, what about Leonardo and his brother, Francisco? Do you know of their whereabouts?" Julie asked, her heart heavy with concern.

"I can only tell you that they are safe. Their families will be relocated and reunited with them soon. Suffice it to say that they are friends of the United States," he said.

"What about the artifacts, Captain?" I asked. "What happens next with them?"

"They're yours. You found them, and filed the proper paperwork," he said. "And, I must compliment you on your move to setup a corporation in the Bahamas. That was a shrewd move, and very legal. You are free to do what you want, and may I offer my congratulations on your discoveries! They were very significant, indeed," he said as he stood from the table and motioned us to do the same.

"Thank you, Captain," we all said. He tipped his hat, and said, "Chow in 15 minutes, sharp. Please don't be late."

"Yes, Sir, Captain. Thank you again," I said.

Little did we know that the crew had prepared a celebratory dinner for this occasion. We were treated as heroes, and the food was absolutely awesome. It wasn't the usual dinner menu the shipmates were accustomed to. The Captain even proposed a toast in our honor for helping the United States avert yet another terrorist effort to disrupt a peaceful nation. The official Belizean Government had also sent a letter of appreciation. The letter stated that we would be welcomed back to Belize as ambassadors of good will and peace should we decide to return, and it was signed by the Belizean President.

As we were finishing dinner, we received a special telephone call. It came to the Captain first, "Yes sir, they are here with me and the men and women of the U.S.S. Kearasage as we speak. Yes sir, we're finished with dinner. Yes, one moment sir. Thank you, sir," the Captain said, and handed the phone to us.

"Ethan, you take it, man," Don said, and all agreed. We were all smiling. Who was on the other end?

"Hello," I said. "Yes, sir, thank you, sir. Thank you very much, Mr. President....

Chapter

37

We had gathered at our townhouse in Asheville. As I had told Carl, it would require more than a cup of coffee to get through the full story. We had decided to make an event of it, and would invite several guests for an evening of dinner and conversation. Recounting the details of our adventure would serve as exhilarating entertainment.

I had stayed at Carl's coffee shop most of the day. My storytelling had gathered an audience. I had called Julie and convinced her to throw an impromptu dinner party of sorts, a very informal affair; and, now, everyone who had been invited had begun to arrive. It was introduced as a *"bring a dish and a bottle"* kind of gathering.

"I cannot believe that you were captured and taken into custody," Carl said. His interest and enthusiasm had not waned. He was high on the adrenalin of the human experience. This had been part of his personality since I first met him. He's an exciting guy to be around, and always sees the positive in life.

"What happened to your two friends, Leonardo and Francisco," he asked with great concern.

"They were reunited with their families in a little town outside of Denver, Colorado. That was where they wanted to settle. It was their dream to live there," I said.

"Have you spoken with them since that night?" he asked.

"No, I haven't. But we received a message through the military services that their relocation had been successful. We were told not to contact them for at least a year, and only with approval from the U.S. Secretary of State's Office," I said.

"Wow," he said, completely mesmerized by the details of the story. "Where are Bob and Lindsey?"

"Right here, Carl," Bob said, as he and Lindsey came walking through the door. They had been at the Grove Park Inn taking a rest before joining us for the round robin questioning they were sure to endure.

"Hey, how are you guys?" he asked. "It's great to see you; and, Lindsey, you're looking especially gorgeous this evening," Carl said.

"Thank you, Carl," she said, taking a seat on the sofa.

"Sit down, Bob. Don and Myra Jean will be here in a few minutes. They were arguing about what to wear," I said.

"Figures," Lindsey said, chuckling. "Bob, will you make me a cocktail, please Sweetie?"

"For you, I will do that," he said.

Bob joined us in the living room as we began fielding Carl's questions. Some of the other guests had arrived, as well. Word had spread, like in Belize... about our tales of adventure.

Don and Myra Jean soon arrived, and we all gathered beside the fireplace. The fun began. The stories would be long and repetitive, but this was part of the adventure.

"Mr. Ethan," the housekeeper said, "telephone's for you," and she handed me the phone. "Hello," I said. "William, man how are you? Yes, it was a hell of a trip. Yep, would love to. You and Elizabeth are welcome anytime. Great! Thanks, good-bye, William. Thanks buddy. Good-bye."

"That was William?" Julie asked.

"Yes, it was. You know that's the first time I've spoken to him since they left so abruptly," I said.

"Wow, that's interesting. I hope we can get together with them soon. We have too much history to lose them," Bob said.

"I agree," I said, as did Lindsey and Julie. Don and Myra Jean were engrossed in conversation with Carl and some of the other guests.

"This all seems so surreal, doesn't it?" I asked.

"Yes, in a way, it does; but, in another way, it's one heck of a tie that binds not only our friendships, but our lives," Bob said.

"Here, Here," I said. "Let me propose a toast then. May our lives forever provide strength to and support for one another! A toast to our esprit de corps," I said. Hands were raised, glasses clinked, and cheers went up in honor of our friendship.

With that, we mixed and mingled with the guests, retelling the stories of adventure. Like Tom Sawyer and Huck Finn, we celebrated our own story of drifting through time on our version of the Mississippi River... the island of Ambergris Caye. Like the tales weaved in many adventures recounted by Mark Twain, the stories of our year on an island, like castaways, lent themselves to each listener's interpretation. One thing was for certain… we were all different; we were all changed from our experiences, and each story had its own impact that was left unexplained.

"Will you go back?" Carl finally asked. We all looked at each other. Bob, Lindsey, Don, Myra Jean, Julie and I, well… we all smiled.

"I never say never," I said.

"Hell, I do," said Don, laughing as we moved to the dinner table. Life is good! Life is good, indeed!

About the Author:

Born in 1957, near Bessemer, Alabama, Hale now resides in Savannah, Georgia, with his wife of almost 30 years. Hale has two children, and five grandchildren. He and his wife have traveled all across the United States, the Caribbean, Central America, and the British West Indies. He has lived and worked in Georgia, Alabama, and Texas. His rural roots and meager beginnings, along with his life experiences, provide the source for his imaginative stories and characters.

In 2006, Hale played the role of Judge Fort in an independent documentary film based in Birmingham, Alabama, about the story and case of Edwin Stevenson and the murder of Father James Coyle. Stevenson was defended by Hugo Black, then a highly renowned defense attorney, who later became a U.S. Senator from Alabama, and who eventually was appointed to the U.S. Supreme Court.

Hale currently teaches 5th grade inclusion at Bloomingdale Elementary, in Bloomingdale, Georgia, near Savannah, Georgia.

Island Castaways is his first novel, and his second book to be published.

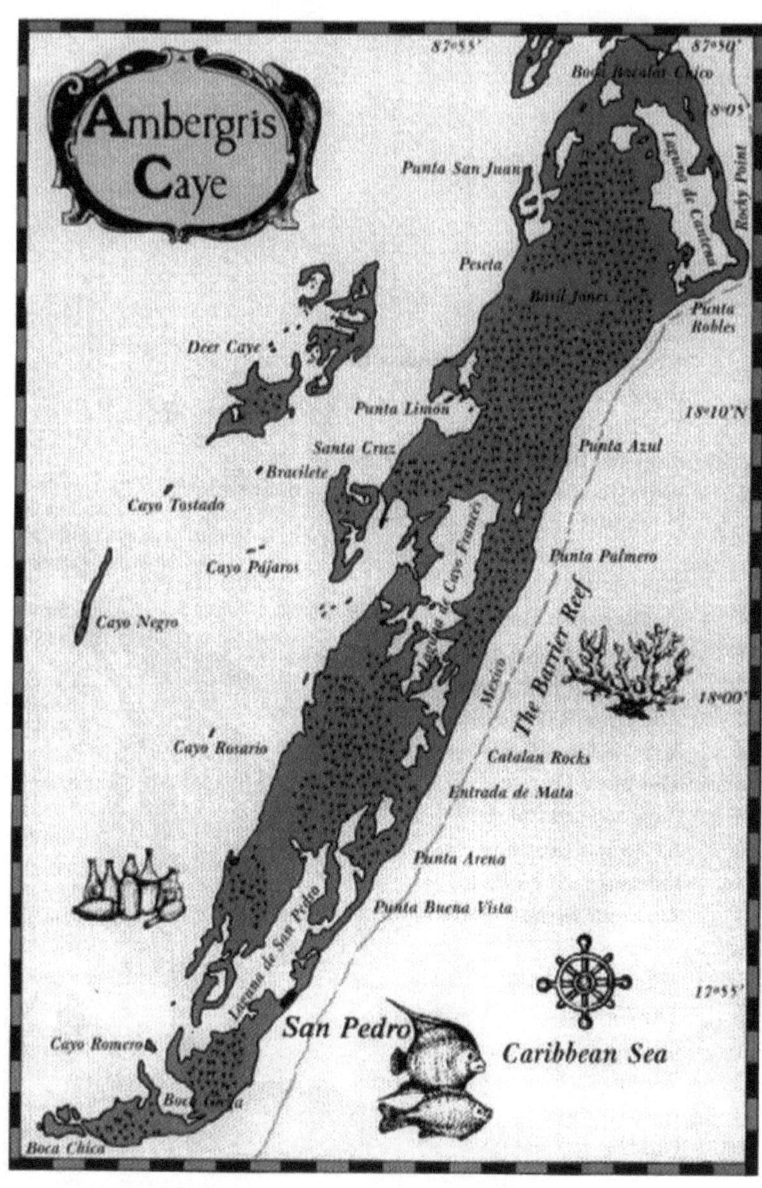
Ambergris
Caye
87°55'
87°50'
18°05'
Punta San Juan
Rocky Point
Peseta
Basil Jones
Punta
Robles
Deer Caye
Punta Limon
18°10'N
Santa Cruz
Punta Azul
Bracilete
Cayo Tostado
Cayo Pájaros
Punta Palmero
Cayo Negro
The Barrier Reef
Mexico
18°00'
Cayo Rosario
Catalan Rocks
Entrada de Mata
Punta Arena
Punta Buena Vista
Laguna de San Pedro
17°55'
San Pedro
Caribbean Sea
Cayo Romero
Boca Chica

www.ingramcontent.com/pod-product-compliance
Lightning Source LLC
Chambersburg PA
CBHW030424310726
48979CB00009B/1610/J

* 9 7 8 0 9 8 3 8 3 7 6 4 0 *